Emerald Hawks Flight

By Patsy Stanley

ISBN 978-1-7332437-6-6

Library of Congress Control Number: 2015907161

Someone once gave me a box full of darkness.
It took me years to understand that this was a
gift.
Warrior Goddess Training book

I am circling around God, around the ancient
tower, and I have been circling for a thousand
years, and I still don't know if I am a falcon, or
a storm, or a great song.
Rilke

We are all children of history and carry its
 imprints in our lives.
Gene Cohen

Table of Contents

Chapter 1. Leavin' Home

They rode through thin, early mornin' sun, over skinny, curving blacktop, coarse cut through ancient hills and the soft green mountains of their generations. They rode slow past coal mines and tobacca' barns with faded advertisements painted on their sides. Once in awhile somebody was outside and thowed' up their hand at them. Mostly they didn't see nobody, just a few milk cows and work mules.

The back of the old green truck they rode in held all they owned. Frayed tarps with knotted ropes tied to homemade side slats kept their belongin's from fallin' out.

Lottie and Emerald set propped agin' the tailgate in a corner of the complainin', creakin' old truck bed, not speakin', watchin' ever thing with wide eyes while the miles passed by. It was the first time they'd seen anything outside the holler where their cabin stood.

The man had stopped at the general store the night before and got what he called a fancy store bought meal ta' take on the road with 'em before headin' up the holler. In the back of the truck set the brown grocery sack he'd carried home. In it was bologna, a loaf of light bread, already warm, a glass jar of mustard, and a table knife. The grocery bag set up agin' a pilla' case holdin' tins of flare', salt, bakin' powder, and a small slab of fatback. A tin of lard set in the black iron skillet next to the pilla' case. Biscuit makin's. They would stop some place for water ta' drink.

Tall, big boned and silent, Thursta set in the middle of the cracked and faded front seat of the truck, holdin' baby Lucy, a sleepin' on her lap. She set weighty and silent between Bolen, the small man a' worryin' the large, black steerin' wheel, and their oldest, West, a' long, tall, boy-man a' gazin' out the winda', watchin' the speedometer, or studyin' the truck's worn gear knobs on long sticks.

The truck engine whined and strained under the heavy load. The hot, damp air flowin' through the winda' swept over the woman's thick, dark hair. Her wide, generous mouth stayed clamped shut agin' anything she might be feelin' as she stared out at the world she was leavin' behind.

Thursta's large hazel eyes stayed shaddered' from seein' too much of an unexpected, unfair life too young. They held an old, well-learned weariness; she'd been seein' meanness since she was too young ta' know how ta' expect and how to unexpect everything but it's dark malice.

The high ridges of her cheekbones stood etched knife sharp in the soft, hazy, mornin' light. They softened from time to time in the dappled shadder's a' playin' over her face as they passed slow out of their old life, all of them a' clingin' to it except Bolen, all a' them both a' dreadin' and wantin' the new world he was drivin' 'em into.

She was thinkin' 'bout the bees. Bolen and the men he drank with had carried a swarm of what

2

they called I-talian honey bees home to her. They brought the bee swarm home ta' her early one mornin' in a warshtub when they come in from layin' out all night. The men he run with included most of her brothers. They gambled, made moonshine, and hunted together.

They got together ever evenin' and laid out til' late. They was allus' a' swappin' for one thing or another. She was used to him bringin' somethin' home ever little while. Generally, it was somethin' she had to take care of.

The men, like they did ever' mornin', went to talkin' and braggin' about their night. They set at the old wood table eatin' the breakfast she'd fixed fer' them. She'd got up at daybreak and fired up the stove and put a big pan of biscuits in the oven. Then she'd gathered big brown hen eggs, fried a dozen of 'em and set 'em ta' the back of the stove.

The men left it to her to do somethin' with the bee swarm. She knowed better than to ask any of them questions. She went out back and studied the rusty old warshtub a' settin' a little ways from the back porch. Somebody had tied an old white sheet over the top of it. She walked around and around the tub ta' hear how the bees inside was a' doin''.

They was calm. She took a' hold of the tub and dragged it across the yard until it set close to the empty bee hive her Pa had made. That ol' warshtub was heavy; she finally quit draggin', stood up and wiped the sweat off her face with her apron.

She glanced up at the top of the hill. Mornin' mist still curled around the trees. It was as cool right now as it was gonna git' all day. She hoped the bees would still be a little slow from the shoemake smoke the men blowed over them when they robbed the bee tree.

She got the hive ready for the bees, then went back in the house. She took her time and pulled on a long sleeved shirt and buttoned the collar up and the sleeves down tight. She put on old jeans and tied her pant legs around her ankles with twine, and pulled on a pair of old work boots. She tied a thin, see through scarf around her head and pulled it down over her face. She nodded to herself. Well, she was as ready as she was ever gonna' be.

She went out back ta' the hive, wearin' a pair of socks over her hands, carryin' the big mash scoop. It was awhile since she'd handled any bees. But the men knowed ta' bring 'em to her 'cause she had a way with animals and birds and bees.

She untied the piece of white sheet around the warshtub' and pulled a corner of it back, makin' a hole for the bees to fly out. She stepped back aways and watched 'em. They come out slow and easy in a steady stream and flew a short ways before returnin' to the washtub. She was in no hurry. It wouldn't do to get in a hurry around bees. They'd jist' git' upset and go wild on ye'.

She watched the bees ta' figure out how they was gonna' act as she edged closer and closer to the tub. They was a gentle a bee as any she'd ever seen. Not a bit of temper in 'em. That feelin' like slow water and old music started runnin' over her. That told her she was in rhyme with the bees, and it would work out jist' right. "Mary had a little lamb..." she crooned, keeping her voice soft and slow. But there was another rhyme she knowed and liked better. She thought they'd like it, too.

"Twinkle twinkle little star..."

She kept her movements in slow motion as she bent over the tub. She was good at keepin' her mind where it needed to be with the bees or any other creature. She knowed what she was a' doin' with them. When she was with the chickens, pigs, or any of the forest animals, she was washed free of the fearful times she lived through in the other parts of her life. The places where her man and family ruled.

She slid the sheet back a little at a time. A few of the bees flew out and lit on her. She didn't mind, not one bit. She pulled the sheet back a little further. When it was back far enough, she dipped the mash scoop into the warshtub, takin' care not to pinch any of the bees or break up the slabs of honeycomb.

She carried the honey ta' the empty hive, scoop by scoop, and when it got down fur' enough, she lifted the slabs of honeycomb out and carried 'em ta' the hive and put 'em in it. She made slow, purposeful trips back and forth between the tin tub and the bee hive 'til it was done.

She backed up a little ways and waited. The bees left the tub and went to their honey. They were still groggy and slow. She pulled the sheet back further and further, 'til the last bee flew to the hive. Then she pulled the sheet back over the washtub quick, and tied it so's they couldn't git' back in. She stepped away and studied the bees. They was placid natured, like regular honey bees. But these bees was much bigger and they had more yella' on their bodies. She admired their bigness and their smooth bodies. She liked the mild sound of 'em and their dignity. They were beautiful. Their honey was the richest, dark gold she'd ever seen.

After they settled into the hive, she went to the house and got Lottie to help her carry the tub up on the back porch. She didn't want to drag it across the ground, 'cause the sound might stir up the bees. They needed people and noise to stay away 'til they got settled in good.

They scooped the rest of the honey out of the tub and let it ooze into pans from the kitchen, then carried it in. Bolen and his friends strolled into the kitchen.

"Ever one of you'ins' take plenty a' that honey home with ya'." he urged, rockin' back and forth on his heels, braggin' about what all he could give away, which was often what little bit they owned.

Thursta studied him. His blond, wavy hair stood tight to his head, so all was well. But that could change quick as lightnin'. When he run his hands through his hair, causin' it ta' stand up, they knowed ta' run. He wouldn't do nothin' much in front of nobdy except them, though.

Small and wiry, wearin' old dark blue work pants from Sears and Roebuck, his great big hands wavin' around, old black, worn work shoes on his feet, he bragged on and on. The men standin' around was all taller and bigger than him and they knowed it bothered him no end. They laughed behind his back about what a cocky litte rooster he was and the big hen he'd caught. The men stared at them with calculatin' eyes. What could they take next? The woman sighed. The man stared at the honey in the pans.

"Where's the rest of it, woman?" He never called her by name. She didn't answer.

"Well," he finally said, "divide it up, woman." She turned away and got busy. The men grabbed the bowls and pans of honey and left. At least they'd bring the pans and bowls back. As quick as the men got out the door, he slapped her.

"Git' the hell out there and git' that honey brought in here!" he shouted. She turned her back to him and waited. She knew he wanted to keep most of the honey and let the bees fend for themselves. But she wouldn't go back out and take it from them, and he couldn't. They would sting him,to spite the smell of him, and he knew it.

Bolen knowed a lot about bees, but he couldn't handle them. They would sting him, 'cause they didn't like him. Maybe it was the constant whiskey smell on him. He thought that was the only reason, but she knowed bees wouldn't put up with bad temper or wildness or unsettled ways roilin' in the sweat of a body.

She'd already reasoned it out while she was a' movin' the bees. She would have her way, for it was for them, not for her. She didn't want them robbed agin'. They would git' ta' keep their honey.

Since he got mad sa' quick and easy anyway, if he didn't git' mad over the bees, it would a' been over somethin' else. Usually 'cause she was sa' much taller than him and it made him mad 'cause she looked down on him. That fact was a constant sorrow to him night and day, and he belittled her by settin' out ever day ta' prove to her he was the boss. She'd already learned that lesson from the men in her childhood.

Bein' a big girl was hard. She shrugged morosely and endured his hits and threats with a stoic face, knowin' he'd lose interest and go on to somethin' else 'fore long. The one savin' grace of the drink. More than anything, she knowed she was saving somethin' from putting up with the misery the man dished out to all things ever' day, rain or shine.

She watched the calm, beautiful bees to see how they was a' farin', and saw they wasn't makin' any honey. That told her they'd lost their queen. They would have to be fed sugar water ever day when their honey run out, or they wouldn't make it through the winter. In the spring, if they made it, they could search for another queen.

Their chance for makin' it without a queen was slim, but she would try ta' help them. She hid most of the honey left in the tub. Honey never spoilt'. She sealed it into quart jars while he was gone, hidin' them in the root cellar behind the cabin. He wouldn't think a' lookin' there. She would use it ta' keep 'em fed when the honey in the hive run out.

She sneaked around and fed the bees ever day after their honey ran out. Fall frost set in, then snow started comin' down. When the honey in the root cellar run out, she carried sugar water to 'em. Ever' time she stepped out the back door with the bowl of sugar water, they rose up in a cloud and come and lit on her and the bowl. She had to walk real slow and set the bowl down careful so she didn't pinch any of 'em, or they would sting her. That was just their natural reaction. They didn't mean anything by it. She waited 'til they were all off of the bottom of the bowl before she set it down.

The man got jealous and tried to feed them a time or two, but they rose up and stung him. The man wasn't one to let his woman have anything that wasn't under his rule for long, but just as her mother had often escaped her father, she often escaped him. She had learned meaning from her mother, who was a rock, and a green willow, who carried the Sight and kept it, even though her father, a hardshell, churchy man, had tried to take it away from her.

Thursta stared out the truck winda' at the mountains they were travelin' through, not seein' 'em. The bees finally died out. They never had much hope of makin' it anyway. The man told her the bees didn't need sugar water, they was fine on their own, once they was settled in.

She let on to him like she believed his lie, but any how, sugar cost a pretty penny, and even though he had an awful sweet tooth, he stopped bringin' any of it home, and she never got to leave the place.

So the bees died out slow, a little bit at a time. She'd watched them and cried a little bit at a time, keepin' pace with 'em. One mornin', she slipped out and looked at the empty hive. They was all gone.

A cold, bitter wind keened a long, low lament through the empty hive, telling her of their end. She turned away and looked up the holler. The wind took on an awful lonesome sound. She climbed the skinny dirt path leadin' up the holler 'til she stood high up in back of their home place.

She stood there awhile, lookin' down at the little brown log cabin and the smooth board porch that stayed cool and soothed her bare feet when she churned butter. She studied the thin metal clothesline strung between two young trees. He'd brought the wire home from the general store and bragged ta' her that they'd never have ta' replace the clothesline agin'. She had to clean the rust off it ever time before she hung clothes on it so the rust wouldn't get on them. Sometimes it got on the clothes anyway, and he raised hell about it.

She watched the ribbon of silver creek water ripplin' shaller 'at the end of the clearing. She warshed clothes in the creek and cooled milk in it fer' the babies.

She leaned forward and keened a little sound of grief. She was verily afraid of him. In a minute, she straightened and stood tall, knowin' at least the bees didn't have to be afraid of him any more. They were free and flyin' wild in a warm field of pretty honey makin' flares', in the good, safe place where bee's go after their life on Earth is done.

Thursta smoothed Lucy's dark hair, so much like her own, over and over with her long, restless fingers. She kept her head turned away from the man as she stared out at the world they were leavin' behind, thinkin' thoughts she would never share with him. His pint of whiskey settled by his hip, Bolen drove on and on, carryin' them further and further away from the life their mountain generations had always known. Neither one of them spoke to, or looked at each other.

Çhapter 2. Thursta

Thursta Plant had married Bolen Hawks because he dared her to. Such a simple trick. But she fell for it.

People in their mountains married young. Her parents married when her mother, Drusa, was fifteen, her father, Stanford, sixteen. They'd been married, with all their children growed up and was a' startin' to grow old together, all set in their ways and prim in their habits, when Thursta come along. She was the biggest surprise they'd got in a long time! That's what they told her, a' laughin' and a' kissin' on her.

Thursta was the baby, the youngest of their many children. She was born when her mother was in the change, the time when women stopped havin' babies. Drusa picked out her name, for her father said he'd run slap' out of 'em. Her name was a blend of the languages from her mother's Cherokee and Irish heritage. When her mother spoke her name, Thursta Plant, it sounded like she was a' sayin' "thirsty plant", meanin' a little green growin' thing, a caress of meanin' they shared.

Thursta's mother and father allus" felt old ta' her. They were tall and slim and quiet anf gray headed. She watched them give each other little grins all the time, like somethin' about life was funny. When she asked 'em what they was a' grinnin' about, they said, "Must be somethin' jist' around the corner."

At night Thursta watched Drusa braid her gray hair into a long plait. That meant it was time to go to bed. In the mornin' bright and early, Drusa heated warsh water and warshed her face and Thursta's with a warshrag, braided Thursta's hair and twisted her own hair up in a tight, gray bun on top of her head. They took baths in the warshtub on Saturday evenin's out back by the well in summer. They took baths in the back room in the winter.

Drusa kept three dresses a' peice for herself and Thursta, two for ever day and one for Sunday go to meetin' at the little white church at the bottom of the hill by the general store. Women wore dresses 'cause the men wore the pants in the family. A woman who wore pants better have a good reason, or she was tellin' she was the boss of her man. No mountain man they knew would stand for it.

Drusa wrapped up her little dab a' grocery money in white cotton handkerchiefs and pinned them inside her apron pocket so she wouldn't lose the money. They never needed much from the general store. Most of their food was canned up from the big garden out past the well. Cabbages and cukes got pickled into crocks and left ta' age in the pantry, meat was put up in lard or hung up in the smokehouse or dried, root crops went down in the dirt cellar at the side of the house.

Drusa's old treadle sewing machine was a Singer she got from the second hand store in town. She sewed up her aprons in plain, serviceable colors, but she was partial to green or blue paisley patterns for her church dresses. Her dresses brushed the tops of her black, pointy toed, lace up shoes. They were styled in the same simple pattern. Three quarter sleeves and a simple round collar. A skirt wide enough to move around in and not show her figure. When she set down, she was all long bones, her hands restin' in her lap like they was ashamed not to be workin'.

Drusa made most of their clothes. Sometimes she sewed for other women. The women come to the house and they drew patterns on grocery sacks or other paper with a pencil before she sewed their dresses up. Thursta liked watchin' Drusa's hands a' movin' over the paper and the cloth when she made the dresses.

Drusa called the fancy dresses frocks because they had extra lace or other trims, shiny buttons, and extra gathers in the sleeves and waist. Stanford called the extra trims gewgaws.

The women brought the material, thread, and trims to Drusa. Sometimes they gave her the leftovers. Drusa trimmed out their church dresses with the extras, and they wore them proudly down the hill on Sunday mornin's.

Thursta's brother Chance was home one day when she was runnin' from side to side of the chair Stanton set in, watchin' his oversized "yers" wiggle, and he told an odd thing. He said that people elsewhere called their "yers", "ears", not sayin' the "Y' before it like they allus' did. Thursta wondered why people would call their "yers" ears. Years had to do with time-keepin', not hearin'. Besides, "yers" was a lot easier to say. So that's what they bcame ta' her, "yer's" ta' hear with and "years" ta' fill.

Thursta had plenty of plain fare ta' eat and a good little twin bed with an iron bedstead in the back room by the kitchen. Her room was once the pantry, but she wanted it, so they moved the things in it to other places. There was a window by her bed. She laid down at night and watched the dark drapin' itself slow like dark snowfall over ever thing. Night fell in shades of gray with slate colored edges. She smelled the memories of spices and picklin' stuff, the lonesome smell of corn and taters once stored in the little pantry. She fell asleep, content to listen to the advice and music the lonesome wind made, a' blowin' through the wild things up in the holler above the house.

Thursta's father and brothers kept the fields plowed around and below the house. They worked the fields all summer. She ran past them while they worked, past the tobacco barn where they hung their allotments of tobacco, past the hay and donkey barn, past the cane field, up into the moving trees and into the shelter of the shaded woods.

Sometimes they shouted at her ta' bring 'em a dipper of cold water and she did. Other times, they waved, and she waved back, her dark hair flyin' in the wind, a young banner runnin' to its true home, wearing the overalls her brother Leon—Onnie'—passed down to her. Drusa and Stanford told her she could could wear britches for awhile yit', fer' she was still a chile' and not a woman. She knowed they'd agreed 'cause she'd been sneakin' britches up in the holler ta' wear and hidin' 'em since she was old enough ta' go up there alone. Thursta didn't care what the reason they agreed was; the overalls pertected' her legs and back side like no dress could. Dresses was useless in the woods. They blowed ever which a' way in the wind and didn't pertect' yer' legs or seat when you set or slid down a rock.

She wandered the woods in the holler up above the house, but she allus' ended up at the little creek. She walked the flat, stacked, gray slate rocks under the sighin' boughs of the green trees hangin' over the creek. She walked, makin' sure there wasn't any snakes a' sunnin' themselves on the rocks 'fore she picked one to settle on.

She'd spent her childhood in these soft, shady, echoing hills. She'd knelt at the creek bank in the woods right above the home place and stared at her dark, lean reflection in the water, tryin' ta' puzzle out who she was. Like a Thursta statue, she'd wait ta' catch a fish in the daincy' merry creek usin' her strong, long fingered hands. She leaned over and listened to the creek, jist' like the sighin' boughs in the trees above her did. They listened together to the songs and stories from other places runnin' over the little pebbles layin' on the clear creek bottom.

Thursta knowed about the fancy copperheads and their mezermerizin' spells. She knowed the old names of healin' plants, and she knowed what the wind was a' sayin' when it blowed a certain way.

She waded the creek, careful to watch out fer' water snakes. She picked up smooth little piated' rocks in her hands and studied the brown and dark red patterns on them. She stacked the rocks ta' make pockets fer' the little fish to swim into, then she caught 'em with her hands. She talked to 'em while she looked 'em over. They flapped back and forth in her hands while she counted the stripes and spots on 'em before she turned 'em loose agin'.

Dependin' on their nature, she'd either slip 'em back in the water so's nobody would know they was ever gone. If they was proud and showy and flapped a lot, she'd splash 'em back into the water so's they'd have a great big fish story ta' tell all their kin. She liked the cool, wet feel of the fish and the way they slapped against the sides of her hands when she put them back in the water and watched them swim away. They'd give her a fish spankin fer' pickin' 'em up. She'd laughed to herself and practiced the sounds the creek made.

She picked wee small wild strawberries with her girlfriends on the high hillsides. They clutched together under railroad trestles while trains run high and loud over the worried wood and complainin' metal above 'em, shakin' the earth beneath them. They dainced on the shakin, ancient earth, all a' them young and full of promise, beleivin' the world ahead was filled with a handsome preacher man, his chilern', a good place ta' live and a garden.

She was content and awful happy, but ever once in awhile, a spell of terrible restlessness come over her. She'd set on the front porch steps, rest her chin in her hand, and study the tan ribbon of dusty road runnin' below the house and the general store.

Stanton picked up the mail. The post office was in the general store at the bottom of the hill. The store stood on a corner where one fork of the the dusty road led out to a two lane blacktop, and the other fork made a skinny lane wanderin' up the hill and across the railroad tracks to their place.

From their front porch, the store looked to be the size of the dollhouse she admired in the five and ten cent store in town. The same old white haired men dawdled on the front porch of the store ever day. They kept a few rockin' chairs next to the door of the store, and watched ever body that went in like hawks. Stanton said it was so's they'd have somebody ta' jaw about.

Next to the general store stood the little church they attended on Sundays. It was painted the same white as the store. The spire on top of it stood proud and high. On Sunday mornin's like clockwork, Drusa got Thursta up and dressed long before church time, so they could stroll sedately down the hill like they was rich folks without a care in the world. They'd play like they'd decided, "Let's not take the car today, it's sa' purty', let's go for a walk, instead." Then they'd laugh til' ya' didn't know which one was the child!

Sometimes when Thursta was a' settin' on the front porch, Drusa passed the screen door, glainced' out at her last child, wonderin' what she was a' thinkin'. But she didn't take time to ask. She'd think to herself. "I'll ast' her another time. At least she's safe from a bad life fer' now."

Railroad tracks circled the hill halfway between their house and the general store. Between the tracks and their house stood a field. On the other side of the tracks stood two fields, then the general store. Her brothers and father worked the fields.

Slow movin' trains passed through once or twice a week, allus' in the day time, circlin' the hill halfway up, metal screeching agin' metal, makin' worn out, weary noises, a' shakin' the ground. Thurst watched the orange, yella' and brown boxcars lumberin' by, makin' their own clackety noises. She tried to ferret out their stories, but they was made of metal, nothin' like a flare' or tree or water.

When she got tired of seein' the world from the front porch, she'd go see sister Wrennie ta' git' her hair brushed and eat some pie. It wasn't' fur' ta' git' there if she walked the railroad tracks.

Wrennie's husband Ben baked pies to make sure Rennie had somethin' sweet to git' her through the day. Most days she stayed wrought up as an old hen without its chicks.

"Wrennie's allus' got pie set back," Thursta would say to Drusa. "Kin' I go on down there?"

Tall, thin Drusa would stop and frown and put her hands on her razor thin hipbones and study Thursta.

"A train might come along and run over ye!"

Thursta scoffed at the idea.

"Don't ye' think I kin' hear it long afore' it comes, and jump off the tracks?" she asked, waitin' 'til Drusa nodded before she took off runnin' down the hill. Drusa, wipin' her hands on her apron, watched the coltish, long legged child-woman run away from their place. She didn't want her to leave, ever. But at least she was goin' ta' sister Wrennie's fer' now.

Sometimes, before Thursta was out of sight, Drusa called upon the Sight of her mother, Fallon Snow and her grandmother, Mercy Webb, askin' 'em to stand with her to watch over their child. Unspoken wonderin' ran back and forth between them, for none of Drusa's other children bore the Sight. No one ever knowed why sich' things happened, nor who the lineage would be passed on to. They only knowed that so far, it was the women in the family who got the Sight and became Healers.

Thursta was the last child. But she was not the new Healer. Thursta was given the beautiful, strong body and constitution of a pioneer woman. The innocence of nature, the learnin' of Nature's ways; she was learnin' organic spirituality so all was easy fer' her. She bore the intuition of a river maiden and was forever filled with feelin's ebbin' and flowin' ever' where.

The three Sighted women, two in Spirit, and one in the flesh, watched their child disappear down the railroad tracks. They hoped she would find a strong man to shield and guide her through life.

They knew there would soon come a time when Drusa would have ta' push Thursta out into the world fer' her own good, or she'd stay forever up in the holler. Thursta would have ta' face the evils and the joys of a world far from her home in her beloved mountains, far from the woods above this place, where nature and Thursta joined forces to keep their life rhythms stocked with magical abandonment and sweet innocence.

Thursta's brothers and sisters were growed and gone. Her mother was too busy to go wanderin' with her. But Thursta felt watched over and kept safe by her mother's sharp eyes and Sight. She was used ta' playin' with the fish and frogs and the other life she come across. Her father laughed an' warned her many a time not ta' talk the fish ta' death.

Chapter 3. Drusa and Stanford

Drusa and Stanford didn't hold with drinkin'. They were strict churchgoers. Stanford set the pace in their marriage and Drusa followed. He believed he had long ago done away with any notion of carryin' forward the "Sight" Drusa had inherited from her Irish and Cherokee ancestors. Though he didn't like to admit it, when they first married, he was rightly fetched by it.

They met in the first grade at the school house up in the head of Mill Creek Holler. The sturdy, one room school house set in a clearing surrounded by trees a few miles between their homes. The school house was full of winda's. The dappled sunlight daincin' through the trees outside threw their shadders' across the wood tops of the desks. The winda's had to be there, even though they were costly and let out the heat from the stove in the fall and early winter. The county paid for them, for ever body knowed mountain chilurn' wouldn't stay cooped up inside all day without being able to look out on Nature. They wouldn't go ta' a school without winda's, and their folks wouldn't make 'em.

A pot bellied stove stood in the middle of the school room. Stove wood was stacked to the side of the back door. Out back, at a discreet distance away, stood an outhouse with a bag of lime inside. A quarter moon was cut into one wall, so's the fresh air could get in all the time. A worn out mail order cataloge to read and wipe with lay on the floor.

The little school closed for most of the winter and part of the spring, so the children could help with the crops at home. The teachers were men, for men were the only ones who could keep the older boys in line. All the teachers used their belts or kept switches to use on the hard cases. Each teacher had anywhere from an eighth grade through a high school education, and were well paid by the county. The little school up in the holler taught through the eighth grade, but it was rare for any body to go past the fourth, fifth, or sixth grade.

Most of them quit as quick as they could. They got married, farmed, or went ta' work in the coal mines. Once in awhile, a student wanted to go past the eighth grade. They had to move to Lexburgh, where the high school was, and boarded with somebody over there 'til they finished.

Drusa did her best ta' resist Stanford's takin' over of her heart, for she was a free bird, one not given to carin' for another very deeply. She wasn't supposed ta', for she bore the Healer's call upon her life, and that kind of carin' belonged to all. Besides, she was already dedicated to the healin' way being the ruling force in her life.

She fought Stanford's old fashioned, courteous ways and his charming respectfulness, his humor that touched her soul. She was scared to death he would cause her to forget her Healer's ways and fill that place in her ancestral heart with his even, white teeth, wide smile, and

the defenselessness he carried about a part of
life.

Everyone said he was a throwback to a former
time, for Stanford was as unlike his family as
blood is to oil. Even as a young boy, he had
bowed over his graceless, ornery mother's hands
when she was distressed and kissed them, and
he sang to her like a Bard from the old world
when she was sad. He was naturally graceful,
standing in such a way that the cast off clothes
he wore fit him like robes of royalty. He sat up
with his sister's miseries without complaint. He'd
whipped a couple of men he didn't like being
around them, but not before he politely asked
them to leave.

Stanford's father was jist' the opposite of him.
A mean man who talked bad about ever' body. He
was mouthy, narrow minded, a know it all, heavy
with both pride and physical weight, miserly with
praise. Stanford didn't like his father or his
manners and cruelties, nor did he approve of his
arrogance, thievery, or bathing habits.

All the while of his growin' up, ever so often,
Stanford had to run to the woods and gasp for
breath for his soul's sake because he'd stumbled
once again upon, and looked at the depth of the
fear he carried at what his father was. His
father's ignorant cruelty, cloaked in self
righteousness, kept Stanford in a kind of
repugnant, visceral horror that left him weak
when the older man was around. After a while, if
he was able to stay away long enough, the
vastness of his fear receded and became
manageable again.

He knew the fear of his father was about more than the whippings he gave him now and then. Those were bad enough. It took him until he was an old man with time to think it out, long after his father died and he didn't mind being ashamed any more at his relief, when he put together that his father's unchangeable, uncurable, absolute cruel ignorance had killed off or limited his sisters and brother's hopes and dreams as well as his own. And Stanford's life and vitality came from hoping and dreaming. Maybe theirs once did, too.

Stanford took the teachings of the church in earnest. He studied them hard, for there were no other philosophies offered in the mountains, and he was forced to settle for what he could get. Infrequently, when time allowed, he wondered about the bigger philosophies working their ways in the world outside of his mountains. He sensed the vast thoughts other men were thinking, and it came to him that different kinds of courage were needed in other places. That only made sense.

He constantly studied the Bible and Nature, learning from both, searching out their deeper meanings. In time he came to understand that both were holy, though he never spoke of it to anyone.

Stanford waggled his too large ears at Drusa ever day and with secret delight, the freckles sharpened over her high cheekbones, though she wasn't supposed to show it, and didn't. He set right across from her most all of their school days. They was both tall and skinny as a couple a' rails.They both possessed long fingers, feet like razor blades, and shoes that hung loose around their heels if they didn't pack them with somethin'. They both jumped ahead of the twenty or so students who came and went in the little one room school house and finished the eighth grade together.

They'd felt jist' alike, and missed the long days in the little schoolhouse, where they studied each other while settin' side by side, and Nature through the windows. They missed a' watchin' rain or snow through the winda's together. They missed walkin' to school together on sunny, clear days, a' seein' the purple lilac bushes a' bloomin' by the outhouse, and they missed a' learnin' together about the big world outside of their mountain homes. They was used to seein' each other ever day, and couldn't stand fer' it bein' any different, so when Stanford turned sixteen and Drusa fifteen they'd married and set up housekeepin'.

Drusa's mother Fallon, heartbroken that her child had chosen not to follow the healer's path, gave her only child her best gravy bowl. She understood that Drusa's heart would have Stanford or die. Drusa's path had taken a turn, so she gave her a little brooch to wear with a picture of her grandmother Mercy in it in memory of the healer's path.

Fallon wept and chanted the familiar, ancient words over Drusa the morning of the wedding day, asking her to keep the Healer's ways above all the other promises she would make to life. But Drusa's heart was full of innocence and love for Stanford, and Fallon saw how it was. A few animals come around, and Fallon bound the future generations Drusa would carry into the Healer's ways with them as best she could.

Then Fallon kissed her daughter, took her hand, and walked their tall thinness out of the forest and back into the light of the meadow, where they picked bouquets of forget me nots to bind into head garlands.

Fallon worked silently while Drusa's girl-woman voice ran on like a small tinkling brook. The field around them was scented with sweet clover and saturated with the energies of many past generations of Healer's who gathered for this time, both men and women. Drusa never noticed, but Fallon took the roll, callin' out their names silent and respectful, while she picked the weddin' bouquets.

But bein' married was different than they'd expected. Plenty of people married at their age, and nobody was agin' it. At the first, they were light hearted with each other, laughin' an' runnin' though' the woods, a' holdin' hands. But the light heartedness went ta' fadin' when the other married men and women went to tellin' the newlyweds how they was supposed ta' pull long faces with each other and not act like chilern' any more. He was ta' be the boss, and she was ta' mind him.

It was the way of things that men in the hills kept a switch to use on their wives when they wouldn't mind them. The men bragged to each other about what size switch they used on their wives. When they asked Stanton what size switch he kept, his big ears got bright red. He shook his head and took a stately stance by pulling out the his pocket watch and looking at it.

"Ain't gonna be no sich' thing in my house. Ain't no need fer' nothin' like that." The men looked at him with pity, like he was a man whose woman told him what to do, whose woman wore the pants in the family. Stanford, who was ever bit as sensitive and nervous as Drusa, didn't try to hold the men's hard stares. He couldn't be stoic and hateful long enough ta' carry it off 'cause hidden deep in his soul, he was a weeping willow and a rock, a twin soul to his beloved wife Drusa. He sighed. So many men like his father. He was surrounded by them. He told the other husbands, to end it, "Gotta go boys. There's work ta' be done."

Even though Stanford held out forever on some things, there were other things he had to give in on. One day Drusa went and jumped in the bed and pulled the covers over her head right in the middle of a busy work day. Stanford said, "What in the hell's a' goin' on?"

Drusa slid the covers back down to her chin.

"We're a' gonna have company I don't want no part of!"

"Who?" Stanford asked.

"That dang Buck and Prissy!" Drusa answered. Stanford shook his head and reasoned.

"They own this house we live in, so git' up, Drusa, and let us go about the work before us this day."

When Drusa was up a' makin' the bed agin', he went back out to his work. Drusa went to the kitchen, but she wouldn't cook a thing for their company. Instead, she cleaned the floor and took the wildflare's' from the table and hid their easy ways with each other behind cupboard doors and the thin calico curtains that did fer' a bedroom door. She changed her apron for a clean one and waited. Just about the time she finished, Prissy and Buck Morgan drove up.

Stanford stopped work and invited them into the house where Drusa solemnly handed them each a glass of water. The couple stared around the little house.They walked to the corner of the livin' room and peeked into the kitchen with a proprietary air. Buck's big, proud voice boomed through the little white clapboard house, while Priscilla's mean little eyes darted ever where, then ever' where else all over agin'.

She asked, "Are you a clean person all the time, Drusa?" Then asked,"Any youngin's a' comin' yit?" Drusa shrugged and stared at the cracked and peelin' lineoleum on the floor. Stanford invited them to set on the front porch. They went outside. Drusa breathed a sigh of relief and watched them from behind the curtain. After Buck and Prissy left, they laughed and held hands like young newly marrieds do, then went back ta' their work.

In a few days, Stanford's father paid him a visit. He called him out of the house to talk to him in the front yard. Drusa watched from behind the curtain with a feelin' of dread. She despised Earl. He was a bully. He was a deacon of a church she didn't like the reputation of, and whupped his boys 'til the very day each of them left his place.

"Stanford," Earl Plant said, "Buck come to see me the other day. He seems to have the idea that Drusa is a little bit odd."

He shook his head from side to side importantly, as befitted his high standin' in the church.

"Her folks set on the porch ever night and drink their nerve tonic." He snorted and shook his head, while Stanford studied the ground hard, his hands fisted in his pockets.

"Ever body knows the "medicine" Doc gives 'em is mostly brandy," Earl said, lowering his voice.

"They say her mother's got the Sight, but she never brings it into the church where it belongs, and shares it with God and the people." He shook his head again.

"She's a' doin' somethin' wrong, somethin' O-cult. Thats what makes that whole bunch sa' high nerved." Earl lectured Stanford awhile, then he got ready to leave.

"You picked her and you had to have her, so you're a' gonna' have to take a' hold and be a man, and keep things right," he said as he climbed in his buggy and drove away.

Stanford was a good man, but he never got finished with his thinkin'. Drusa watched him a' ponderin'. She wondered what was on in his mind here lately, causin' him to stop and stare off into nowhere. She waited, not a' worryin', fer' they was gonna' to have their first baby, and she knowed he was thinkin' of somethin' solemn and good about it. Maybe a fine name.

Finally he told her what he'd been thinkin'.

"Drusa," he said, "I believe you'd better hide your..." he stopped and looked around as though searching for a word. "You're a' gonna' hafta' hide the Sight you and yore' Ma got, away from the chilern' we're a' gonna' have."

He kept talkin' while she smoothed her hand over her belly to pertect' their child from his words. She let the words pass by, not snatchin' them out of the air nor a' spellin' em in her mind like she usually did when he talked. Her own man was sayin' she should hide the Healer's ways passed down to her through her mother's generations.

Her mind flew to Fallon and Mercy. She remembered them tellin' about the time Old Billy Barnes went crazy with his gun, a' shootin' up their place while their men was gone. He didn't git' ta' kill nobody, cause' Mercy got the Sight of it happenin' before it did. They was all hid up on the hill by the time Old Billy come into their yard, a' wavin' his shotgun and a' roarin' at them to come out so he could shoot their devil souls for bewitchin' his woman into leavin' him.

The woman he was hollerin' about was a girl he abducted from some place. He stole her when she was twelve and kept her ever since. Nobody ever went to out to dirty Old Billy's place, and the girl's people had forsaken her. He'd kept her for nigh' on three years when Mercy give her the jar.

Fallon shook her head in disgust at Old Billy Barnes and Mercy shrugged and smirked at her from their hidin' place on up the hill.

"That girl's finally got away from that filthy old bastard!" Fallon heard the joy in Mercy's whispered words. "I got it in my mind to give that poor little girl a clean quart jar with just a little piece of new honeycomb in the bottom. No lid or nothin' to it, and I did it!"

Fallon stared at Mercy. In her minds eye, she watched Mercy waitin' for the stolen girl on the path to one of Old Billy's fields. She watched Mercy step out from the brush and hand the jar ta' the cringin' little thing without speakin' or lettin' on she noticed the ragged girl's bruised, dirty face and warshed out eyes. At the last minute, Mercy pulled the pretty pink ribbon out of own her thick brown hair and tied it around the jar for the little thing. A few days later, Mercy found the clean, empty jar a settin' on a stump out back of their house. There was a big, dead poison spider a' layin' beside it on a little square of white cloth. She knowed it was done, then. The girl was gone.

She knowed Old Billy would show up, for the girl never put the pink ribbon back with the jar. Mercy carried the dead spider in it's little square of cloth up to the old shoemake bush on the side of the hill. She'd buried it under the west side of the bush, way down in the roots to keep old Billy from a' goin' after and findin' the girl agin'. She placed a piece of dried bitter root in the hole with it, to make sure Old Billy got what he deserved.

Old Billy went in their empty house and shot
it up while they hid out on the hill. After he left,
they crept down the hill and went in the house
and looked it over. There was holes in the walls
and things broke all to pieces, but the iron skillet
still set on the stove. They all pitched in and
cleaned ever' thing up. They knowed Old Billy
would think their men would come home and
find out what he'd done, so there was no danger
of him ambushin' them agin' at their house. He'd
hide out for awhile, afraid their men would come
after him.

By the time the men got home, they'd covered
the shotgun holes in the walls with tacked up
pictures from the Sears and Roebuck catalogue
and was a' fryin' cornbread and fatback and a'
hummin'.

Old Billy left home ta' find the girl and git' her
back, but nobody' ever heard or seen from him
agin'. Only two women ever knew that he
stunbled over a shoemake root when taking a
short cut home, and fell into an old dry well
nobody ever went near over on a corner of Deck
Parson's land. He'd wailed and cried and cursed
and died and not one soul ever knew the
difference. Only the three of them knew what
happened.

Drusa brought her mind back to Stanford's
words. He was still a' talkin'. She sighed. Her
heart cast itself low in her chest, searchin' fer' a
deep hidin' place while his words kept tumblin'
and tryin' ta' swirl around her. She found it. The
rest of whatever he said didn't matter any more.

She looked in his eyes, pressed her mouth together, nodded, and turned away.

She couldn't have a baby with a strike agin' it, jist' like he said. Stanford watched her walk away. He knowed somethin' was forever taken from him, and it was true. He started to go after her and take it all back, but his father's words sprung into his mind. He stopped and mashed his mouth down on his true feelin's, and turned away.

Drusa went to the kitchen and stood in front of the stove. She looked down at her long, spare hands. He was right. But she would never give up being a Healer. The Healer would have ta' live alone in the woods, away from him. So she hid her "Sight" from then on, and never shared her knowings with the church or him, until the people around believed she had forsaken the old, sinful, odd ways that kept her family from fully embracing their God.

But while all that was goin' on, they were still young. They held hands and laughed when no one was around. He took her hand in his and bowed over it, and kissed her hand and pressed it to his chest right in front of people.

Then the babies started comin', and they were called on to set righteous examples in the raisin' of 'em. They were too busy makin' what little livin' they could ta' tarry along the way. But ever once in a while, Stanford come in and set down with Drusa. He took her busy, hard workin', long, thin hands in his own long, thin hands and rubbed them and smiled his wide smile at her, and their love went on, runnin' like a stream, over a few rocks here and there, down through time.

Drusa left the Healer's ways of herself, her mother, and her grandmothers Fallon and Mercy behind and raised her children. Not a one of 'em had the Sight. Jist' about the time they were growed up and gone, ever one married and proper actin' and church goin', jist' when Drusa was feelin' all dried up inside with only husks of her old self left, along come little Thursta.

When Drusa looked down at the baby in her arms, her last child, she already knowed her name. A peculiar thrill run through her. She heard a drummin' sound, the likes of which she hadn't heard since she was a girl. She heard the faraway shouts of her grandmother's people and the sounds of their big, bare feet a' daincin' on the Earth.

Thursta seemed to hear and claim the sounds too, for she looked up at Drusa and smiled. Drusa stared down into ancient baby eyes that would turn hazel, green and gold, with little bits of brown lookin' like leaves floatin' in 'em, like water in a round pool, like heaven on Earth.

"Her name is Thursta," she said to Stanford.

"Never heard it before, but it sounds okay ta' me," he said, putting his seal of approval on it.

Chapter 4. The Healers Sight

Thursta first saw glimpses of her mother's
Sight when they stood together in the garden and
Drusa sniffed the air and spoke low to her, so no
one else could hear. Her mother "learned" her
things when no one else was around. Drusa
taught her which tree would blossom first, and
what kind of talk the wind was a' havin' and why.
Thursta learned to recognize the waitin' turn of
her mother's head when somethin' or someone
was near, but not in sight yet. She learned the
uses of witch hazel and plants, how to dry them,
how to make poultices from mustard.

The burden of work Drusa once carried alone
was mostly gone, and she could devote extra time
to Thursta. Her countenance and step lightened,
and she found acceptable reasons for her
absences while she carried Thursta all over the
hills and up and down the hollers.

Drusa led her through the ancient, steep, tree
filled green hills, teaching her to see them
through their ancestor's Visions and Words.
Thursta learned that her mountains was full of
Ferns and Mystery. Green Cheer. High and
Hallow-ed, songs of God and Earth a' blowin'
eternal divinations down through the hollers and
into the mountain people. Songs wove into their
souls, carried by the invisible winds and the
prophetic voices of the singers in the little white
churches below the mountains where some kind
of knowin' they didn't understand often come to

the people, and they carried the burden of it into the churches where speaking in the tongues of their Biblical ancestors turned the weight of it into good.

She learned to walk soft through the muckel druin, the layers of leaves and knowin' little bones layin' hid under shade trees. She dug up the black dirt and smelled it, standin' in the ever shadowed woods beside May apples and trillium. She stood in misty valleys, and climbed dry, high, sunlit places on the sides of hills combed with plows for generations. They dug three pronged gensing in the fall, buried the seed pods, twisted the tough stems and hung it from nails in the rafters in the little back room for the roots ta' dry for herbal use.

"All other herbs like a little bit of gensing ta' be with 'em," Drusa instructed her.

"Why?" Thursta asked, willowy and dark haired, young and sure of her world.

"Ta' be their companion," Drusa answered. "Sang' is full a' fire's life and strength; that makes it constant hungry ta' share itself with others. It's a strong companion."

From then on, Thursta always carried a little bit of 'sang with her.

One day Drusa said, "I was married 'fore I had a chaince' to learn ta' distill and make rock rubs and learn more of what my mother knew. And ever body kept a' dyin' off all the time..."

She looked off into the distance, a Healer seein' things, her restless fingers plucking at the rope on the well bucket.

"What'd they die of?"

Drusa caught herself at Thursta's question.

"Oh, the pox and the fever, and ever thing else you kin' think of."

She turned and walked away.

As she grew older and began to understand more, Thursta realized her mother saved this kind of learnin' jist' fer' her. Thursta watched her mother's face soften and her eyes grow wise and full of light when they was alone in the hills. Drusa held Thursta's hand and run with her.

Sometimes, when they was a' settin' under a tree a' restin', Thursta thowed' her arms around her mother's waist. Then scared to death and barely breathin' for the great risk she was takin', she slowly inched her head down on her mother's shoulder. In those rare times, Drusa treated her like she did the hummin' birds. She become still and waited, like she did for them, their roarin' little huntin' song stilled while they set on her open palm in the garden by the hollyhocks.

When the sounds of the wind quit rompin' through the grass and the trees quieted down, Drusa raised her hand and let her long fingers trace their way across Thursta's face, and flow, smooth and quick, through her thick, straight black hair.

Thursta kept her eyes closed, peaceful in knowin' her mother's face would never once turn to look at her. Her mother's eyes would be lookin' straight ahead, out at the Nature in front of the two of them, her eyes full a' green lightnin' and glintin' gold, so Thursta could show the feelin's runnin' across her face without anybody a' shamin' her. Sometimes her heart swelled and

she cried. Her mother never let on. Her mother
had the best manners of anybody in the world.

But Thursta hardly saw any ease in Drusa
around the home place. Drusa taught her
housekeepin’ in a dry, quiet way. Thursta
knowed not to mention what they did. It was
theirs alone, the only time she saw her mother
bein’ easy in life. Sometimes she wondered how
her mother ended up livin’ like she did, tall and
slim, all prim and proper, a’ mindin’ Stanford.
The wonderin’ made her proper sad, but she
didn’t know why.

Drusa knew the time would come when she
would have to turn Thursta over to the rest of the
world for other kinds of learnin’. Thursta wasn’t a
Healer like Mercy or Fallon and didn’t carry the
Sight, so she would never have that knowing,
that instinct to help her. She hoped the learnin’
of Life wouldn’t break her little girl’s heart, and
so she called on the mournin’ doves to watch
over her child.

Chapter 5. Leavin' Nature's Church

As she grew up, the rules Thursta's father and brothers and sister's put on her kept changin' and gettin' stricter. Then her mother broke her heart on purpose. Thusta couldn't believe it. It like to have killed her. Thursta never forgot how it happened. First, Drusa drawed away from her and started pushin' her away. She stared out over Thursta's head instead of bendin' over graceful like so Thursta could look into her deep green eyes and renew herself.

Drusa spent less and less time with Thursta in the hills. She was forced to spend more and more time with her brothers and sisters, a' settin' in the little church at the bottom of the hill. She was bein' weaned from her mother and the unseen ways, and she knowed it and didn't like it one bit. She'd seen it done ta' Ginny the calf and to Toots the runt pig. They'd squalled and bellered for a long time. Now she knowed why they'd cried sa' much- 'cause it hurt sa' bad!

After awhile, losin' the way to learn the secret, holy knowin' of her mother's magic made her sick. Her heart got hot and heavy. Ever day, so she could live though' it, she went to the creek up in the holler and waded in, and set down. She poured handful after handful of cool water over her breast. She trickled and patted the thin water and poured it down the center of her breast through her mournin' fingers ta' take away the ragged edges between her and her mother. They was now apart, one on each side of the other.

Sometimes she laid down in the cool, shady creek and let the shalla' water run over her, and let the talkin' water go on all around her. She listened to the water's words, hopin' it would say somethin' to help, but the water sang its songs and run right on past her. All it told about was bein' restless and where the fish was. She wished it wouldn't keep what it knowed to itself at the wrong times.

She knowed she had to get better or die, and she wasn't goin' to give her mother up, and she wasn't gonna' run away. She laid on the bank, watchin' the patterns of the leaves wavin' above, dapplin' the world around her with movin' lights and shadders'. At night, layin' in her small bed, clear up to the dawn's early call, she could hear the mournin' doves a' cooin' to her. She couldn't understand their words, but at least their sad talk let her know she wasn't' alone.

Weeks went by. The odd pain eased up, and some way or another, there was things she couldn't remember any more. She and Drusa, together or alone, would never walk the old paths again. She set in the water and searched her mind for the unremembered parts of her life while Mercy and Fallon kept unseen watch over her from the creekbank.

The veil Drusa once told her about had been drawn over her so she could stand life as it would be. She knowed it when she went to the creek and set in the water, and found herself a' waitin' on the place in her breast to bleed some more.

But it didn't. It give up. She looked down at her heart, seein' through skin and blood and bone. The edges where it split apart was covered with somethin' like jelly. Tender and pink, almost a clear color. She stared down at the pink edges for awhile. They wept like sores sometimes did, pink fluid drippin' down into somewhere, she didn't know where. Sadness come over her, and she cried for her losses. Now a part of her familiar world would forever remain a stranger to her.

She wandered over to a tree with grass under it and laid down. She was plumb wore out. She put her arm over her face and closed her eyes. Later that day, when Thursta and Drusa were busy in the kitchen, Drusa turned to her and grabbed her shoulders with both hands and looked down into her eyes.

"Don't be sa' fashed over this," Drusa said. Thursta looked up at her, her own wide mouth, so much like Drusa's, tremblin'. "Don't make too much of it. Go on with it."

Drusa's eyes reddened. They filled with silent tears as her hands swiftly picked their way across Thursta's high cheekbones and around her eyes. She flung somethin' away before she turned to go draw water from the well.

Thursta watched her leave. Somethin' was gone. Somethin' was finished. She felt the sadness of it in her soul. She stood swayin' on the worn lineoleum kitchen floor in the little white clapboard house perched up on the side of the hill.

After awhile she stepped out the back door. Drusa stood by the well with the empty water bucket. She turned her back to Thursta. Thursta looked at her, and knowed her mother was a' cryin'. She sighed. This partin' was hurtin' both of them sa' bad!

Thursta looked past Drusa and out to the future. She walked past her mother and stopped, so Drusa could see she was a' doin' well. She looked at the garden and nodded. It spread out from close ta' the well. That way, they could carry water to it, easy.

Her eyes roved over the hollyhocks rimmin' the back fence of the garden, and she drawed the smell in. All summer long they'd be thick with hummin' birds. Henrietta, her best friend, and the rest of the girls would run the hills, a' pickin' tiny wild strawberries and eatin' 'em. They'd stand under the railroad trestle while the train rattled across the rails on the high wood bridge above them, and not tell a soul about it. The apple trees would blossom, an' the wrens and bluejays would stay busy like always. Some things passed, and some things was for always. It would have to be enough.

Her eyes traveled up the hill to the cane patch. When the tall, tough stalks started to turn yella' in the fall, the men would cut the stalks off a foot from the ground and run 'em through the mill press. The light brown juice from the mashin' would pour down into the big, flat metal pan beneath the press.

She'd watch the men turn the big crank on the press. She'd watch the women skim the foam off of the cane juice and pour it in the pots hung over the fire to boil down into cane syrup. The mashed up cane stalks would be fed to the mules and cows, with some left over for the chickens to pick at. The mule's was bad to hang their heads over the fence and bawl for more mashed stalks for a week or two after the sugarin' was done.

She turned her head and studied the way the wind. It was ripplin' the grass beyond the cane patch. It was callin' to her. Up there, in the cool quiet, was her creek. She would go to it and bathe in it, and let it wash away the rest of her hurt in the Blood of the Lamb, Amen. She started up the hill, doing a little hop, skip and jump ever now and then to make her waitin', watchin' mother feel better.

She wasn't' at the creek long when she heard a new sound on the wind. She follered it over the ridge. She walked easy, knowin' nobody would bother her on her father's land. She kept a lookout for copperheads, for her mother had explained how they could charm ye' and mesmerize ye', so you'd let 'em come right up and bite ye'.

In a little core of wild grass under a tree was three young, brown wrens in a fallen nest, a' hollerin' fer' all they was worth. She reached down into the nest while the birds hollered in fear and flapped against her hand. She felt beneath them and knowed right then what was wrong. The nest had fallen into scrawgrass and the scared baby birds had writhed around 'til their tiny legs and feet got caught in it. Scrawgrass held onto to rabbits and snow in the winter, and birds, and whatever else it could get a' hold of. The more you tried to work it loose, the tighter it got.

She started hummin' to soothe the baby birds. She worked their legs and feet loose, then the nest, then put the nest back up in the tree with them in it. To keep her scent off them, she barely touched them. If her smell was strong on them, their parents wouldn't take 'em back. Being sa' little, and not flyin' yet, they'd surely starve and die if a critter didn't find 'em first.

She hid and watched until the babies and their parents were back together. Then she went back the way she come, tarryin' a little, satisfied and feelin' purty' good. She walked over the hill and strolled to the back of the house. It had to be close to supper time, for she was mighty hungry.

She stopped by the well to warsh up. She sniffed the air. Somethin' shore smelled good! She warshed her hands and face and neck and arms in the warsh pan, usin' the bar of lye soap for cleanin' up after field or garden work. She rinsed her face and dried with the towel hangin' from the metal hook on the side of the well.

She opened the back door and stepped in. The table was set like it was fer' company. It was sa' full of good food, it looked like the middle would cave in! Her mother stood there, smilin' at her, lookin' greatly satisfied.

"Who's a' comin' over?" Thursta asked. "Nobody," Drusa answered easy, still smilin' at her. She stared at the table, her mouth a' waterin'. She was big eater, and she shore' was hungry! Ever thing she liked was on the table. Drusa's special corn cakes made up of cornbread batter, 'cept it had sweet corn and pieces of fried bacon in it, and it was fried in small spoonfuls on top of the stove. She dropped spoonfuls of the batter into hot bacon grease in the iron skillet, turnin' them over when they got brown on one side.

Mashed taters, a big heapin' bowl of 'em settin' on the table, high and white as the snow on Sawyer's Mountain, with rich, yella' butter, fresh from the cow, drippin' down the sides. Golden brown fried chicken was piled high on the white platter they used for company. There was green beans cooked with a slab of salt pork, corn on the cob, sliced tomatoes and cucumbers, and a bowl of milk gravy and big, fluffy biscuits.

Stanford come in about that time. "I cain't believe my eyes! What have you done, woman, cooked ever thing on the place? Who's a comin' over? Maybe I better go to the garden and see if anything's left."

He grinned and made like he was headin' out the back door. Drusa didn't answer him. Stanford shook his head and set down at the table and didn't say any more. Drusa said "Child, set down and eat." Thursta looked at her fer' a minute. Her mother never called her child in front of anybody. They set down and went ta' eatin', payin' no attention to Stanford's talk about how the plowin' was goin'.

Drusa kept on tryin' ta' get Thursta to eat more. Ever time her plate looked close ta' empty, she piled more food on. They kept lookin' at each other and eatin'. Stanford finished eatin' and stood up. He grinned down at the two of them and nodded.

"That's the finest meal I believe I ever had. Don't know why ya' cooked it. But there it was, and I'm grateful fer' it."

He groaned and patted his lean, flat belly and ambled out the door. Drusa ignored him. She grabbed a big spoonful of mashed taters and plopped them down on Thursta's plate. Thursta was so full she hurt, but it was a different kind of hurt than she'd suffered lately. When they couldn't eat one more crumb, they jumped up from the table and rushed around, clearin' it, puttin' ever thing away, not lookin' at each other. They warshed the dishes, and dried 'em. Then Drusa sent Thursta outside while she finished up.

Thursta set on the porch, full and content. She watched the evenin' make its slow, steady fall. The stars come out before she went back in the house. She fell into bed and was asleep before she could turn over. The next mornin' Drusa handed her a packet of food wrapped in a clean cloth before she went up the hill to the creek. She took it without a word, and when she was far away from home and hungry, she opened it and ate cold fried chicken and sweet corn pone, and dipped cool water from the creek to warsh it down.

Chapter 6. Brothers and Sisters

Thursta's brothers and sisters took up where her father left off. They yammered at her all day long, never seein' who she was. They wanted her to be who they wanted her to be. She stayed mad and scared and argued with them. They didn't like it. There was no understandin' of who she was, and most were jealous of her being the baby, a' gittin' sa' much of Drusa's attention.

Samuel, her oldest brother, was tall and well set up. He was a beautiful man, with high cheekbones, flashing black eyes, and black hair. Samuel could strike a pose of ease and high regard any place he went. He knew how to lay things off with his hands. He used them to do his talkin' for him. Samuel knowed he was so handsome he spellbound people. His skin was as reddish brown as a polished acorn, and he thought he was a big shot 'cause he sat on the jury in town.

Jury duty was a permanent position. No woman ever set on the jury. A man got put on it because he had good judgment and a history of always bein' fair minded. Samuel waited it out, and let the people in town talk him into settin' on the jury. The twelve men settin' on the jury tried cases whenever there was one, which wasn't very often. Samuel liked to sign his name in big letters, Samuel Plant, across any "official" papers, but at home, they all called him Acorn.

He didn't like it, but he put up with it, and chose to ignore it.

Thursta's brothers were as different from each other as daylight and dark. Solemn was tall, thin and fair skinned, with straight brown hair and blue eyes. Thursta didn't know him very well because he married before she was born, and moved up into the head of Branch Creek.

When Solemn came to visit, he set on the porch. He wouldn't go in the house. He talked to Stanton while Drusa made a plate of food and carried out to him. He always turned it down, and Thursta watched her mother's mouth droop each time she carried the full plate back in the house. But he always drank a full glass of whatever Drusa stirred up for him. Down to the last drop. Sometimes it was sassafras tea. Solemn liked it best.

Solemn never stayed long, but he always hunted up Thursta if she was around. Before he went home, he'd ask her what she'd been a' doin'. He always listened intently to what she said. Sometimes he laughed. She didn't know why, but she liked makin' him laugh. His smile come on slow, but it was like watchin' the sun break over the hill in the mornin'.

Leon—Onnie—was short and stocky, with big ham hands and feet. He wore his light brown hair in a military cut. He got ever thing done in a hurry. He had a good sense of humor and jist' laughed when people made up stories about how much he could lift. They said one time he picked up a mule and set it out of his way.

Brewster, nicknamed Chance, was chancey. When someone asked him a question or for help, he got sa' nerved up that whoever asked him was a' takin' their chances on him. Chance was tall and gangly and couldn't be still one minute. He was married to a little woman who thought he hung the moon. She was sharp and practical, and he let her manage him, and they lived very well.

Sister Minnie was married before Thursta come along. Nobody saw her very often, for she lived ten miles away. It took a long walk to get up to Grass Creek, the holler she lived up in. Minnie was always kind to her. Thursta liked her smooth face and soft voice. The thing she liked most about Minnie was how she picked out her words slow and with care. That was a gift Thursta didn't have.

Two sisters, Fern and Viney, were best friends. They were married to brothers and lived beside of each other not far from their family home. They run in and out of their mother's house, proud churchgoers and busy, proper women, cacklin' like hens all the time, correctin' ever' body on the home place. Thursta took a leaf from her mother and didn't get mad at them. Drusa and her just watched them and stayed quiet when they rushed in, pecked at them, and then rushed back out.

Sister Wrennie was beautiful, with a child's wide eyes and round face. Her husband Ben thought the world of her. They lived just down the railroad tracks from Drusa and Stanford. Ben took care to overlook Wrennie's faintin' spells and the big shines she sometimes cut, poutin' and a' cryin'. He cooked and cleaned while she wore dark purple and red velvet robes and set in front of her mirror, combin' her waist length black hair, and a' smilin' at him now and then.

Drusa kept back a little sweeting in the cupboard for Wrennie fer' when she come to visit, 'cause Wrennie cried over ever' thing. Nobody could tell what might set her off. A joke might set her off as easy as a tragedy. Drusa told her old time stories to keep her from her constant sorrow.

Brother Johnson and sister Geraldine lived in Ohio. The one room school house had carried them through the eighth grade, then they moved to Lexburgh, finished high school, and ended up livin' and working in Ohio. They come to visit once in awhile, and both of them acted like it was time to leave before they got there. Geraldine sometimes brought her man with her, and he crossed the hills with her brothers, playin' cards and drinkin'. Johnson had a busy little wife who could never come with him because she was always stove up with somethin'.

Ever one of 'em bossed Thursta around and told her time and agin' jist' how her life was supposed to be. They ordered her not ta' run the hills any more. They wanted her to be "devout" during church, and insisted she had a bad habit of lookin' around and not listenin' to the preacher. They wanted her to wear dresses, and not put on the old cast off britches they left at the house for their mother to cut up and make into quilts. She was supposed to wear a smile and be settled all the time, when everybody knowed her feelin's run across her face like water crossin' a creekbed.

Her sisters told her that someday she'd have a husband to mind. They said she had to accept that fact, that she'd come to like it in time. But there was nothin' she liked about most of the men she knew outside her family. They none knowed about the wind and the sun, and how to climb a tree without hurtin' it. She had watched men. They were allowed to be mean whenever they took a notion to, without being called to account for it.

But Stanford was different, milder and always a' jokin'. He didn't like to hunt and he put his boys to doin' it as soon as they could handle a gun. He didn't stand around with other men and talk bad about women or other men. Thursta never saw him ever offer to whip Drusa. People said he was a dry man, one who didn't have much to say about anything, but Thursta knowed he owned a talkin' poet's heart.

She'd run through ever book in school, readin' the books quick, doin' all the work with ease, so they put her to readin' long stories and poetry from borrowed books. That's how she knew the words for what Stanford's heart was like. Gracious and Generous.

The men outside her family made fun men that wasn't like themselves and they held grudges. They tolerated the men who were different from them because it made them feel superior, or they had to put up with them to make their livin'.

But girls and women, that was different. Anything out of the way with them met with a switchin', and more. Thursta's fear kept on a' growin', right along with her mind and body.

Chapter 7. Love Crosses the Mountain

Thursta met Robert Polk when she was fifteen. He was a well set up young man who came over from Hap's Mountain to visit their church. She met him on a Sunday mornin' when the sky was purple and gold on their walk down the hill to the church. She was wearin' a new dark purple dress Drusa had made. The dress was the color of the lilacs bloomin' on the tall bush agin' the side of the porch.

She liked to set in the back of the church with her girlfriends so they could roll their eyes at each other while the preacher hollered on and on about hell fire and brimstone.

Her best friend Hen, short for Henrietta, set beside of her. They were whisperin' about going strawberry pickin' after church when Robert walked in and set down in the pew right across from them. They both stopped talkin' and stared at him. After awhile, he looked across the aisle at her. She looked back and thought, "His eyes are jist' like brown velvet. The dark kind that ya' brush different ways, and ever time the color jist' gets better." She stared into his eyes, not thinkin' about what she was doin', searching for patterns like the little piated rocks in the creek. There was copper and ambeer' a' settin' deep in his eyes. But it wasn't a' waitin'. It was a' restin', calm and sure.

Suddenly she realized what she was doin', jerked her eyes away from his, tucked her head down, and pretended she was readin' her Bible for all it was worth. When church let out, she strolled by him. He was talkin' with some people, his back to her, friendly and a' smilin' and a' shakin' their hands. She stopped and turned back after she got past him. He smelt like angels must smell, she thought. She stepped closer to his back and sighed. He smelt like cloves and gensing and air and woods. Clean and sweet.

She sighed again, and he turned just a little bit, craning his head around. She looked the other way, like she was watchin' fer' someone. He studied her a minute, then he broadened his back, squared his shoulders and stepped his feet farther apart before he turned back to the people he was talkin' to.

She stepped closer and sniffed his back some more, until she saw her mother comin' towards her with a frown on her face. Drusa grabbed her arm and led her out of the church. "What do ye' think you're a' doin?" she scolded.

Robert saw somethin' in her, she didn't know what, and he started crossin' the mountain regular to see her. He was good and kind and calm, and older than she thought. Her parents approved of him because he owned a good business and went to church. Thursta didn't care. She liked the smell of him, and he was taller than her. She was already taller than most of the boys and men she knew. And she was still a' growin'. Her family didn't pay much attention to it, but the other men and boys didn't care much for big women. Whenever she was around, they got meaner, and handled it by sayin' behind her family's back, what a good worker she'd make for a man someday.

Robert visited on Sundays, and they walked down the hill to church with Stanford and Drusa. Thursta liked the smell and feel of him a' settin' beside her. After church they strolled back up the hill to the house. Robert set on the porch with her father while Thursta and her mother made Sunday dinner.

After dinner was over, the men set around and talked farmin'. They traced their generations back in these hills from the time they were settled. When the Sunday dinner leftovers were put away and the dishes done, the women came out on the porch and set in silence near the men for a short time. Then they went back in the house, as was proper.

Robert was allowed to take Thursta for a short walk before he left to cross the mountain back to his home.

"Thursta?" he always asked her, pulling her arm through his while they walked, smoothing his warm, strong fingers across hers. "Have you enjoyed a good week?"

She always nodded and said, "Yes."

Then he always asked her, "What did you do this week?"

She always answered pertly, "Oh, a little of this and a little of that."

He'd grin down at her and ask what she thought of the preacher's sermon. She would turn her head away and roll her eyes up to heaven. Robert just patted her arm.

But one day he grew solemn and said, "Thursta, time will change you and me. These little frolickin' ways will leave us, and we'll take on new ways." She never knew what he meant when he said things like that, but it shore' sounded sad.

Her family planned her future for her without ever askin' her what it was she wanted. Her brothers stayed out of Robert's way, for he didn't drink or gamble, and her sisters dressed in their best and brought their husbands over to meet him. She didn't see any other way out, except to go along with them.

She accepted her fate, but the burden of it made her restless. Robert was a fine catch, but she needed more time. She took to wanderin' the hills and the creeks and standin' under the railroad trestle. Fall set in, and she still felt like a trapped animal. The leaves turned color and fell to the ground.

Čhapter 8.   The Trickster Comes Callin'

Then Bolen come along. He was back home from workin' in the lumber camps in the northwest United States, and he planned on leavin' the hills as fast as he could. But then he saw Thursta walkin' with Robert one Sunday afternoon. He figured the man with her was her boyfriend or husband because her arm was tucked through his. He nodded his head and passed them by without a word. He crossed on over the hill to the moonshine stills hiding place. But he'd already got a good look at her. He thought about her high cheekbones and big, generous mouth. He kept thinkin' about her long, thin legs, and the smooth, easy way she moved her large, tall body, and her black hair. He recognized the trapped look in her hazel eyes and saw the way she pulled away jist' a little bit from the words the man was a' sayin'.

He couldn't get off her off his mind. Lightnin' had struck. He was hasty and high tempered and hot blooded, and he didn't give a damn about the man the girl was with. He only cared if they were married or not. If they wasn't, he wanted her fer' his wife.

He asked around and found out her name was Thursta Plant, that she was spoken for, and goin' to be married soon. That made him mad, but he hid it. He made up his mind he was going to stop it from happenin'.

He took up going to the church she went to so he could meet her and her folks. It cost him most of his patience because he despised church goin'.

Before long, he was acquainted with her parents, actin' like a good feller around them. Then he made friends with her brothers and started runnin' around with them. Then he started droppin' by to visit Stanford and Drusa, slippin' in questions to learn Thursta's habits.

Pretty soon, ever where she was, there he was. He talked all the time. He kept talking. He told her he knew she wadn't gittin' to do anything she wanted to, he knowed she didn't want ta' git' married yet, and he thought she shouldn't have to until she wanted to. He was careful ta' never let her know his true intentions.

Robert was a physical and mental match for Thursta. He was tall and dark and big boned. He was thoughtful and picked out his words, makin' them count.

She didn't like Bolen. She was uneasy around him. His light blue eyes followed her ever where, and she felt the ice in them, but didn't know what it was. Bolen's pale blond hair laid in hard, sharp waves over the top of his head. He was small, mouthy, wiry and quick. Ever' thing she didn't like or know anything about. He was much older than her. She felt slow and stupid around his quickness, and she towered over him. But he was friendly and mild to her, and she started gittin' used to him, for he was always around.

He talked about himself to her, tellin' her only things that would make her think he was a good feller. He said he left his home the first time

when he was fifteen. He come and went as he
pleased, and he was his own boss, and allus'
would be. He intended for it to stay that way, and
someday, when he was ready to marry, his
woman would have those freedoms right along
with him.

He wouldn't tell her anything about his family.
But she'd heard plenty about them. His father
was said to be a quiet little man, and his mother
was said to be the meanest mouthed woman in
the county.

People said Bolen was a loud, mean drunk.
They said his father, Ben Hawks, farmed his land
and was an expert plant and tree man and went
all over the state graftin' people's plants and trees
for them. Grant Hawks, Ben's father, taught Ben
how to do it. Marthy Hawks, Bolen's mother, was
a strong, stocky, opinionated, fiery tempered
woman. She had a big crop of thick blond hair,
icy blue eyes thay stayed wide in permanent
anger, and a mouth so busy it would wear out a
saint's patience. It was told around that ever'
Sunday mornin' she went down the hill to her
church and hollered amen, while the preacher
thundered on about hell fire and damnation. No
one dared cross her. No one liked her.

Ben Hawks was a quiet man. He let her have
her way in ever' thing, but Bolen wouldn't do it.
Marthy prized Bolen above all else. He was her
only son, and she fixed what little carin' she had
for anybody on him. But he stayed away from her
all he could while he was growin' up. He spent
most of his time down the hill at her folk's house
where he could come and go as he pleased. His

nature was such that he slept better outside on the porch with the blue ticks and beagles than he did in the house.

He left home at an early age. People said he was a rollin' stone, mean as hell, and a bad drinker with a mean mouth like his mother. Thursta listened to the talk, but it didn't seem to fit the man she was learnin'.

Robert wasn't around much, and Bolen was, and he was as good to her as his nature would allow. Sometimes a swift feelin' went through her, and she felt like she was being charmed by a copperhead. But the feelin' passed sa' quick, she couldn't hold on to it. And she didn't want to keep that feelin' for long, for Bolen opened up the world to her in way no one else ever had.

He was beginning to seem daring to her. He'd done things the people she knew never even thought about. He'd traveled to different states and worked at all kinds of jobs. He described the places he'd been, makin' them seem bigger and better than they was. After awhile, she started thinkin' he was just a little bit good lookin', with his blue eyes and wavy blond hair. She started tellin' him a few things about her life, and how it stifled her. The words were new, she stumbled over them. She wasn't able to say them to anyone else. He encouraged her to tell him more, and her words poured out like a river. He listened and nodded and acted like he cared.

Then, jist' as winter was startin' ta' set in good, and the first snow fell on the ground, her mother started workin' on her weddin' dress. She was to marry Robert right before Christmas. They would be goin' away for a week on a honeymoon trip, right after the weddin'.

Stanford and Drusa had grown cool to Bolen. They warned Thursta to stay away from him. He knew he didn't have much time left. One day he went to her house while ever body was out of the way. He set down at the table where she was peelin' taters.

"Thursta," he said, in his high, mild voice, "why don't you take a little ride with me sometime? Any time you say. You set the time. We could ride over to the next county and get married real quick. Binnish' they're sa' set on you gittin' married, you may as well marry me."

He waved his arm to indicate her family. "It's the easiest thing you ever done. It only takes a few minutes. Then you wouldn't have to go through with anything you don't want to ever agin'."

He nodded and smiled at her.

"My woman's gonna' be free, like I said. You can be your own boss then. Nobody can order you around. We'll travel to all them places I told you about."

He kept on talkin', weavin' his words with care.

"And if you don't like bein' married, we'll jist' part ways. Either way, nobody'll be able to tell you what to do again!"

She listened while she peeled the taters. He kept talkin'.

"I'd like ta' persuade ye!" he said. Then he dared her to run off with him. He knowed she liked a good dare. He made it sound like a lark they would be goin' on, and they would jist' be friends again after it was over, if that's all she wanted.

Before she could think it through, it was done. One Saturday mornin', she slipped out of the house and met him. They rode across the hills together and were married by the Justice of the Peace on Fall Mountain.

She stayed with him for three days. Then she tried to go back home, but Drusa and Stanford couldn't take her in. The law said the man had all the rights to his woman, and all of them knew it. She'd married him, and now she was his property. Drusa was heartbroken.

"Pray for him to stop the drinkin'. He might be a good man without it," she said sadly.

They were helpless to stop him. Bolen came and got Thursta, and jist' laughed a drunken laugh when she cried, carryin' her belongin's away with her. He took her back to the little cabin up in the holler he had found for them to live in. She was sixteen years old.

Bolen didn't keep a switch like her brothers and the other men did, but he drank ever day and hit her to make her mind. As long as she cooked and kept everything clean, and didn't sass him, he didn't drink sa' much, and he even smiled at her once in awhile. Sometimes he set down and tried to talk to her, but she turned away. He run around with a couple of her brothers and gambled with them. They'd betrayed her. She wouldn't look to any of her family fer' help or friendship again.

Bolen worked hard and played hard. He was used to keepin' what money he made for his self and he liked it that way, but he also liked to live well. He traded for a milk cow and a pig ta' raise for meat, and he put out a little garden. He liked to hunt almost better than he liked drinkin', and he brought home squirrels and rabbits and other game for her ta' clean and cook.

Bolen and some of the other mountain men liked ta' run the hills at night. They liked the dark, and wasn't a bit afraid of it. They moved swift and quiet, dark ghosts travelin' through the hills at night. They left their women and chilern behind, peerin' out through the small circles of light cast into the darkness by the kerosene lamps lightin' their forest homes.

Bolen spent most of his time drinkin' and huntin' and makin' moonshine with his friends. He drank plenty and sold the rest. He hid moonshine in holler stumps and under tree toes. He didn't work a regular job, for there were few jobs in the mountains, and nobody would hire him anyway, fer' he was a bad drinker. He farmed a little, made moonshine, gathered gensing and blood root and sassafras bark with the other men to sell by the pound down at the general store.

It was a hard time in the country, for the Great Depression had set in. Hardly anybody in the mountains had enough money or food. Sometimes one of the desperate men cheated by addin' weight to his herb sack, but he soon got found out.

Bolen allus' started off with plenty, but in no time, he drank it up or traded it away. They lost each place they lived in because of his temper and drinkin' and mouthiness.

Finally they settled down in a cabin up in the head of Crow Holler. The only way to git' up the holler was walkin' or ridin' a horse or a mule. By then, the babies started comin', and the little bit of freedom Thursta gained when he was gone growed less. Her time was took up with tryin' to feed the babies and pertect' them from him and his friends. Her heart ran with unceasing tears, her feet with hard work.

The solace she once sought for her soul had caused her to run off and marry him. She'd made the biggest mistake of her life, and she knowed it. Listenin' to the moonlit creek talkin' and a' runnin' free in the woods was a thing gone forever. And she'd never see her beautiful Robert again, except standing in the love light of her heart and mind forever.

Thursta's Lament

To another I should have wed,
but now I've made my marriage bed,
I've lost my way and turned to clay,
and I cain't go home no more.

The callin' of the mournin' dove,
speaks to me of throwd' away love,
it tells me what I should have known,
and I cain't go home no more.

Now the yearnin's past recall.
all that's left is flesh and bone,
my heart has gone and turned to stone,
I speak to the angels of my love
and I'll never go home no more.

Thursta glanced over at West. He would help Bolen with the drivin'. West was born late summer in the first year they were married. He was tall and thin, with Bolen's light blue eyes and wavy hair. His mouth was like hers, wide and generous, his teeth large and straight and white like hers.

West set by the window, starin' out at nothin' as they moved steadily north. He could set still for hours and never speak a word. He was thinkin', but nobody would ever know what he was thinkin' about. Anybody asked him, he jist' shrugged and said, "Nothin'."

His long fingers moved restless along the rolled down window edge, his fingers sayin' all the things he never did. West was a crack shot, as good a hunter as Bolen was. Bolen had poured the whiskey down him from the time West started walking. Like Bolen, West couldn't stand bein' in the house very long. He was an outdoor man.

Thursta smoothed baby Lucy's hair back. West flashed his fine white teeth at her.

"She'll be rubbed bald by the time we get there, if you keep it up."

Thursta laughed and Bolen smirked at her. They were both secretly delighted any time West joked, for it wasn't very often.

West and Lottie, their first boy and girl, walked and talked in their sleep. West ground his teeth in his sleep ever night and dreamed about huntin' and Lottie dreamed she was holdin' a baby.

Lottie rode in the back of the truck with Emerald. Lottie was tall and slim with fine, thin, blond hair. She stayed nerved up and couldn't help Thursta with anything. "Like brother Chance," Thursta said, ignoring that Lottie's ways might have something to do with Bolen pouring the drink down her too. Emerald, their next girl, leaned against the rickety tailgate of the old truck, watchin' the world passin' by. The miles rolled slowly by on the hot, black topped highway.

Thursta didn't like havin' babies. It was hard on her. Because she was a big woman, people thought birthing ought to be easy for her, but it wasn't. Women in the hills didn't go to doctors when they were havin' babies.

Emerald was born to the rhythm of her mother's fearfully drummin' heart and the rhythm of her scared, painful cries. Aunt Bonnet, who was helpin' and known to be as dry as old sawdust, shook her head and said, "That baby will carry that fearful introduction into this world all her life!"

Bolen was drunk and pacin' around the outside of the house the afternoon Emerald was born. He named the babies. He shook his head gravely at the extra responsibility he carried, now that there was another mouth to feed.

He staggered around, sayin', "Hmm.... Should I name her Penelope? Biscuit? How 'bout Gravy?" He staggered and pointed around him. "Er' Tall Tree or..." he pointed at the dogs, "er' Blue or Dollie?"

One of the women came out the door to fetch more water from the creek.

"Name her after a flare er' a rock er' somethin' ya' damn fool!" she shouted at him.

Bolen stared at her for a minute, then his mind took a whole new direction and he proudly named the new baby Emerald. Then he left to brag to his friends and tie on a week long drunk.

When Emerald was a week old, Old Doc Hall, eighty years old, rode his mule up the creek to make out her birth certificate. He signed the birth date as bein' the same day he showed up. Thursta didn't dare correct him. He stayed until they give him a quart of moonshine and a dressed out chicken. Then he rode back down the creek.

"At least I won't have to contend with Marthy fer' awhile," Thursta thought, as the truck strained along under it's heavy load. She lifted Lucy to her shoulder. "The farther away from her, the better!"

Bolen's mother Martha never stopped bein' mad at her for takin' her boy away from her. The children never counted in Marthy's tongue lashin's. They didn't matter to her. She'd been fury and hell rolled into one voice, loud and hateful, all agin' her. Bolen thought it was funny and jist' laughed about it.

Right after they were married, Bolen announced "I don't plan on stoppin' travelin' jist' 'cause I got married!"

He'd left on his first trip not long after West was born. She didn't know where he was, and Marthy blamed her for his leavin'. Soon he was gone for a month or two at a time.

Bolen and some of the other men who traveled the country durin' the Great Depression left when they pleased and never sent back any word of where they was or any money. He kept right on takin' trips while Thursta and the chilurn' stayed to themselves up in the holler, living on the edge of hunger and isolation. After awhile, they got used to his leavin', and they started makin' little ways of bein' they couldn't have when he was around.

When Bolen got home, he looked for the ways they changed while he was gone. He got in the habit of comin' back mad so he could knock their independence out a' them and make them mind him again.

West, Lottie, Emerald, baby Lucy, Thursta and Bolen rode north in the old truck. None of them knew the world they lived in, the tall green trees and the gray shale rocks, the busy wind blowin' its talk down through the hollers, and the days of wadin' in the cool, singin' creeks on the mountains, was gone forever from them. Gone was the voices of the languages they understood. The holler was as noisy as a big city, if a body cared to listen. The time of known family voices, their people and the way they spoke their words and the old stories they passed on about their kin, their life heritages, told for good or bad in their mountain language, was gone.

They rode north in the old green truck with bald tires a' singin', ragged old tarps tied over the back, holdin' ever thing they owned in place, while the dust of all the roads they would ever travel, lay ahead of 'em...

Never More

High up in the mountains,
rain's a fallin' down,
the flowers and leaves and branchin' trees,
are sighin' with the sound.

Way up in the holler,
the bluebirds flight is gone,
the mournin' doves and flowerin' gloves,
have passed along their song.

The rain runs down the drippin' eaves,
of the empty house below,
it taps the porch with loneliness,
and runs off in a flow,

Inside's a silent cradle,
outside are paths well worn,
where voice and play and light of day,
gave way to night and morn.

No feet will run these rugged hills
Nor hunters range nor stay
The old homestead will crumble ill
til' others find their way

So blessed be the angels,
all cryin' and forlorn,
their babies are all gone away,
they'll see them there no more,

Yes, high up in the mountains,
the folly's played out it's time,
now ever bodys left this place
and it's memories far behind.

Chapter 9. The Wanderers

The Great Depression and World War Two
ended, taking the old ways of being with them.
People all across the country were tryin' to find
new places to settle down and new ways to live.

Thursta and Bolen joined the migration of
southern families traveling north along the
"hillbilly highways" to find work during the late
1940's. Many of the mountain men, like Bolen,
had hoboed around the country. They had turned
their hands to any work they could find, any
place they could find it, to make it through the
hard times.

The men natured like Bolen, left and came
back again and again. Each time they fiercely
claimed their wives and children back. They did
whatever it took to force their families be loyal to
them and to remember their rights while they
were gone, though they never sent home a penny.
The women dared not look to another man while
he was gone, fer' he would likely kill both of 'em
when he got home. He would git' away with it too,
for she was his property by book and unwritten
law.

Other mountain men who hoboed, wrote home
and sent money. The wives and children and
relatives of the men stayed in the mountains,
pickin' gensing, gatherin' blood root and other
plants to sell to the traders in the small towns at
the bottom of the mountains.

Mountain boys learned to hunt at an early age. The women dried or salted down the meat they brought home. During those hard years, poor people wandered all over the country. A steady, small stream of them traveled up into the mountains where Bolen and Thursta lived. They were people sa' hungry they'd lost their pride. They would steal anything the mountain people didn't hide.

During World War Two, the rationin' of sugar, butter and other staples left the mountain people, poor in good times, even less to work with. But they were practical people. They built lean to's up against their houses and hid their pigs and chickens and cows behind the walls. They growed gardens and tobacco allotments behind walls with no roofs on them so the sun could shine down on the crops.

They kept their cows and horses and pigs and chickens inside lean to's at night, and took their dogs and carried guns to guard them in the day when they let them out into the runs.

When the hard times were over, the people took the lean to's and the runs down and spread out again. But by then, another generation or two of children were born, and the mountain people were even more used to keepin' ta' their selves. Tendin' to family and keepin' other people away was a habit born out of survival, a mountain way of life they became used to.

They kept company with who they lived with, and who they went to church with, and they were used to having few friends. They kept their distance and watched the different branches of the families living around them. Over time, each family learned the character and traits of the other families.

The men knew the signs of who'd been through the woods before them and whose family they belonged to. They knowed what each man's character was, and what he would stand for and what he wouldn't.

The women recognized each other's sewin' and cannin', and cookin' and kids. The men hunted, worked, and drank together. The old men hung over checkerboards in the little grocery stores that dotted every corner. The women and kids socialized at church.

When the hard times ended, some men came home to stay. They picked up their lives and went on. Other men who came home, had seen somethin' of the outside world and wanted better jobs and a better livin'.

Many of those men took their wives and children and moved north to find steady work in the car factories. Others followed the vegetable and fruit crops, and became migrant workers.

Some women and children left their mountain homes with broken hearts and draggin' feet, while others went with a lively curiosity about their chances in the outside world. But all of their lives was made harder in new ways, for they were givin' up the nature of the hills and valleys and hollers their generations had adapted to many ages before, and the people who understood their ways.

The Roamer

I'm leavin' home, but I'll be back
I'm headin' down that railroad track
You stay right here, and keep my place
It'll be awhile 'fore you see my face

When I git' blue, I got to go
Down that road, this old hobo
my restless feet, they got to run
along this life til' the day is done.

I know that you'll make out somehow
Jist' feed the hogs and milk the brindle cow
If I end up dead or gone too long
Jist' grow the garden and sang' me a song

Git' you pappy's mule and borro' his plow
I got it all figured out fer' ye' now
So you jist' mind me close and good
do what I say cause' I'll be back some day

They stayed in different places so Bolen, Thursta and West could work the migrant farms to make money to live on. They lived and worked out of the old green truck or stayed in empty shanties they found. They worked while Lottie watched Emerald and baby Lucy. They kept wanderin' north and eventually settled down on a migrant worker's farm.

The migrant worker farm was five miles from the small town of Grant. Their house was one in a cluster of tiny gray houses huddled together in the center of a worn, bare field. A few feet behind each house stood an outhouse. In front of every fourth house stood a water pump. There were no grass or trees or flowers around the houses, just dusty tire tracks worn in deep grooves right up against each house.

The owner saw to it that his worker's didn't pile up old junk sofas or cars around the houses. His workers didn't dare leave anything out in the yard to set on. They were ordered to carry their garbage to the dump over the hill behind the farm.

At one end of the fields stood long metal storage sheds and equipment to work the fields. Onion and mint fields stretched out in three directions as far as the eye could see behind the sheds and the little gray houses.

Chapter 10. The Red Stripe

Ever body climbed out of the truck and poured into the tiny gray house. Emerald climbed over the tailgate and stood in the hot dust, holdin' on to the tailgate. She had to have something to hold on to since all she'd known was gone. She was afraid all the time now. She was used to the truck; it was the only thing that stayed steady in her world. It stayed with her no matter where they went. She rode in it and studied its green paint, dusty fenders and rippled bed as it carried her to new bad things and then away to more.

Her heart pounded with dismay at this new bad place. It was the worst one. Her eyes watered as she sucked in the strong, sour smell of the muck ridin' under the sharp, bitter smell of mint and onions growin' in the fields around the ugly, worn out, tiny gray houses.

None of them stayed in the house. They came right back out and went ta' talkin' with people. Emerald stared at the strangers they were talkin' to. Their mean, dark looks scared her, even though Bolen said he knowed them from back home, and this was the place to come to, a place where he knowed somebody. The men, women, and children reeked of dirty clothes, sour sweat, fear and whiskey. She sensed somethin' worse stood waitin' under the sunshine the hot sun was pourin' over them.

She shuddered with fear at this new darkness suddenly staining their lives. She looked to Thursta for help. Thursta was standin' with the bad people, a' holdin' Lucy pressed to her chest like she didn't want her to see. Thursta's mouth was pressed down into a thin white line. No help there. As usual.

Emerald stared at the ground. She scrubbed her bare feet through the tan dust. The dust felt hot and dry and painful, not cool or comforting. She wanted Thursta to tell Bolen they had to leave this bad place right now, to git' in the truck and move on again, but she knowed better than to say anything. He'd beat Thursta if she did, fer' she looked jist' like Thursta's people.

While ever body was a' talkin' and a' shakin' hands, pretendin' to be laughin', Emerald slipped into the little house to look around. Maybe there was help in it. Somebody had done a little cleanin'. It smelled of failure, fear, Clorox, booze and grease. She wasn't allowed to say the "booze" word in front of Bolen. The livin' room wasn't big enough, and it was too hot to catch her breath in.

She peeked into the tiny kitchen. There was one small winda' and no cupboards, jist' a short wood shelf nailed above an old white two burner stove on legs. The cracked linoleum coverin' the kitchen floor was worn down into a black path runnin' between the chipped white sink settin' crooked on four spindly legs and the cookstove.

Beside the cook stove set an empty cardboard box for wood. Off the kitchen was one tiny bedroom. She climbed the rickety ladder leadin' to the other bedroom up under the roof. She stood in the hot, stuffy little attic and looked at the pointed ceilin', bare rafters, unfinished walls, and the one little winda'. She smelled the tiredness and the whiskey, and felt the desperation of the people that had slept there. The house was too small for all of them, the ugliness lurkin' outside was too dirty. She shuddered to think of how it would be.

She crept down the stairs and went back outside and stood in the hot sunshine, a small, thin shadow pressed up against a wall of the ugly little house. She was afraid some of the bad people might notice her, but they kept right on talkin' to Thursta and Bolen. She knowed they'd git' around to her in time. They knowed it, too.

She listened to the sound of the people's voices comin' from inside the houses. She heard the angry slam of screen doors, and the weary, loud and mean voices of the people outside the ugly little houses. Their voices stabbed at her like sharp knives. She felt the violence the place was steeped in and the complete absence of anything gentle in the bare, crude rawness surrounding her.

Panic welled up in her. The inside of the hot little house repelled her and there were no trees or plants or livin' rocks outside to fix her mind on like there was back home. She longed for the shade of the trees specklin' the creek with reflections of their leaves. She longed for the sweet smell of the wind a' blowin' down the holler and the soothing, cool calls of the mourning doves.

Thursta had taught her to run to them places when Bolen come home with his drunken friends. Where could she go now? She looked around in desperation. There was no goodness to hide behind in this evil place. She pressed up against the wall and walked carefully around the little house, tracin' it's life with her fingertips. Her eyes hunted over the gray walls until she saw the thin line of red paint somebody once painted around each of the little windows. The thin red line was no wider than a pencil mark, as though it was a' hidin'. She sighed with relief and ran her finger along the red line. It stayed bright and happy and didn't seem to be sad about bein' there.

"Somebody put that paint there for somebody like me to see," she said sadly to herself. "Somebody without a tree. Somebody who wants to go back home." She wanted to find whoever had done it and run away with them.

They settled into the little gray house. West slept upstairs and Thursta and Bolen slept in the tiny bedroom downstairs with Lucy. Lottie and Emerald slept on a skimpy pile of clothes in a corner of the kitchen.

The Migrant Field Worker Blues

I got a field sack slung over my shoulder,
two big holes in my thinned down shoes.
I got cold pinto beans on cold corn bread,
and a great big onion or two.
I'm headin' out,
to work in them fields.
I got a wide brimmed hat on my head,
a pair of fresh oiled shears in my sack
I'm headin for the fields this mornin',
It'll be late when I gi't back
Yes, I'm a' headin' out
to work in them fields.

Got sleeves buttoned down agin' the sunshine,
my old shoes are tied up real tight,
ten cents a crate, so' I cain't be late
pick my pay up this Friday nite.
Yeah, gonna' top them onions
in them ol' onion fields.

Walkin' past a line of little gray houses,
I know there's a Bible in each one,
by the porch sets an old rusty car,
waitin' for us men to be done.
Yes, I'm a' settin' out now,
Got a' thing or two to git' done.

My whiskey bottle sets a' waitin',
sourin' in the noon day heat.
hidden in the shade of an old farm tree,
I'll slip in a drank or three.
It'll be sundown fore' this days work is done.

Tell the boss I'm a' comin' right quick,
I got a thing or two to get done.
cause' night falls a'waitin' fer' us fellers,
to ride around and drank some rum
Yes. I'm a' headin' out, to work in them fields.

In the spring the workers carried the onion sets from the sheds to the fields in burlap sacks slung over their shoulders. They got down on their hands and knees and crawled along, planting the sets in neat, straight rows, one at a time in the black, scratchy muck. As the onions grew, the workers weeded and hoed them by hand.

At the end of the short northern summer, the onions were ready to top. Day after day, the workers crawled through long fields of straight green rows with a pair of metal onion shears, dragging a crate or an onion sack behind. They gathered as big a handful of onion tops as they could and pulled them out of the ground. They swung the handful of onions over the crate or bag top and clipped off the tops with the shears. The onions fell in the crate or sack and the workers tossed the tops down on the ground. When the crate or sack was full, the worker hauled it to the truck where the boss marked down a credit on their card and handed them another empty crate or a burlap sack to fill.

The workers planted the mint by hand, but it could not be gathered by hand; the oil in the full grown mint plants was too strong. The owner drove his equipment across the fields collectin' the mint, brought it back to the sheds and dumped it into the back of trucks waitin' to carry it away. Smaller fields of tater's and mater's were worked by hand.

Life settled into a routine. Thursta come in from the onion fields, made water gravy, fried taters and cornbread. They eat beans and biscuits and onions in the mornings. The men and boys eat first, leaving very little if any, for the women and girls. There was never enough, and they stayed hungry 'til Thursta cooked again.

Lottie found a job as a waitress in town. She hated the migrant worker farm. She started spending most of her time away from it, workin', and runnin' around with her new friends in town. Thursta was secretly glad of it, for the farm was a bad place to live.

West had drunk so much all his life, he barely worked or ate. He spent his time ridin' around in old cars with other drunks or passed out on the bed up in the hot little attic room. Bolen and Thursta let him do whatever he wanted. Bolen had started him off on the drink when he could barely walk and he knowed that's why he was in bad shape. They both provided for him without a word of blame to each other about how he got that way.

West volunteered to watch Emerald while they worked the fields. Emerald loved his smile and his beauty, but she was terrified of his mean, crazy spells. She knew he was a busted up human being, that Bolen's the one that done it, and Thursta let him. Mostly she knew they never told him no.

Lucy stayed with an old woman in another little gray house. Lucy never wanted ta' leave the old woman. She cried ever day to stay with the her when Thursta picked her up. It hurt Thursta's feelin's, and she declared, "That old woman ain't got nothin' to do all day 'cept hold her and rock her. She's a' pettin' her to death!" Every mornin' they ordered Emerald to stay in the house and not go outside until they got back.

The Migrant Farm Men's Club

Most of the men on the farm worked hard in the fields and drunk up their paychecks. They made their women work right along side them and used her money to buy food for the week and ta' live on. Late Friday afternoon, the men picked up their wife's and their own paychecks. By dusk, they was drunk and drivin' their old cars in closed, tight circles right up against the houses. They reached out and beat on the thin gray house walls with their fists and laughed at the scared women and kids huddled inside.

The men solemnly admired each other as they took turns drivin' around each house. They passed their whiskey bottles to each other, getting louder and meaner as the night wore on. The women and children stayed trapped inside of the little gray houses. Once in a while the men got into fights with each other. But the real beatings were saved for the women and girls.

Emerald kept her head down when the farm men or boys was around. She stayed as invisible as she could. She couldn't stand the look of burnin' hates and filthy hungers trapped in them. The only peaceful time was early in the mornin' when the air was cool, after the drunks passed out.

The men took their anger out on their families, went to sleep and got up the next mornin' like nothin' happened. They ignored the broken hearts and the broken noses, and the blood it cost their families. They thrived on the fear they had over their families, for it gave power to powerless men.

The Children's Gang

Children of all ages lived on the migrant worker's farm. Most of them stayed sick from neglect, hunger, and lack of cleanliness. They liked it that way. Small children were left alone in their house to fend for themselves. Emerald hid behind the tiny windows of the gray house. She trembled in disgust and fear as she watched the older kids that quit school and wouldn't work wandering around in a gang. They wore filthy clothes, their hair was uncombed, they had snotty noses, bruises from beatings, and sores on their faces and arms from playin' in the black muck.

They quit school at sixteen. Many of them quit school before that and their parents hid them from the truant officers.

They were divided into two gangs by the time they quit school. One bunch quit and worked in the fields. They kept their mouths shut and stayed clean and sober. They hoped hard work and a little money saved up would get them off the farm and into a better life.

The bigger gang stayed angry and dirty and hid out from the truant officers and the law. They wouldn't work, they liked the farm, and no one was gonna' tell them what to do. They sneered at books, school, and cleanliness. All day long they wandered around the little gray houses, fightin' with each other and using foul language. But when the men come in from the fields they disappeared.

Emerald and the other small children learned to stay in their house. The gang of bigger boys and girls waited and watched for them to come out when they needed to use the outhouse. They hurt them, like cats playing with mice. Sometimes they tore off their underwear and laughed at their nakedness. Once in awhile a father got mad about the bruises and blood on his child and went lookin' for the guilty parties.

But the gang always stuck together and said they didn't know a thing about it. If the little kid named them, they called that kid a liar, and took revenge the next time they caught them outside alone.

The men and women who didn't work in the fields stayed in their houses and minded their own business. They shut their doors and their minds and hearts when the gang of big boys and girls got a hold of one of the little ones.

West stayed in the house most of the time, drinkin', nursin' a hangover, or sleepin'. He wanted the house completely quiet. He ignored Emerald unless she made noise. She learned not to make a sound when he slept, or he would tie her hands behind her, thow a blanket over her head, tie it around her neck and stand her behind a door. She stayed quiet and still and away from him, whether he was asleep or awake.

Thursta took to comin' home at noon to see if West had done somethin' to her while she was gone. But Thursta never told him not to do anything to her, and bitterly, Emerald knew why.

West spent his evenin's ridin' in the cars circlin' the houses and drinkin' with Bolen. Then he found a girlfriend on the farm, and she started takin' up most of his time. He spent the days up in the attic bedroom sleepin' while his girlfriend Jan worked the onion fields. On Friday night, she handed him her paycheck and he spent it and stayed away from the house. He grinned and said she wouldn't know what to do with a dime anyway. Emerald didn't care. She was glad. She liked Jan because she kept West away from the house.

Time was square, and Emerald kept bumpin' into it's sharp edges. There was fast time and slow time. Fast time was when Thursta was home. It was listenin' to her voice, knowin' she was there. It meant she had comfort and safety. Not much and not for long, but it was all she had.

Slow time meant West and Bolen comin' in drunk and mean. It meant they might bring their friends in the house, and she would feel the danger in ever place there was in the small world she was trapped in.

She grew practiced at watching Bolen for signs of his quick anger. It was scary enough to hear his loud threats and demands and to see his face red with anger, but when his friends came in the house, she was almost mindless with fear.

The migrant farm made Emerald heartsick. Her spirit started wastin' away. She dreamed constantly of walkin' up to the highway and headin' back home to the green hollers. Her legs became thin sticks as her heart became a shriveled searcher that couldn't find what it needed to survive. She lost her fire and muted down, barely speakin', intent on becomin' ashes. She stopped eatin', but no one noticed.

One day when West was gone, she crawled upstairs into the hot little attic room. She staggered to the tiny bare window. It was closed. Suddenly she couldn't get her breath. She shoved her palms against the window edge, her body tryin' to get air.

A picture of a fish West caught one time flashed into her mind. It was a' gapin' for air, jist' like she was now. Mouth open, she looked up at the blue sky through the little winda'. She just had to get back to the green hills of home and feel the edge of her grandmother's apron in her hand and look up into her calm, green eyes. She wanted to feel the cool wind up in the holler a' runnin' over her in waves. This little house was allus' sa' hot. She never wanted to be alive in this kind of world again. It was time to die, and she was verily glad of it. Amen. That's what her grandma used to say when she really meant somethin'. She slid down to the floor and lay there, staring up at the blue sky outside of the little winda'. Slowly she started dying on purpose.

She left and went some place. A place without sound or pain. There was no purpose in that place. She recognized the wordless concept throughout all of her being, and moved steadily deeper into that place, unafraid.

Then she heard somethin'. It drew her back, stealin' her attention away from the door openin' ahead of her in the distance. The swishin' sound of Grandmother Drusa's skirt and her quick, sharp steps drew Emerald's soul back into the hot little attic room. She'd know that sound anywhere.

She opened her eyes and stared at the tops of her grandmother's pointed black shoes. Her eyes traveled up the tall, bony woman lookin' down at her. They wandered over the wide mouth and high, hilly cheeks with little holes in 'em, 'til she looked into squinty eyes glintin' with green and gold faded lights. Her grandmother's hair was pulled up into the gray knot on top of her head, like always.

She remembered bein' jogged up and down on Drusa's bony lap with her a' smilin' down at her back home in the cabbage rose papered livin' room of her grandparents little house. Drusa's voice allus' sounded like it was comin' from a deep well. Her grandmother was old before she was born. The sounds and smells and look of her oldness started pourin' wisdom and beseechin' kindness into Emerald's soul.

Drusa studied Emerald, then smiled down at her. She knew exactly what Emerald was up to. Hot tears seeped from Emerald's eyes. She felt her grandmother lean over her, her breath a comin' and goin' like a feather across her face.

"Emmy! Listen to me! Nobody wants ya' to die, foolish Little Moon Girl! They want ye' to live! The Gifts of Rudimentation and Sight have been passed on to ye', and it must be carried forward, no matter how hard it might be!"

Her voice became scoldy and stern.

"Emmy! Ye've been called to the ways of the Healer, and there's ones waitin' fer' ye' and nobody else kin' do their healing fer' 'em, so it cain't end now!"

She stopped scoldin' and started croonin'. "The little Lord Jesus is with you ever minute and forever more."

Emerald's tears dried up. She looked up into the most beautiful smile she'd ever seen. It bathed her in light. Drusa stood above her holding a snow white trillium in her hand. Trilliums were Emerald's best flare'. They growed in the shady woods back home. Grandmother Drusa once told her the stars cried at night for their beauty. She drawed in the earthy, cool, damp smell of the trillium and the starched, ironed scent of her grandmother's dress. She knowed it was dried out in the sun on the clothesline back of the little white house she lived in. She drawed in the familiar smell of the leather oil her grandmother used to polish her black shoes.

"Emmy! Let's go home and visit fer' jist' a little while, but you got ta' come back here purty' quick, and stay!"

Drusa's voice grew stern.

"No more of this tryin' ta' die off jist' 'cause life's hard! There's too miny' dependin' on ye' fer' that!"

Emerald reached up for her grandmother's hand and fell into an instant, deep sleep as her soul ran back to its home in the mountains.

With her heart healin', and an infusion of the steady, livin' knowledge flowin' through the sweet air from home around her, she woke up after awhile, crept across the room and down the stairs.

Thursta walked in while she was creepin' down the stairs. Never one for words, she planted her hands on her hips and watched Emerald. She pressed her wide mouth down into a white, thin line and piled some clothes into a corner of the livin' room and ordered Emerald to lay down on them. She draped one of Bolen's old shirts across her and left.

Emerald sniffed the shirt. At first, all she smelled was whiskey and cigarettes, but an underneath, a faint smell growed stronger. She sniffed it in and sighed. The love and remorse Bolen hid from everybody had scented his whiskey sweat and stained it into his shirt. She felt his sadness and his inability to change the wrongs he kept doin'. Maybe it leaked from him like the wound in the side of Jesus leaked in the picture her grandmother had on the wall in her livin' room. She started to cry for him, but a scent of trillium wafted across her, and she fell into a deep sleep. Later that evening, she eat a few pinto beans and a small peice of cornbread.

She felt Thursta watchin' her the next few days. One day, Thursta come in early from the fields. West was off somewhere. Emerald was by herself. Thursta grabbed her hand and rushed her out the door. She run with her to the back of the peppermint field and shoved Emerald down into the mint and dropped down beside of her.

"Shhhhh!" she said, her finger over her lips. She studied the ugly little houses off in the distance. Then she said, "Nobody seen us."

Quick as anything, she grabbed Emerald and rolled her over and over in the mint. Emerald laughed while Thursta rolled her back and forth. The strong mint felt good, like water made out of fire.

"We're gonna' git' them clothes off a' ye' and then we're gonna' rub ye' down with the mint." Thursta announced.

"Ta 'git' rid of all them ugly thoughts and all that bad stuff all a' them bad people on this place has thowed' on ye!"

She pulled Emerald's clothes off until she stood in her underwear. Then she jerked up handfuls of mint and scrubbed her down with it and tossed it away like it had somethin' bad on it. Emerald's heart beat madly in her chest, for Thursta's hands were all over her for the first time since she could remember, and because the fresh mint carried liquid green fire, and, because she believed her mother had finally seen her. At last she heard Thursta's patient question. She didn't know how many times it had been asked.

"Are ye satisfied yet, are we done?"

She nodded, and quick as lightnin', Thursta pulled her over to the little creek behind the mint field. She thowed Emerald's clothes in the water and pulled a bar of soap out of her jeans pocket. Emerald followed the clothes into the water. Thursta soaped and rinsed Emerald, the clothes and herself, even though she was fully dressed. She did it quick, and soon they sat in a grassy spot in the hot sun, dryin' off.

"Whew! Pon' my honor," Thursta said. They both laughed. Emerald looked down at her mother's blue jean cuffs. The cuffs were still wet, but they were neat and evenly rolled up. Thursta knew how to do that. Her mother knew how to make them exactly right, like the thin stripe of red paint around the winda's nobody ever noticed. In a few minutes, their clothes were dry. Thursta pulled Emerald to her feet and rushed her back to the house. Then she hurried back to the onion fields.

Thursta was scared into being mad. She couldn't forget Emerald almost died because of the awful place they lived. The cotton cloth that flour sacks were made of wore like cast iron. Women all over the country washed the empty flour sacks and made dish towels and dish clothes out of them. Them some of the women began buying dyes to color the flower sack material and sewing up pretty, useful things. The flour companies discovered the women were using the sacks to make dresses and curtains and other things. Each flour company started printing tiny stripes and other designs on the plain white sacks, trying to outdo each other for the women's business.

When Thursta had saved enough patterned flour sacks, she borrowed a treadle sewin' machine and made Emerald a new dress. Then she got someone who owned an old Brownie camera to come and take a picture of Emerald in her new dress. Emerald squinted up at the camera, a wide grin on her snub nosed, pointed little face. The bright blue sky and a crop of fresh green peppermint was the background of the picture.

One morning, Thursta took Emerald with her to the onion fields. Emerald was glad to get away from the hot, tired little house. The owners paid ten cents a crate for topped onions. Thursta showed her how to gather the onions tops in her hand, pull the onions out of the ground, hold them over the crate and clip the tops off with a child's pair of onion shears. They got down and crawled along in the black muck, dragging a crate behind them. Emerald liked the strong smell of the onions and the cool breeze that come along once in awhile. She felt safe and useful. She kept thinkin' about the dimes she was earning. Thursta said, "Emerald, you're doin' doin' a good job!"

She worked in the fields the rest of the week, dreamin' of the glass bottle of cold orange pop and the jar of pickled pig's feet she would buy with her dimes. Thursta stood in the pay line on Friday afternoon with Emerald and picked up their pay. Emerald waited for her to give her the dimes she'd earned, but Thursta put all of the money in her pocket.

"Mom! I want my dimes!" Emerald wailed.

"I thought you was a' workin' to help put food on the table!" Thursta scolded her. Emerald started cryin' and turned away. In a minute, Thursta dug in her pocket and pulled out a dime.

"Here's a dime." she said. "That's all you git'." Emerald grabbed the dime. The next mornin', Lottie visited and walked her to town to buy an orange pop.

She liked goin' to the onion fields, and she liked to work. It made the time pass. Sometimes the other women smiled at her. Their smiles gave her a confused, happy feeling. The work kept her protected from the dangers of the house and farm gang, and she got to buy orange pop on Saturday mornin' with her dime. But most of all, she was near Thursta.

Then a day come when the onions were all harvested. The fields lay bare. Most of the farm workers moved on, but Bolen was kept on for the winter at a low pay. His pay was barely enough to cover the house rent and pay for food. All of them were cooped up together in the ugly little gray house for the winter.

The small coal stove sat in the middle of the tiny livin' room floor. The heat it give off was used

up by Bolen and West and their drinkin' pals.
The men slept on the floor by the stove, while
Emerald and Lucy shivered on their pile of rags
in a corner of the kitchen floor. Bolen and
Thursta slept in the little cold bedroom.

Chapter 11. Lottie

A swain can be plain
he's not to blame
it's just a gift, one of thrift
look past it and you'll see
he's just the same.

A few of the women from the farm went to the
town dump ever so often to pick over it, looking
for things to keep. Ever time Lottie come home,
she wanted Thursta to go with her to the dump.
Emerald listened to Lottie tryin' to talk to
Thursta on the way to the dump. "Mom," she'd
say, and laugh. "I made the best soup at the
restaurant the other day."

"Did ye?" Thursta would answer coolly, with
reserve in her voice.

"But it wasn't as good as you ever made on
your worst day," Lottie would say. Thursta would
look proud and not answer.

"My pies ain't much good yet," Lottie said.
Thursta didn't answer.

Emerald watched how Lottie looked at
Thursta while they walked. She always come in
the house a' talkin' away with a big smile, but by
the time they got to the dump, Lottie's smile was
all gone.

They searched through the garbage while
Emerald wandered up and down the hills around
the dump. After awhile, Lottie'd grin at Emerald

and set some trash on fire. That was the only place Lottie could burn something up and not get in trouble. Emerald grinned back at her. Thursta just turned her head away and acted like she didn't see the fire. That was the signal for them to go home.

Lottie's birthday fell right after the leaves turned gold on the trees. Thursta waited 'til Bolen and West was gone someplace before she took out the things she'd hid and baked Lottie a birthday cake. Emerald, Lucy, and Thursta sung Happy Birthday to Lottie. Lottie's wide smile of pure joy flashed at Thursta. In that instant, Emerald saw how very deeply Lottie loved their mother.

Then all that changed. In the middle of the winter, Lottie caught pneumonia. The weather turned cold and ice covered ever thing when she took sick. She come home to Thursta and moaned all the time 'cause she couldn't get her breath.

"I cain't stand this!" Bolen said to Thursta. "Do somethin' with her!"

Thursta watched out the winda' as Bolen's old car slid across the ice and out to the highway. He refused to take Lottie to the doctor before he ran away. She wrapped Lottie up in quilts and carried her five miles through the snow and ice to the little hospital in town. The hospital had half a dozen beds and two doctors, a father and son. They made up a bed for Lottie, and Thursta left her there.

Lottie spent over a month in the little hospital, hovering between life and death. She'd been goin' ta' church with a couple named David and Mary before she got sick. They stayed night and day with her at the hospital. They spelled each other so she'd never be alone. They set by her bed and prayed for her to live.

Thursta walked to the hospital twice the first week Lottie was there, but in a coma, and she couldn't stay 'cause Emerald and Lucy was home alone. Bolen just shook his head and went his way when Thursta told him how worried she was about Lottie.

Thursta ground her teeth and cried when an ice storm blew in and Lucy and Emerald got the mumps. She managed to walk to the hospital when the worst of the blizzard was gone, but they wouldn't let her see Lottie for Thursta had a bad cold. She asked them to tell Lottie she'd been there, and left. Bolen stayed away from home, sayin' he was afraid of gettin' the mumps, he never had them, and he intended on stayin' a man.

The weather kept them iced in. Thursta stood at the stove, makin' water gravy ever day. There was nothin' else. No food, no bread, no beans, jist' flare' and lard, and Bolen and West wouldn't come home and help. The days drug by, and in spite of stayin' cold and hungry, Emerald and Lucy slowly got well.

A month passed before Lottie came out of her coma. Ever time she woke up, Mary or David was settin' in a chair beside her bed prayin'. They smiled and held her hand and fed her what she could eat.

Each day Lottie waited for Thursta to come and see her, for she loved her mother more than anything else in the world. But she never did, so Lottie changed each day Thursta didn't show up. The doctors told Lottie she'd lived through an illness that kept her hoverin' between life and death. They said she was lucky to be alive.

But Thursta never came to see about her and Lottie was forced to believe Thursta didn't love her like she'd always hoped. Actions speak louder than words. Lottie's heart broke. Her devotion to Thursta began ebbing away. Her heart hardened against her mother in hurt self defense.

Thursta didn't see Lottie 'til David and Mary dropped her off. They did their best to talk her into goin' home with them, but she needed Thursta in spite of it all. It was snowin' when Lottie walked in. Thursta turned from the stove and looked at her. She helped Lottie take her new coat off. "My, my! What a purty coat!" she paused, "...and new boots and a hat and a muffler and mittens!"

"There's food in the sack," Lottie finally said, and they went on with their lives. Their stories came out piece by piece to each other, so they could stand it. Thursta stood at the stove, boilin' taters and onions with a scrap of fatback from the grocery sack Lottie brought.

She stirred water into a bowl of cornmeal, then glanced over at Lottie.

"The girls got the mumps, and I caught a bad cold. I walked to town ta' see ya', but they wouldn't let me in, they was afraid you'd catch my cold on top of the trouble you already had. Then I fell down and got hurt."

She stared down at the skillet while Lottie assessed the familiar bruises with her eyes. The smell and sound of the milk gravy bubblin' in the black iron skillet and the sound of her stirrin' went on and on 'til Lottie nodded, acceptin' her words. She would never know if she really fell, or if Bolen beat her up.

"There ain't no damn phone on this farm, so I couldn't call the place ta' see about ye'!" Thursta complained. She bowed her head again over the gravy skillet. Another long silence wore on between them. At last Lottie said. "Well, I shore' missed ye."

Little by little, she told Thursta pieces of what she remembered. She spoke of David and Mary, and how they prayed over her and never left her side. Thursta cried a little with her back turned so Lottie couldn't see her, and praised them silently for doin' what she wanted to do, but couldn't.

They talked in fits and starts, each tryin' hard ta' reach the place they once held with each other. But something had changed that they couldn't get back, and they both knew it. Thursta had disapproved of Lottie too long, and her lengthy illness had made it too late for them to forge the bond of love Lottie needed from her mother. Lottie began to replace Thursta's needs with her own, one at a time, so she could go on livin'. Now she would have to find someone else to love her.

Chapter 12. Movin' On

I hate this place, I'm a' movin' west
Where cowboys live, and Gabby jests
As soon as I turn the tv off
Just watch out world
and I'll be gone.

Thursta hated the migrant farm and the people on it. Spring finally came. She searched desperately and at last found an old run down house standing on a rise in a hayfield. It was off on a side road about three miles from the migrant farm. It had stood empty for many years and never did have electricity in it. Rain and sun and snow had poured through the broken winda's and rotted the floorboards and walls. The roof leaked, and part of it had caved in over the back of the house.

But there were gnarled old trees giving shade around the house. Wild flowers bloomed ever where, and there were woods behind the hay field the house set in.

Thursta studied the old house. No more drunken men in old black cars circlin' right up tight agin' this place ever night, getting madder and madder 'til they jumped out of the cars and stormed into the houses where their children and wives were hidin' in terror of 'em. No women a' screamin' in pain and fear, no cussin' and slammin' doors, or gangs to hurt her kids.

She planned it out. She could walk the three miles to the migrant farm to work the fields.

"I kin' use kerosene lamps fer' light and heat the house with that little wood stove them people give me when it gits' ta' be winter," she explained eagerly to Bolen.

"The stove kin' set in the middle of the livin' room floor, and I kin' nail up blankets over the walls. That way, the heat'll stay in, and the cold'll stay out. We kin' chop wood for the stove from the trees in the woods behind the house. We kin' fix the stair steps and roof as we go along. We lived without them things before, back up in the hollers. We could do it again, easy."

She stayed desperate. She would do whatever it took to get away from the migrant worker farm. She kept on talkin' to Bolen, tryin' to persuade him to move to the old house. But Bolen liked being contrary. He said he liked the way things were on the farm, and he twisted her arm and slapped her and ordered her to shut up. But Thursta kept on a' standin' up to him.

It was comin' on ta' late summer when he figured she'd paid enough so they could move into the old house. She was black and blue by then, and her broken collarbone was mendin'. Bolen griped and complained and hit her constantly, but that was no more than she expected him to do 'cause she stood up to him and he let her have her way.

Bolen and West wouldn't stay at the old house. They laid out at the migrant farm. They left Thursta to work on it and to figure out how they were gonna' live and eat. The little bit of money Bolen gave her for food trickled down to almost nothin'. Ever body except Bolen and West went hungry. They drunk their whiskey and rode around together and bought themselves food. Neither one of them could eat much 'cause of the drink. Sometimes they brought home jars of pickled pig hocks or orange sodas and tossed 'em out the car windas' and laughed and drove away.

Emerald didn't care what they did. She could breathe again. It was warm outside and there were trees everywhere. There were bushes and woods to explore and hide in, like there was back home. It was safe to be alive again. She could step out the back door and walk to the outhouse without fear.

There were white snowball bushes on each side of the back steps. She set on the back steps and talked to them and felt their cool petals and smelled them. The feelin' of being a trapped animal abated as she explored the fields and the dusty road in front of the house.

The thing she liked best was bein' able ta' see' who was comin' down the road before they turned onto the path through the field and up to the house. She saw them long before they got there. She could hear and see Bolen and West before they got home. She had time to hide somewhere outside, away from them and their drunken friends.

She watched Thursta pacin' the outside of the house, sniffin' the air like she was pleased with somethin'.

But a few weeks into summer, somethin' else went ta' botherin' Thursta. Emerald followed her around, tryin' to figure it out.

Thusta finally make up her mind to somethin'. Emerald and Lucy filed into the kichen and watched her pull out the flour sack, bakin' powder and salt and set them on the table. Then she herded them out the door and they headed for town. They set on the scrolled stone bench in the town square to wait while Thursta went in the grocery store. She came back out carryin' a brown grocery sack. She went down the street and into the restaurant where Lottie worked. In a few minutes she came back out carryin' the grocery sack and a flat, snow white piece of cardboard. They went home, carryin' the cardboard, the sack of groceries, and Lucy.

They watched her set the sack down and start a fire in the cookstove. She fed the stove pieces of kindlin' until it was burnin' steady. The kitchen got hotter and hotter. She propped the back door open with the broom.

"I'm a' bakin' my mother a birthday cake," she announced importantly to them.

"When it's done, we're gonna' take it to the post office, and mail it ta' her!"

She took the groceries out of the brown sack and lined them up on the table. A little bag of pure white sugar, a small square of snow white lard, a little brown bottle, and a can of evaporated milk. They'd never tasted cake, or seen one baked. They watched Thursta open the lard carefully and grease the round biscuit pan. They watched her sift flour, salt, sugar, shortenin' and bakin' powder together and set it aside. She broke eggs into a bowl, poured the evaporated milk in, then whipped them into a froth. Emerald watched her pour the eggs and cream into the flour mix and beat it all together. When she was done, she set the bowl down and opened the small brown bottle.

"Ooohh!" Emerald exclaimed. "It smells sa' good! What is it?"

"Vanilla," Thursta announced proudly, pouring some into the batter and stirring it. They swayed with the delightful smell of vanilla while she poured the batter into the greased pan and put it in the hot oven to bake.

After the table was cleared, Thursta grabbed a bowl and handed it to 'em.

"Go out back and pick me some a' them blackberries!"

They raced out the door and came back quickly with a bowl of ripe berries. She warshed the berries and wrapped them in a clean cloth. She squeezed the purple juice out of them into a clean bowl before she took the golden brown cake out of the oven and set it aside to cool. While the cake cooled, she beat lard and sugar into a stiff frosting. Then she divided the frosting into two bowls and colored one part purple with the berry juice and left the other one white. She smoothed the white frosting over the top and down the sides of the cake. Then she made a funnel out of a piece of clean white sheet, spooned the purple frosting into it, and squeezed out purple flowers on top of the white frosting. When she was done, she handed them the bowls and the spoon to lick. The cake was beautiful, the kitchen filled with heat and magic.

"Grandma Drusa's birthday cake!" they chorused. Thursta boxed up the cake. She took the little stub of pencil from its hidin' place, found an old envelope and tore it open. She scratched out a few words on it, folded the envelope, placed it under the cake plate in the box, and closed the lid. She laughed in little bits and pieces while they walked back to town, carryin' the cake. Emerald carried Lucy.

"Mother's birthday's is jist' a week away. The cake should git' there right on time for her ta' eat it on her special day!"

She laughed and said, "This is what Mom'll do." She pretended like she'd jist' got the box in the mail. "What's this?" she asked with big eyes. She made motions like she was openin' the box. Her eyes widened in surprise, and a big smile poured over her face. Then she wiped her eyes.

"If I was back home, she'd thow her arms around me, and hug me to her breast, fer' I'm still and always will be her own youngest. I know that's what she would do!"

But the man in the post office said he couldn't mail the box.

"You can't send perishable food through the mail, and besides, it's not in a good, strong box or taped up, either."

He tried to hand the cake box back to Thursta. She gave him a hard look.

"You mail it! I don't care how you have to do it. It's for my mother's birthday, and she will have it!"

The man studied her for a minute. Then, quick as could be, he found a sturdy brown box and announced "That'll be an extra quarter." She nodded. He placed the bakery box with the cake in it inside the brown box, packed newspaper around the bakery box, and taped it shut. When he was done, he shook his head at her and warned her.

"It'll probably be all smashed up by the time it gets there."

She didn't answer. She wrote the address on the box with a pencil, paid him and stalked out of the post office, her head held high. On the way home, she sung a couple church songs she'd learned back in the hills when she was a girl.

After a long wait, a letter arrived from her mother. Emerald watched her open it, a daughter waitin' for a mother's love to thow' it's arms around her, using words. But Drusa's mind was on the coal miner's disaster that happened earlier in the month. In the last part of her letter, she complained about the cake. She said she didn't know what it was. She didn't mention the letter Thursta wrote.

Thursta cried. Then she got mad. She wadded up the letter and thowed it away. She went outside and stood in the yard, looking' south, until her yearnin' ta' be warm and young and pure again stopped, and started fadin' away once more.

Chapter 13. Dark Days

Thursta ran out of bakin' powder. She gathered Emerald and Lucy up from their play and they walked to town to buy more. The day was warm and sunny. They dawdled along under the shade trees. At the end of their road they turned left and strolled out to the blacktopped highway runnin' past the migrant worker farm. They took the grassy path runnin' alongside the blacktop. The path wandered around bushes and up over a small hill and down under trees. Ever body from the farm used it to walk to town.

They were crossin' a small hill when Thursta heard a man's voice holler at her from the road. A carload of the new bums Bolen had started runnin' around with was drivin' by. Thursta turned her head away from them, disgust written on her face. The car turned around and drove by again and the men in it made like they was goin' ta' stop.

Thursta ignored them, but she grabbed Lucy away from Emerald, and walked faster. Emerald had to run to keep up with her. The men were pleased to see she was scared. They started laughin' at her. The car followed her, the men in it hollerin' dirty names and ugly threats. Thursta turned back towards home and started runnin'. The men's voices faded as she turned the last corner and their old house up in the field came in sight. She stopped, bent over, breathed hard in and out for a minute, then took off for home agin'.

"Them bad men are sich' fools, they might take it in their heads ta' come back'!"

Emerald recognized the carload of nasty men. Bolen didn't generally run around with them. He'd brought 'em home with him a couple of weeks ago, though. Her skin had crawled when stupid Bolen let them in the door. She'd felt faint from the evil stench they carried. But as usual, stupid, drunken Bolen didn't notice a thing.

Thursta had gone as white as a sheet. They'd looked at each other, filled with foreboding. The forebodin' they'd both felt that day, was back.

Life was forcin' Emerald to learn about different kinds a' beatin's. Women and kids bent over, black and blue, shufflin' along, heads bowed, not lookin' at anyone. Shamed and a' hurtin', the man who done it proud and a' darin' anyone to speak agin' what he had done.

A kid on the migrant worker farm a' wantin' to go to school, the bus passin' by, his family laughin' at the lost look on his face for losin' his chance. The nasty names people called her sister Lottie was a beatin'.

She shrugged the thoughts away with her thin shoulders and hurried on. Too many kinds ta' count, and they might kill her if she kept on.

They hurried to the house. Thursta loaded the shotgun and ordered her to take Lucy and hide out in the woods back of the field. Emerald set on the back steps between the snowball bushes with Lucy, rocking back and forth, torn between wantin' ta' stand by Thursta, and a' mindin' her.

After awhile, she took Lucy's hand and wandered across the back yard to the edge of the field. She hunted out a hidin' place in the tall grass, and sank down in it with Lucy.

There wasn't a noise on the place for a long time. Then she heard Bolen's car drive in and stop. A car drove in behind him. She listened to the car doors slam, and heard the voices of the men who had chased them, laughin' and cocky. She listened ta' 'em go in the house. Lucy stood up and looked at her with big eyes. She pushed Lucy back down into their hidin' place.

"Ya' stay right here and wait fer' me, or I'll whip ya' when I come back!"

Lucy started to laugh at Emerald, but Emerald knew what would scare Lucy.

"The boogyman will come out of yon' trees and steal ya', if you don't stay as still as mouse right here." Lucy's mouth quivered. She hid her face in the grass.

Emerald slipped up to the house and peeped through the kitchen door. Bolen and the bad men were settin' at the kitchen table, drinkin' and smokin' and laughin'. Thursta stood at the sink with her back to them, peelin' taters and makin' coffee. She'd put on a clean pair of blue jeans with the cuffs evenly rolled up, and a clean work shirt. She looked clean and white and frozen, like the people Grandma Drusa took Emerald to see in the funeral parlor.

She opened the screen door, walked through the kitchen and stood by Thursta. Thursta glanced down at her, then went back to peelin' taters. The kitchen was hot with the stink of the dirty, drunken men. The coffee was on the stove, percolatin'. Emerald turned her head sideways and stared at the five men settin' at the table. The men was watchin' her and Thursta with hot, avid eyes. What they knowed that Bolen didn't, was makin' them laugh at ever thing he said. Bolen was rared' back in his chair. He thought they was laughin' at what he was sayin', and he talked faster and drank faster from his whiskey bottle.

Emerald glared at him. She felt such contempt come over her that Thursta had to nudge her with her elbow. Just about that time, Thursta poured the hot, fresh coffee into cups. Emerald sniffed. She didn't like coffee, but she knew the exact smell. This coffee smelled funny, different. It smelled rich and fruity in the humid kitchen. Thursta turned back to the stove and set the pot down. Then she poured Bolen a cup from a hot pan on the back of the stove, shieldin' her actions with her body. She put more wood in the stove and give Emerald a long look, then jerked her head at the garbage can in the corner. Emerald strolled casually to the sink and picked up a handful of tater' peelin's and carried 'em to the garbage can.

She stared down at the empty bottle of Fletcher's Castoria Soothing Laxative Relief and covered it with the tater peelin's. The men drunk the hot coffee right down and Thursta poured more. Then she put the skillet on the stove and the aroma of sliced taters filled the kitchen. Next she pulled out their last skinny strip of bacon and carelessly and expertly sliced it, pretendin' the men weren't watchin' her with hungry eyes. Emerald knew it was the time of day they liked to eat when they was drinkin'.

Nobody ever had any extry' meat to share. They all hoarded it for their own families. But these drunks was glad ta' eat somebody else's. Bolen kept on actin' like a big shot, braggin' on the meal they would all be eatin' in a few minutes. Thursta put the bacon in another skillet ta' fry, and refilled their coffee cups. She set the coffee pot back on the stove and went ta' makin' biscuits. The men set there, talkin' loud, waitin' for the food to git' ready.

Jist' about the time the taters, bacon and biscuits was almost done, the men's guts started gurglin'. The sound was sa' loud Bolen stopped braggin' and stared at them.

"What the hell?!"

Their guts groaned louder. Two of the men grabbed their bellies and started groanin'.

"What the hell's the matter with ye'?" Bolen hollered.

Thursta kept her back to them. Calmly, she took the golden brown biscuits out of the oven. She took the crisp, succulent bacon out of the skillet and began makin' milk gravy while they watched, guts gurglin' and groanin'. They was sa' close ta' eatin!' The house smelled wonderful. Emerald was droolin' in spite of her fear. Bolen puffed up with pride and hollered at the men.

"Set down! Ya' all eat a bite. It'll be ready in a minute."

He shot Thursta a stern look. She looked back at him innocently as the men collectively rose from the table like a swarm of bees and run out the door towards the outhouse. The screen door slammed behind them. Bolen stared after them.

"Well, I'll be damned!"

He jumped up and ran out the door after them, wavin' his whiskey bottle and shoutin' at them to come back. Thursta grabbed the empty bottle out of the garbage can and shoved it in Emerald's hand.

"Git it gone right now," she said under her breath. Emerald ran out the back door and past Lucy's hidin' place. Lucy jumped up and ran after her. When she reached the edge of the woods, she threw the little brown bottle as far as she could into the woods. The men jumped in their cars and took off in a hurry.

Bolen munched golden biscuits topped with milk gravy, slices of crisp fatback and crunchy fried taters', wonderin' out loud where his drinkin' buddies got the runs from.

"Why, they couldn't none eat a bite."

He shook his head mournfully back and forth, like it bothered him that they didn't eat all their food up, knowin' and not willin' to let on that he knowed Thursta used up the last of their scant food to make the feast before them.

"Must a' bin' somethin' they drunk."

Emerald offered innocently. Thursta shot her a warnin' look. Bolen didn't notice. He speculated on the kinds of whiskey they drank. He couldn't figure out why he didn't git' the runs, too. Thursta interrupted him and offered him more coffee. He nodded his head yes, off ruminatin' somewhere in a deep alcoholic fog. This time she poured it straight from the coffee pot into his cup. The fruity smell filled the air. Emerald didn't dare look at Thursta, or she would have busted out laughin'.

A few days later, the bad men come home with Bolen again. Thursta started the coffee pot without a word. Somebody had left some Dexlox, Designed to Make You Relax and Let Go in the cupboard. Thursta poured the coffee, and soon the men run out the door agin'. Bolen told Thursta she better check the well water and see if somethin' was wrong with it.

In a few days, the men come back again. This time Thursta set a box of D-Con rat poison on the counter, right where they couldn't help but see it. Bolen asked her what the rat poison box was a' doin' on the counter, and she said she needed it to kill some rats that had got into the kitchen.

He accepted her explanation without question, but her challenge made the men mad. They took to pullin' in the driveway and settin' when Bolen was gone, actin' like they were waitin' for him. Each time the men pulled in, Thursta shooed Emerald and Lucy out the back door and ordered them to hide until the men left. Sometimes she hid with them.

Emerald asked her, "Why don't you tell Bolen on them?" Thursta glared at her like she was stupid.

"He'd kill me first, and then them."

"But you didn't do anything!" Thursta nodded her head with finality.

"That's whad'd happen, fer' shore'."

Emerald thought a while, then nodded. Ye' didn't have ta' be a bad woman ta' get in trouble with men.

Thursta run out of beans and flour. Bolen wouldn't drive her to the store. "What's the matter with yore' legs? They broke or somethin'? Yer' a' gittin' lazy!"

She didn't answer. After he left the next mornin', she put on clean blue jeans, rolled the cuffs up, and put on an old blue workshirt. Then she shooed Emerald and Lucy out the back door and ordered them ta' hide 'til she got back from town. They watched her edge along the side of the field and then out of sight from their hiding place. A long time passed.

Then Flint's old car pulled into the driveway. Their cousin Flint was Thursta's brother Leon's son. Thursta and Lottie were in the back seat. West was in the front with Flint. Ever body got out and reached into the trunk of the car. They pulled out a couple a' shotguns and two rifles and carried 'em in the house. Emerald raced in the door. "What ya' doin?"

They all turned to her at once and shouted.

"Don't you say one word about the guns to Bolen or anybody else! You hear us?"

She backed up, hands up in front of her.

"All right! Ya' gonna' kill somebody with 'em?" she asked hopefully. They ignored her question and hid the guns while she hugged Flint.

"Flint Plant, are ye' stayin' awhile this time?" she asked him, hopefully. Flint grinned down at her. He was tall and lanky, like grandfather Stanford. He'd been best friends with West back in the hills, and he missed West, so he moved north at the start of summer. But they'd gone their own ways over West's drinkin'. Flint hated the farm as much as Thursta did. Flint was ambitious. He wanted to get ahead in life and own a good car and a house. After a few days on the farm, Flint left to work in the fruit orchards in the west part of the state. They didn't see much of him, just a weekend here and there. When he come home, he stayed with Thursta and Bolen.

Bolen and West behaved when Flint was around. They knew his high temper. He wouldn't put up with any wrongdoin' or beatin's a goin' on with kids or women or stuff like the bad men comin' in and drinkin' in their house. They could stay drunk out in their cars where nobody give a damn, where they wasn't able ta' bother any body or eat up ever thing on somebody elses place, leavin' the women and kids ta' starve. Not while he was around. Emerald and Thursta loved him the best of all the men they knew.

In the next few days, the work on the migrant farm ran out. The onions and mint crops were harvested. The farm owners let Bolen and the other workers go for the winter. West moved in with his girlfriend on the farm, so Bolen lost both his job and his drinkin' buddy. He pouted up and left town without a word. He left Thursta with no money to buy food or pay rent. In a few days, the last of their food ran out.

Flint drove into the yard and got out of his car. It was Friday night. He was down for the weekend from the orchards, and planned to run around with West and Lottie. He got out of his old car and went to the trunk. He opened it and set out two bushels of ripe peaches. Emerald and Lucy ran to the peaches and started eatin'. Flint watched them a minute and shook his head. Then he went in the house.

Flint was ornery natured, but he was still their hero. Thursta counted on Flint when he was around, even though his tongue was like a surgeons knife, his words often making her flinch.

Peach juice run down Emerald's chin as she listened to Flint's sharp, chastisin' voice and Thursta's apologetic one. She heard Flint say, "It's jist' as well Bolen's gone. You're better off without him."

Flint carried the peaches in the house, then he went to town and come back with Lottie. They brought food. Bologna, bread and milk. Taters. Flour, salt, lard and bakin' powder.

Flint cleaned up and went to find West. Thursta figured they wouldn't see him 'til late Saturday night. On Sunday, she'd feed him her best before he went back to the fruit orchards.

Not long after Flint left, a carload of the bad men turned into the driveway and rolled to a stop. One of them shouted out his winda'.

"Yer' old man's gone now!"

The men laughed, opened their car doors and started to get out. Thursta ordered Emerald to run ta' the woods with Lucy before she eased the barrel of a shotgun through a livin' room winda'. "Boom!" went the shotgun. Gravel scattered at their feet. They jumped back in the car and tore out of the driveway, shoutin' threats at her.

Early the next afternoon more cars turned into the driveway again, the men in them enraged, shoutin' filthy words. Out stepped West, Flint, Lottie and Thursta onto the front porch. From her hidin' place, Emerald heard the screen door slam, then the sounds of shouts and shots. The bad men's old cars tore out of the driveway, leavin' no threats lingerin' behind in the air.

"I don't reckon they'll be back after that!" Flint said. "If they do, we'll git' 'em!"

They'd been very careful where they aimed so they didn't hit any of the men, or anything that would keep their old cars from runnin' so they could make a getaway. Flint came home the next weekend to check on things.

"They drove by twice, but didn't pull in," Thursta told him. Flint frowned, got in his car and left. He pulled into the driveway early the next afternoon. Thursta met him at the door.

"Ever thing okay?" she asked nervously. Flint nodded his head and spoke mild, like he was sharin' the latest gossip.

"I heard last night that some a' them no good sorry excuses for men are mad about their cars, 'cause fer' some reason, they won't run. They cain't' go nowhere in 'em. And none of them no account bastards can remember any thing they been doin' wrong. Drinkin' kin' cause a man ta' lose his memory jist' like that!" he announced woefully, snapping his fingers.

"Too bad, ain't it?"

Thursta looked around. "What'd ya' do to 'em?"

"I guess somebody might a' put a little somethin' in their gas tanks, but they'll never know about it."

He shook his head in mock sadness.

"Nobody knows what happened. They jist' know their cars won't run. And they shore' cain't' go no where with a car not runnin'. That means the sorry bastards cain't' drive into a body's driveway, cause' their car won't run ta' git' there. Or go up and down a road where they know an unpertected' woman lives without her man, cause' their cars won't run."

Thursta laughed in admiration. He grinned at her and she grinned back. "What ya' want ta' eat? Anything I got on the place is yours!"

Chapter 14. School Days and New Love

Lottie was still waitressin' at the restaurant and livin' in the little back room. She planned it all out. She'd live at the house and go to school and work at the restaurant weekends and summers. When summer came, she'd move back into the little room behind the restaurant and work full time. She planned to quit school as soon as she could; she was no good at it. But the truant officers were zealous, and she had to go or spend time in a juvenile penitentiary or reform school.

School started. Emerald and Lottie walked down the dusty road each mornin' to the one room red brick schoolhouse out by the black topped highway. Emerald liked school the first few days. The milkman delivered milk in small glass bottles with cardboard tabs on the tops. She'd never seen brown milk and didn't like the look of it. They called it chocolate, but it was brown like dirt. Lottie talked her into tastin' it, but Emerald favored the bright orange drink that came in little glass bottles.

The teacher was young and nice, but the days were long, and Emerald wasn't used to mindin' anybody or havin' to do or think about anything in particular, like the teacher was tryin' ta' make her do. She was used to being watchful, fer' she never knowed when trouble might show up. The orderly, safe world inside the schoolhouse calmed her, bored her, and the safety of it put her to sleep. She didn't want ta' learn to read or to count. She wanted to sleep.

One afternoon she asked ta' go to the outhouse, escaped outside, and wouldn't go back in. She climbed the apple tree near the outhouse and ate green apples. The teacher came outside to find her. Emerald refused to come down and hollered, "Go to Hell!" at the teacher.

The teacher sent Lottie out to get her and take her home. She told Lottie to tell Thursta that Emerald wasn't ready to start school yet, to start her again next year.

"I'm ashamed of you!" Thursta scolded. Emerald hung her head and pleaded to go back to school. "I'll be good this time and mind her, Mom!" but no one would let her go back.

Another Chance at Love

Bolen stayed gone. Thursta had to have money. She found a job cleanin' and cookin' for a man across the fields. "His name is Nate," she explained to Emerald and Lucy. "You'll have ta' stay by yer'selves ever day. Emerald, you'll have ta' babset Lucy. You know how she is, so jist' let her keep on decoratin' her little nests."

They both turned to contemplate Lucy. Lucy grinned back at 'em. She didn't like to go outside. She liked to stay in the house. All day long she hummed or sang little bits of songs comin' from somewhere in her head while she moved the little bunch of stuff she gathered starting at the beginning of each morning, to another place.

Lucy was quick tempered and short sighted. She couldn't see anything past the end of what she wanted right now. She went into fits of hysteria if she didn't get her way, or if Bolen was too loud.

She trembled and turned red faced and screamed in such a high voice that Thursta was afraid she'd break ever winda' in the house. Nobody could make her stop. She'd fight 'em like a devil. They had ta' wait the storm out.

When Lucy wasn't havin' one of her frequent fits, each object she took notice of became the most important thing in the world to her, whether it was a string, a fork, a plate, or a dish rag. She arranged and rearranged her little hoard of bright gum wrappers, soda and beer bottle caps. If anyone tried to take one thing from her little stash before she was through with it, there was hell to pay. Thursta frowned at Lucy as she studied her.

"I cain't make up my mind if she was over-scared of bein' in this world when she was born, er' if she ain't got sense enough to be scared." Emerald looked at Lucy.

"Cain't' we go with you?"

Thursta shook her head no.

"He lost his wife, and they never had any youngin's. He ain't used to 'em."

Thursta crossed the woods and fields behind the house out to the blacktop to get to Nate's house. She worked five days a week. She cleaned his house and cooked him a hot dinner and left it in the oven for him, so it would be warm when he got home from work.

Indian summer set in, and Thursta walked with Emerald and Lucy to the carnival on the edge of town. Emerald liked the way Thursta was lookin'. She wore a black pleated skirt and a white blouse to the carnival instead of her usual cuffed up blue jeans and work shirt.

It seemed to Emerald that Thursta wasn't worryin' sa' much about Bolen comin' back any more, or how they would fare this winter.

They set out in the late afternoon, crossed the hay stubbled field the carnival was in, and strolled past a tent. Suddenly they were surrounded by a world of magic and beauty, noises and sounds Emerald never knew existed.

Emerald held on hard to the few scraps of security and beauty in her life. The green of Thursta's eyes, the sound of her voice, the smell and feel of clean clothes dried outside, the thin line of red paint around the gray house, the white snowball bushes. The perfume Lottie wore, the taste of orange soda, the sound of rain, the smell and look of a skillet of fried taters, pinto beans, golden crisp corn bread, and her grandmother's birthday cake.

She stood in the dusk, a small, thin stick of a child. Her soul began to dance with joy. She sniffed the sharp, sweet smells of cotton candy and browning, tender hot dogs. Above the tents, the colors of the neon lights on the Ferris wheel blended into the setting sun.

Thursta counted out five nickels each into Lucy and Emerald's hands and turned them loose. They rode the merry go round and ate cotton candy. They picked out a plastic duck at a booth. There was a number on the bottom of each duck, and they got the prize that went with the number. They ate their first hot dog and wanted more. Thursta had a black and white picture of herself made. The picture cost twenty five cents. They were proud of how pretty she was in it.

Thursta kept on lookin' pretty. She was happier than Emerald had ever seen her. The first snow fell, and she crossed the fields to her job while Emerald stayed behind with Lucy. Her work hours grew longer.

She told Emerald and Lucy about Nate's nice house and how she liked workin' in his big, warm kitchen. She said she liked the house so much she stayed a little longer to bake somethin' special for Nate's sweet tooth.

She brought home pies and cakes she baked for him. Each one was missin' a peice or two. She said he told her to take them home 'cause he couldn't eat the whole thing. They waited for her at the kitchen table ever afternoon. She cooked them somethin' as soon as she come in from work. Then she set down and talked while they ate. Like dry little sponges, they soaked in the smiles and funny stories she told them.

One day she came in lookin' pretty, carryin' a lemon pie. She stomped the snow off her boots and hung up her coat. She cut Emerald and Lucy each a big peice of pie. A prayer was in her voice when she spoke.

"It may be that you kids can go to work with me purty' soon. You'd have to mind, and not talk too much. Would you like that?"

They nodded yes, their mouths full of pie. She
was makin' enough money from her job to buy
the food and fuel they needed for the winter and
she seemed easy about it.

Emerald overheard Thursta tellin' Lottie about
Nate. She heard Lottie tell her ta' git' out and go
ta' him as quick as she could. Emerald's heart
filled with hope. She went to sleep on the pile of
clothes under the window, dreamin' of a new
father instead of Bolen, and a new home where
nobody stunk or drank, or beat on women and
kids and sometimes each other. They'd eat good
dinners together, Thursta would stay pretty, and
they would have a real bed to sleep in.....and best
of all, Bolen would never come home again.

Then Thursta turned sad and quiet. She
stopped goin' to Nate's house to work. She
stopped talkin' about Nate, and she stopped bein'
pretty. Emerald and Lucy' begged her to take 'em
to Nate 's to live.

"Take us over there ta' live! We'll be good!"

Thursta's eyes watered and she clamped her
mouth down hard. West spoke with calm
certainty from the doorway.

"None of us ain't got a chaince' of a snowball
in hell, that's all there is to it." He turned away
and left.

Emerald and Lucy sneaked across the fields
and looked through the window of Nate 's house
to see what went wrong. All they saw was a
grandfather clock and a rug on the floor of a
long, polished hall. A cold wind blowed across the
white porch of Nate's big house. They left, filled

with a new kind of hopelessness neither of them understood.

Emerald overheard Thursta tellin' Lottie she was gonna' have a baby. She said she'd counted it up, and she was that a' way before Bolen took off. Neither one of them knew it.

Winter set in. They spent most of their time huddled around the little pot bellied stove in the middle of the livin' room floor. They slept on the floor as close ta' the stove as they dared. Thursta cut wood in the woods behind the house. She got up ever few hours to feed the fire. The blankets she nailed over the walls and doorways didn't keep the cold out. They all had coughs and runny noses.

Thursta walked to the migramt farm and got onion culls. She buried them in the hot ashes in the bottom of the stove. When the onions were cooked, she pulled them out and they peeled and ate them. On good days they had fried taters' and beans or corn bread ta' eat, but there was never enough, and they went hungry.

Thursta bought her groceries from the McKee Grocery Store on Main Street in Grant. They were the only grocery for miles around. The Mckee brothers were big, jolly men, always jokin' with their customers. They heard about Thursta's troubles and wanted to help.

The Mckee brothers knew plenty about pride, and whether it was too much or too little, or at the wrong time, but they still didn't like proud people goin' hungry. They figured out a way to handle Thursta's excess pride. She allowed their plan to work. When she come in the store, they'd begin jokin' with other customers. Then they'd notice her and slip an oyster or some odd thing in her pocket as a joke.

She'd stick her hand in her pocket, bring it out and laugh. She let one brother hold her attention with his talk while she pretended she didn't see the other brother slipping extra food into the bottom of her grocery sack. She left the store with all kinds of foolish things in her pockets, and extra good, sensible food in the bottom of her grocery sack-with her misplaced pride intact.

Hank was born towards the end of winter. Thursta had to go to the little hospital in town instead having him at home. After Hank was born, the doctor told her she shouldn't have any more babies, it might kill her. She agreed, and they did the surgery to stop her from having any more.

Bolen came home a month after Hank was born. There was a deep snow on the ground. He'd been gone seven months. But he never came straight home. He looked up his drinkin' buddies first. They got drunk together and told him the stories about Thursta havin' Nate Saxton's baby.

Thursta had made the back room into a bedroom for her and Hank. She nailed blankets to the walls and opened the door to the livin' room so the heat from the stove could get in. Emerald was sittin' on the bed holdin' Hank. All of a sudden, somebody started poundin' on the back door and cussin'. Thursta jumped like she was shot. She recognized Bolen's voice.

"Emerald, grab Hank and run!" she shouted. The shoutin' scared Hank. He started screamin'. Emerald wrapped the blanket around him and run in the other room and hid behind the door with him and Lucy. It was too cold ta' hide outside. Bitterly, she wished he'd died off some place.

Bolen kept on shoutin' threats and poundin' on the back door. Thursta shoved the dresser in front of the back door.

"When I git in there, I'll kill you, you old whore! Runnin' around on me was ye? I'll see ye' dead in a short time!"

"Yore' at the wrong door!" she hollered, hoping he'd never make it around the house in the condition he was in.

"What?" he shouted.

"Yore' at the wrong door, ya' old fool!" she shouted through the door. She hesitated a moment.

"You're scarin' the new baby to death with yore' hollerin!"

"I'll kill that youngin' an' you too!"

"How come?"

Thursta put a deliberate whine in her voice.

"Hit ain't mine, that's why!" he shouted.

"Why, Bolen, that's a damn lie!" She allowed fury to enter her voice.

"You was gone before I knowed I was a' gonna' have this youngin'! Why, I've had a hell of a hard time makin' a livin' 'cause you took off on me!"

"Yeah, well I heard you made more'n a livin' off a' Nate Saxon!"

"Hank ain't his, ya' damned old fool! He looks enough like ye' ta' be yer' twin!"

A big silence fell. Emerald looked down at Hank. He looked up at her. He looked just like Bolen. Emerald sighed. Thursta sighed. Lucy sucked her thumb in the silence. Bolen finally spoke.

"Ya' named him Hank?"

"Yep!"

Thursta let weariness creep into her voice.

"Cause a' me a' likin' Hank Williams sa' much?"

"Probly'."

Her voice said she'd had enough. Another long silence fell.

"It's colder than hell out here! Open the damn door!"

"I cain't open it, Bolen. It's iced shut, and snow's on top a' that!"

Her voice held the deliberate patience one practices with fools, and Bolen heard it.

"Well. Come on out here, woman, and help me git' in the house!" he commanded loudly. Thursta let out a breath. It wasn't as bad as she had feared. She put on her coat and told Emerald to stay out of the way with Lucy and Hank until he passcd out.

In a few days, Bolen counted it up, and decided that Hank belonged to him. Thursta had been in thc family way before he left. He never mentioned Hank not being his again. And that was his last trip.He didn't tell the big stories about where he went like he usually did.

Something had happened, but nobody asked what or give a damn, except for West. And Thursta never told him about the surgery.

> Somethin's over, I don't know
> I jist' know my feet won't go
> around the bend ta' the road no more
> places are a' waitin', I'd like to go
> but somethin's over I don't know
> and I'm home ta' stay once more

Flint and Bolen argued and Flint left. It was Bolen's fault.

"It's comin' on spring anyway," Flint said to Thursta, who was cryin'. "Time fer' me ta' go back to the fruit orchards."

He stayed some place else when he come home, but he always stopped by to see Thursta and the kids. The rest of the time he spent runnin' with Lottie and West.

Spring came again. The farmer let the field the old house stood in go to hay. Thursta was busy with Hank, so Emerald and Lucy wandered around outside, lookin' at flowers and bugs. A few weeks into summer, Bolen decided to house hunt since he wasn't gonna take any more trips.

Chapter 15. A Good Home

They moved to a house out in the country on a gravel road ten miles the other side of Grant. Flowers and bushes grew in the front yard. A small porch on the side of the house led into the kitchen. A water pump stood over a white enamel sink in the white kitchen. Emerald looked up in wonder at the light bulb hangin' from a wire in the middle of the ceilin'. Bolen saw her lookin' at it.

"We got eee-lectricity," he crowed in satisfaction. Above the kitchen was a small attic. The kitchen led into a living room with two bedrooms behind it. The outhouse stood a good distance behind the house with wildflowers growing around it. Two red barns, one tall and thin, the other long and low, stood behind fields on the other side of the driveway. The farmer they rented the house from stored his equipment and hay in the barns. They were to stay out of them. Behind the fields were dense woods.

West helped them move in. Emerald forgot to be quiet around him. She grew bold because both Thursta and Bolen were there to stop him. She ran in and out of the bushes growin' up against the front of the house. A wild kitten hidin' under the bushes ran from her. She didn't know anything about cats. She chased it and grabbed it up in her hands. The kitten went wild, bitin' and scratchin' her and sunk a claw into the top of her right hand. She screamed in shock and pain and and slung the cat away.

She ran to the kitchen. Thursta treated the bites and claw marks on her hands and arms with peroxide. The kitten left a claw in the top of her right hand. Thursta pulled out the claw and treated the wound, but it was deep, and in a few days, pus pockets formed in it. It took weeks to heal, and for years, every time her hand bothered her, she remembered what West had done to her. And, that no one did one thing to stop him. In fact, they supported him in it.

As quick as Thursta got done treating her hand, West jerked her into the livin' room, grabbed the long switch he'd cut while she was in the kitchen and whipped her with it. She shouted in pain and screamed for help. At first she thought they hadn't heard her. He whipped her until he was satisfied, then he shoved her down on the floor. She sat in the frozen silence slowly realizing it was deliberate. They would do nothing to stop him.

Something in her changed permanently. She distanced herself from all of them. She found a quiet place inside, and fled there. She sat in the center of it, waiting for the shock and hurt that returned time and again to surprise her at not being rescued-on purpose.

She set in the same spot for three days while West set in a rockin' chair and watched her, his switch a' layin' ready by the chair. If she moved, he switched her with it. Bolen carried whiskey to him. Thursta carried food to him. West went away for a few minutes sometimes, then come back. She didn't move while he was gone. She knew better.

Everyone walked back and forth through the house, movin' their things in. She heard Lucy's voice and Thursta's and Bolen's. They walked past her, talking to each other like she didn't exist. She heard Thursta cookin' in the kitchen and smelled food.

She prayed for Flint to come home. She knew he'd make West let her up. Flint and Lottie didn't know about the things he did to her, like tying her up and almost smotherin' her. If they found out, they'd whup his ass good.

She peed on herself, for she didn't dare ask to go to the outhouse. He whipped her hard with the switch when he saw the puddle of pee spread out from underneath her. At the end of three days he let her up.

Everybody disappeared. They hid from her. She knew they hid out of guilt they would soon get over. They didn't want to talk about what they should have done. They were going to pretend it didn't happen. She was angry in a way she never was before. It was over, but she wouldn't forget it, either.

She went to the kitchen and drank water. She wrapped the few greasy cold taters left in the skillet in a piece of light bread. She went outside and walked to the edge of the woods, turned and stared back at the house. She hid there 'til dark. Then she edged back to the house, slipped into the little back room, and laid down on the pile of clothes on the floor beside Lucy.

She cried in the night. She'd never feel the same again about her family. They were cowards, people who wouldn't stand up for what was right. Her tears had waited to be rescued, hot and ready in the bottom of her belly, but nobody stopped him. There was no way to leave and nobody to go to if she ran away. Grandma Drusa was too far away. There was no way out yet. She'd have to endure it for now.

They all took up their new routines. Bolen still worked at the migrant farm. He was almost mild at home. He had no patience or a steady stomach. His nervousness had to go somewhere, but for the first time, he took part of his temper out on his drinkin' buddies.

Out of the blue, he brought home a cow named Bessie. She had a calf named Bossie. They were put in the low red barn. Thursta milked Bessie and Emerald and Lucy rubbed her warm sides. They loved Bossie's nose snufflin' 'em, and the rough lick of her tongue. Thursta's glass churn had a wood paddle in it. She kept it on the porch and churned butter from Bessie's milk. Emerald and Lucy turned the crank and helped her make butter. Bolen's favorite drink was the buttermilk left over from the churning. It soothed his stomach that stayed hot from the drink.

West didn't feel good, and he wasn't getting along with Jan, his girlfriend, so Thursta made the little attic room above the kitchen into a bedroom for him. Emerald practiced being a silent ghost around him and the rest.

Lottie started comin' home. Emerald watched her followin' Thursta around, talkin' in a low, pleadin' voice so no body else could hear. Thursta pressed her lips shut, turned her head away, and didn't speak. Emerald thought, *"Ya' favor West, but not Lottie. Is it because she's a girl, like me? Well, we know our prospects now."*

Emerald and Lucy played in the yard with Hank. They stayed out of the house as much as they could because of the hell always going on in there. They crossed the road and found a small gravel pit and wandered up and down the roads scuffing their toes through warm dust.

School started. The long yellow bus picked Lottie and Emerald up in front of the house each morning. It delivered them to the big red brick schoolhouse in town. All twelve grades went there.

Everybody in Emerald's first grade class was scared of the teacher. Mrs. Port was all sharp edges, from the black dress covering her tiny, thin frame, to the black lace up shoes tappin' hard and loud across the wood floors towards them when they did somethin' wrong. Her eyes were like little black beads, her thin patches of dyed black hair pulled up into a tight little knot on top of her head. She held her lips in a thin, straight line they could barely see. Her sharp voice rang through the class room as she stalked back and forth, slapping a ruler on her palm all day long.

Emerald got off on the wrong foot with Mrs. Port the first day. She'd never seen a clock. She was used to eatin' and sleepin' around Bolen's drinkin' habits. People came and went without plannin'. No one questioned any of it. When food was there, they eat. When it wasn't, they did without. The same with clothes and shoes and coats. They didn't go to church on Sundays. Thursta, Emerald, and Lucy didn't have any friends. Only Bolen had friends. Lottie, Flint, and West had friends away from the house.

The first afternoon, Emerald grew tired of sitting in the classroom. She stood up, ready to go home. Mrs. Port asked her what she was doing.

"I'm a' goin' home," Emerald announced. Mrs. Port pointed to the clock on the wall, and told her it wasn't time to go home yet. Emerald stared at the clock. She'd never seen one before. What did that thing have to do with her goin' home?

Mrs. Port ordered her to sit down. She shook her head no. Mrs. Port rushed down the aisle between the desks, grabbed her hair and danced her down the aisle up to the dunce chair. She pushed Emerald on to the tall chair, then ordered her to hold out her hand. She tapped Emerald's open palm with the ruler a few times. Then she ordered her to sit there and think about mindin' the teacher like she was supposed to. Emerald stared at her palm. What jist' happened? Mrs. Port tapped on her palm with the ruler to punish her. But the hair pullin' hurt worse. The ruler was supposed to hurt, but it didn't.

When she got home, she declared to Thursta, "I'm not goin' back to school ever again!"

She didn't want the new dresses or underwear Thursta and Lottie had made her. She didn't want the new shoes, either. They hurt her feet. But the next mornin' she got on the bus. It was either that or get a bad whippin'.

When spring came, Bolen and Thursta went back to workin' at the migramt farm. They got home late each day, and Thursta went to cookin'. They dropped Hank off at an old woman's house on the farm, and left Emerald and Lucy at home. West was supposed to watch them, but he was back livin' at his girlfriend's house. Emerald was damn glad. They rarely saw Lottie any more, and Flint was off workin' in the orchards.

Each morning, Thursta packed their lunches, gathered up Hank, and they drove away in the old black car just as the sun came up. Thursta ordered Emerald to take Lucy and hide outside somewhere 'til the drunks left.

At first, Thursta did the dishes and cleaned the house up before they left for work. But as the summer wore on, the drunks stayed longer and longer, and Thursta left more and more of the work for Emerald.

Emerald stood in the yard, watchin' Bolen and Thursta holdin' hands, walkin' out to the car. Thursta held Hank in one arm. She had a black eye from the beatin' Bolen give her the night before. Bolen swaggered along, carryin' his battered black metal lunch box in one hand. All the food they had in the house was in it. Emerald watched them get in the car and drive away without a backward glance.

Hate for Bolen rose in her, followed by contempt for thursta's putting up with him. Her feelin's all mixed up, she slipped back in the house to get Lucy and hide outside until the last of the drunks left. As soon as Thursta come home, she went outside again and stayed. Thursta called for her to come and help, but Emerald pretended she didn't hear.

The summer stayed long and dull. Bolen and his drinkin' buddies set around the kitchen table, braggin' to each other at night. They were all high tempered and proud of the way they run their families. They bragged mournfully about how their women folk forced them to treat them bad.

Bolen and his friends didn't believe in men or boys doing what they called "women's work". Men held down jobs and hunted. Men took care of their cars. Men drank if they took a notion to. No one else had a say in the matter. Men cleaned their guns and threw their cigarette butts, beer bottles, whiskey bottles, and plates down wherever they damn well pleased. They demanded food when hungry, and if there was no food, or it was poor or skimpy, their woman was to blame. It was her job to cook for the men of the house and know how to make do with what they provided. They wasn't made of money.

The men he ran with wouldn't allow their women to learn how to drive. Their women couldn't go to the store unless their husbands or sons drove 'em there. When a woman was sick and couldn't do her work, other women did it for her until she got better and could do it herself again.

The men set in their old cars in the yard. They rode up and down the back roads, drinkin' and braggin'. Men and boys ate before the women and girls. Bolen felt ashamed when he couldn't feed his friends. He liked 'em to think he had ever body that belonged to him under his control. If any of his friends was havin' trouble with his womenfolk, Bolen advised him. After they left, he'd follow Thursta around, shakin' his head sadly at their plight.

"It's a sorry man who cain't' make his woman mind. Sometimes a hard hand is a good thing."

He followed her around while she worked, explainin' his philosophy to her. The dishes and pots and pans slammed into the sink and into the cupboards while he explained his version of life to her. He smirked at her with watchful, cunning eyes while she kept her head down and got busier to keep from answerin' him.

Emerald and Lucy slept on the floor under a window in one of the back bedrooms. They slept in their clothes, on top of a small pile of clothes. Thursta made sure the window opened and closed easy. She made Emerald practice opening and closing it, in case Bolen got past her when he was beatin' on her, and tried to hurt them. It was Emerald's job to open the window and pull Lucy through it to the outside. Then they were to run down the road and hide under the bridge. That was Thursta's instructions.

Everybody ran when Bolen went on one of his rampages. They cut across the yard and headed down the road to the bridge, runnin' as fast as they could, while he staggered out into the yard and shot at them, or threw knives and rocks at them. They hid under the bridge and waited.

They knew he'd go back in the house and unscrew the light bulb in the kitchen. Then he'd set in the dark with his gun loaded, waitin' for them to come back so he could shoot 'em, 'til he passed out. If Lottie spent the night, she had to run too. But Emerald noticed that Bolen never did it when Flint was around.

Chapter 16. Lottie's Adventure

Lottie got a job sellin' magazines in the spring. She left town on a bus with a bunch of other young people. They were going to travel the country, sell magazine subscriptions, and get rich. She returned in a couple of months and moved in with someone in town. Then she changed her mind and moved back home.

Emerald was glad Lottie was home. She'd grown taller and she wore her hair longer. She was still willowy and thin and wore pretty plaid dresses. She had a ready laugh, but had always been unsure of herself behind it. Emerald knew Thursta could see it, but nothing made any difference to her. She still turned her head away when Lottie spoke. Emerald was growing to dislike thursta more and more.

Lottie didn't stay long. One day she took Emerald outside and asked her to keep a secret. Emerald nodded. Lottie started cryin'. She said she was gonna' have a baby, that the father was a man she'd met when she'd been selling magazines in another state.

Emerald went with Lottie to tell Thursta. When Thursta heard Lottie was "caught", she said she was surprised it didn't happen sooner. Lottie and Emerald got mad. Lottie moved moved back in town and started waitressing again. Emerald moved a little farther away again in her feelings for her mother.

Lottie met Sam. She told Emerald he was the love of her life. She told him about the baby, but he didn't care. Sam was married. He left his wife and got him and Lottie a place. Bolen and Thursta stayed mad and ashamed of her. When she stopped by, Thursta scolded her.

"It's bad enough ta' have a baby ya' don't even know the father of, and not be married, but to take someone else's man right in front of ever body we know! That's the worst thing you could do ta' us! I won't be able ta' hold my head up in town any more."

"You oughten' ta' be able ta' hold yer' head up over what ye've already done ta' us kids."

Lottie answered bitterly. Thursta slammed off. Lottie was scared to death from bein' in love and goin' to have a baby. She kept comin' to see Thursta 'cause she needed her, but she never stayed long before Thursta run her off.

Fall came, and West drove Thursta, Emerald, Lucy, and Hank to the carnival. He parked at the edge of the field and pulled out a fifth of whiskey.

"I'll wait in the car," he said.

The dread the winter months brought, when going outside meant freezin', and stayin' inside meant figurin' out how to not be seen and stay alive, dropped away from Emerald for a little while when she stepped inside the ring of brightly lit tents.

School started. Emerald went by herself. Bolen didn't quit drinkin' just 'cause school started, so they still hid under the bridge when he went into his rages. The house stayed cold. The heat from the stove in the livin' room didn't go into the bedrooms. Emerald dressed quick and run her fingers through her hair in the freezin' cold. There was never a comb around. She slipped into the kitchen and grabbed whatever she could find to eat. There was never much, and most times, nothin'. They didn't have a clock, so Emerald watched for the bus through a window in the living room when it was empty. She watched from outside when the drunks spent the night on the living room couch and floor.

In a shame laden voice, Thursta urged Emerald over and over, "Act like nothin's wrong when ye' git' on the bus! Don't tell nobody nothin'! Tell 'em ya' aint hungry, if they ast' about lunch!!"

It took Emerald awhile each mornin' to thaw out in the classroom. The teachers and pupils took it for granted she went well fed, from a warm house to a warm bus, then into a warm classroom, like they did. They had no idea she needed to get warm before she could think straight, then she had to try to think about school books, instead of the food she needed.

At noon, she forced herself to look away from the other kid's lunches and pretend to be interested in somethin' else. Sometimes the waterin' in her mouth got so thick she couldn't swaller' it all, the drool ran out, and she wiped it away with the back of her hand. The teacher ordered her to bring lunch to school. The teacher sent notes home to Thursta. Nothin' changed, and the teacher quit bothering with her.

There were mornin' and afternoon recess. On nice days, there was a long lunch hour outside. The kids played Red Rover and other games. Priscilla, a huge, hulking sixth grader, was the bully of the school. When they played Red Rover, she hurt their hands and knocked them down. Emerald quit playin' with the other kids because of Priscilla.

Instead, she spent her time makin' people and rooms out of twigs under a big tree she nicknamed Elmer who stood on the edge of the playground. Sometimes Priscilla came over and called her names, but she never looked up or answered. Elmer was her only school friend. She studied the bark on Elmer's trunk, counted his layers, and decided the bark was Elmer's coat. The leaves on Elmer limbs were different sizes and shades of green and brown. She watched how the sun touched him and the ground around him. He was always warmer where the sun shined on him. Sometimes she slipped behind him where the other kids couldn't see her, and hugged him. In the classroom, weary, tired, and always hungry, Emerald stared out the window's and day dreamed about food and a better life.

Pissy Frog

Lottie had her baby. She named him Neil. He was a Thanksgivin' baby, and she called him her little turkey. She brought him over so they could see him. Then she started droppin' him off at their house. Neil spent weeks at a time with them. Lottie came to see him when she wasn't workin' or runnin' around with Sam. They quarreled and Sam went back to his wife, but they still couldn't stay away from each other.

Thursta half heartedly tried to make Lottie spend more time with Neil, but she loved him so quick and so much right from the start, she stopped complainin', and accepted him. He became her new boy and she doted on him, even though Bolen and Hank were jealous.

Neil had a strong, wiry little body, thick, frizzled blond hair, green eyes and a wide, full mouth. His teeth came in big and white and straight. They were the largest teeth anyone had ever seen. Thursta asked Lottie if his father had big teeth, if that was why she'd fell fer' him. Lottie snickered and said, "Yes!"

Neil smiled all the time with his big wide mouth. Ever thing was funny to him. He was a happy go lucky little boy with a rugged troll's face, shaggy hair, and huge grin showin' oversized teeth.

Emerald loved him as much as Thursta ever could. Thursta bragged that Neil was gonna' grow up to be quick and smart. Flint laughed ever time he saw him, then nicknamed him Pissy Frog.

When Thursta got home each day, she grabbed Neil up and hugged him like she was gonna' squeeze him to death. Hank and Lucy watched, jealous and complainin'. Emerald hung back. She wasn't jealous at all. She didn't want hugs or anything from Thursta or Bolen. She just wanted to survive them, grow up and get the hell out. Thursta put Neil down and turned to them.

"Ahhh!'" she scoffed at them and opened her arms.

> "Little Star, you came to us out of the night
> You made our pathway dance with light
> you smiled your wise love into our souls
> and forever you'll live in our hearts."

The first Christmas in the new house passed, with snow on the ground and a fried chicken dinner with mashed potatoes and pinto beans. Spring came. Bolen and Thursta went back to work at the migrant farm. At the old house, Bolen used to make Thursta walk to the farm while he rode past, laughin' at her. Now they drove ten miles to get there. They left Emerald in charge of Lucy, Hank, and Neil for the summer. The drunks were told to stay away. Bolen made 'em get up and leave before they left for work. Emerald didn't know why he made 'em leave or care.

She dished up stale fried taters and pinto beans in the middle of the day. They took naps in the afternoon. There was no way to stay cool, so they spent time layin' around, talkin' about ice cream and kool aid.

Hank was walking, and Lucy was good as long as she had her decoratin' pieces to sort through. Emerald changed enough diapers to know why Flint nicknamed Neil Pissy Frog. Thursta showed her how to make a fence of chairs between the kitchen and the living room. She ordered Emerald to keep the three of them in the livin' room until she got home, but she no longer minded Thursta.

Emerald and Lucy carried Hank and Neil into the woods behind the house and into the barns. They explored the gravel pit across the road, and met the red headed neighbors. But when Thursta got home, they were always in the livin' room, smilin' at her with innocent faces.

Chapter 17. Lottie's Man

Lottie married Lester late in the summer. Lester was a huge, oily, hulking man with thick, curly black hair and black eyes. He exuded stinky oil and smelly sweat and laughed and talked without ceasing.

Thursta said dryly, "Wherever Lester is, there dwells noise."

Lester was partial to the Bible, chicory coffee, ham, and food of any kind. He drawed money for havin' a bad back and he spent his time cookin' and eatin' and blabbin'.

They rented a house a couple of gravel roads over from Thursta and Bolen. Lottie took Neil away from them and took him home with her. She was gonna' have another baby, and she said she wanted Neil with her. Neil didn't want ta' go, but she took him anyway. Thursta and Emerald missed him like the dickens.

Bolen and Thursta still worked on the onion farm. Lester, Lottie, and Neil started comin' over ever day while they was gone, saying they was there to help Emerald babysit Hank and Lucy. Neil played with Hank and Lucy, while Lester went straight to the kitchen, put on the coffee pot and went ta' eatin' and cookin' up ever thing in the house.

Lottie didn't have any friends, and Emerald could tell she didn't much like Lester. She talked to Emerald about all kinds of things while Lester was in the kitchen. The words poured out of her like a river. All that was in the house they lived in was a couch, a bed, a stove, Neil, and a big stack of detective magazines. Emerald didn't know where the detective magazines came from. They were filled with pictures and stories of dead women, mostly with their heads cut off. The stories told about detectives who tried to find out who killed the women and bring the murderers to justice, but mostly they never did. It was a mystery that never would be solved. The detective magazines talked a lot about women who flirt and ask for it, and get it, and there isn't anything can be done about it.

The stories scared Emerald. She went to Thursta and told her about the magazines. They stared at each other with a sense of foreboding.

"Somethin's bad wrong..." Thursta stated.

"I'll find out what I can." ......

Then Lester and Lottie joined a Pentecostal church and Lester became determined to save Thursta and the kids souls from peridition. Thursta didn't like Lester.

"He's lazy and no good. All he thinks about is eatin' and another thing I won't mention. There's somethin' else wrong with him I don't know yit', but I'll find out 'fore its over."

She snapped out the words and rolled her eyes in anticipated retribution. When Lester told Emerald his intentions of saving Thursta, she said, "Why don't ya' try savin' Bolen instead of Thursta?"

Lester shook his head solemnly. "Bolen's a lost cause if there ever was one! Cain't nobody help him now! He's gonna' fry in Hell!"

Emerald listened with interest as Lester went into a lurid, enthusiastic account of what Bolen was gonna' suffer in Hell. When he finally stopped to draw breath, Emerald said "Sounds real good ta' me!"

Nothing could stop Lester from trying to save Thursta's soul. He became obsessed with the notion of it. Thursta snorted when she heard what he was up to. Lester always swaggered into the house, thumpin' a Bible, letting it lead the way.

West drove drove by real slow, but never pulled in if Lester's old black car was there. Emerald watched West's car disappear in a cloud of dust down the road. She knowed exactly why he didn't stop. He couldn't stand noise and would try to stop Lester's preachin; he was too damn sick to make him stop.

Early one mornin', Lester drove into the yard. He swaggered into the house, but fell back a step or two when he saw Thursta was home, and not at the onion fields. He wasn't gonna' git' ta' cook and eat ever thing today or bother the kids!

Emerald, Lucy, Hank and Neil were in the kitchen with Thursta. Lester got his second wind and swaggered on into the kitchen, his Bible leading the way. He thumped it down on the table, expecting Thursta to listen to him. After all, he was a man with a Bible.

"Set down, Lester," Thursta commanded. He did. She served him her special coffee. It always give him the runs, but he drank it all, and come back for more. He laughed and said ever body needed a good purge now and then. Thursta washed the dishes with her back to him while he set on the chair, shoutin' Bible verses, rollin' his black eyes up towards heaven. Emerald watched him, wonderin' when he would receive the outhouse call.

He kept on readin' 'til his wavy, oily black hair stood straight up on his head. Greasy sweat rolled down his slick face like a river. Emerald, Lucy, Hank and Neil leaned against the kitchen wall in a row, watching Lester preach at Thursta's back. Finally he thumped his Bible down, declared he was a new man, he would never be the way he was before. That did it for Thursta. She whirled around.

"How are ye' new, Lester?" she demanded. "Yer' all built up this mornin'. Ya' come here that way. What did ye' have planned besides eatin' us out of house and home? Ya' know, I heard a little somethin' 'bout ye' doin' somethin' ye' shouldn't a' done here while back...and gittin' away with it! But that won't happen here," she stated grimly.

"These here is nice little chilern' and I'd kill anybody who does one little thaing ta' 'em."

She swept her hand out with the biggest butcher knife she owned in it. Lester blanched.

"I guess I'd murder any pervert who bothered my grown chilern, too," she stated matter of factly.

"I don't like what I'm a' hearin' ya' got in that house yore' a' holdin' my girl captive in. I'm a comin' over there later, and them damn magazines better be gone fer' good. And I'll tell ye' somethin' else. If I tell West or Bolin on ye', they'll shoot ye' without thinkin' twice about it. The only reason I'm a' holdin' back, is on account of Lottie.

Now, you got a damn good reason to pray fer' yerself' instead of anybody else, and you better start right now! Looks to me like you need to quit eatin' sa' damn much, and keep yer' ass out a' the bed! We ain't gonna' provide extry food fer ye' at this house not one more day! Yer' off the dole! And we all could stand fer' ye' to find something to do besides preach! That ain't gonna' git' ya' any money! Unless you got a church ta' run, ya' need ta' git' off a' yer' lazy ass and git' a damn job! And don't come over here agin' with me gone!"

Lester jumped up and hollered, "Sorry for takin' up yer' time!" Then he rushed out to his car like the devil was after him and tore out of the driveway.

"Ain't that jist' like that damn fool! Gotta' have the last word, even if it was ta' git' him killed!"

Thursta looked at the row of kids standing again the wall and turned back to the sink. She started mumblin', talkin' ta' herself, like they wasn't there. They grinned, for they'd seen her do this before.

She grabbed up the dish towel and strolled over to the chair Lester's empty chair. She plopped down in it and pulled her hair up straight until it stood up on her head. Then she mopped her face with the wet dishrag, and rolled her eyes up to heaven, beggin' fer' forgiveness of somethin', they couldn't tell what, 'cause she was a' mumblin. But the tone was exactly Lester's.

Humble and sneaky. She rolled her eyes over at them.

They all started laughin' and imitating Lester. They kept it up until they heard someone come in the door. Thursta jumped up and went to the kitchen sink. They jumped up from the floor where they'd been a' stabbin' and a' buryin' Lester, sendin' him straight ta' hell, and acted like there was nothin' goin' on.

"Jist' remember ta 'run ta' the woods and hide if he comes here. Don't set one foot in this house 'til his car is gone awhile," she told 'em.

They hoped they was done with him, but Lester kept on comin' over, followin' ever body around, talkin' about magic and God. He spouted Bible verses in his loud voice, his oily black hair standin' up and his face slick with a river of oily sweat. The kids watched him like he was a televison show. Thursta ignored him until he started bellowing out church songs.

She went to West. "There's somethin' bad wrong with Lester, more than you know."

West knew she meant more than she was sayin'. He listened real close.

"Yer' a' gonna' have ta' keep an eye on him, and pertect' the chilern' from him. I don't know what he's thinkin' ta' do to 'em, or to somebody one of these days. It'll be bad, that's fer' shore'! He's crazier than a best bug!"

She studied West a minute.

"An' see if ya' cain't git' him to stop singin'. It's a' peelin' the damn paper right off a' the walls!"

West said Lester was a fool, 'cause he didn't know when to be afraid or when to shut up.

Lester started talking about the Bible and healin' magic. Emerald let him look at the warts on her wrist. He showed her how to get rid of them. She was to rub a penny on each wart and wrap the pennies up in an old rag and bury it. He said she had to believe in it, or the healin' magic wouldn't work. She did it, and the warts went away like magic.

She thought hard about it. Maybe somethin' bigger than Lester was at work in the world. Maybe Lester had got a hold of it, maybe he hadn't. Whatever it was, she saw that he was determined to mind it, and not do bad things any more. The book called the Bible told all about it. It was about a big shot named God. He was old and skinny, with long white hair and a long white beard. He had blue eyes the color of the sky at noon in summer, and he set up on a throne way up in the clouds. He took a' hold of Lester and changed him through fear, after Thursta went over there and cleaned house on 'em, and burnt the bad magazines up. Now Lottie seemed happier and Lester treated her better.

Lottie was a' gonna' have another baby. Now she had Neil and Billy, and another one on the way. Thursta shook her head when she heard the news. "Stairsteps!"

Emerald went to church with them and set on the front pew with Neil. She clapped her hands and sung and watched people get slain in the spirit. She liked speakin' in tongues, and she walked on the bed of coals they laid down at the front of the church. But she wouldn't go near the poison snakes when they took them out of their cages to handle them.

She was still learnin' about putting her hands on people to heal them. She knew she'd always be learnin' about healin' ways. People in the church started turning to her to help with healings. They told her what needed to be done, and it was natural for her to find the Healers' place Mercy, Fallon and Drusa still dwelt in.

Çhapter 18. Cracklin's and Corn

Bolen took up quarreling with his drinking
buddies. He bought a hog and him and a bunch
of men butchered it out by the barn. Thursta and
the kids hurried back and forth, carryin' big
slabs of fresh meat to the house ta' be warshed
and cut up. Cracklin's sang in the heavy iron
skillet on the stove all day long, makin' ever
body's mouth water. Thursta and Lottie piled the
crisp brown cracklin's on platters. They didn't
have time ta' cool off before they was gone. Bolen
went in and out, grabbin' a bite now and then,
nodding his approval.

Thursta and Lottie cut the meat up into pork
roasts and chops, fatback, ribs and
bacon.Thursta made the kids stay away from the
hot kettle of rendering fat on the fire outside so
they wouldn't get burned. She made sausage and
boiled the cleaned pig's head, and made head
cheese. She packed the meat into barrels and
poured lard over it so it wouldn't spoil. The hams
were hung up in bags in the low red barn to cure.

A few days later, Bolen brought home ten
bushels of corn for her to put up for the winter.
She canned corn and dried corn. They eat fried
corn, pickled corn, corn on the cob, and corn
fritters. Bolen never cared before if they eat or
not. They didn't know what ta' think of him.

School started. Marlene lived at the corner of
their road. She rode the bus and was in the

same class as Emerald. One Saturday mornin',
Marlene's brother Clyde stopped at the house to
ask if anyone wanted a ride to church the next
morning. He stood waiting for an answer outside
the screen door while Thursta scowled at him.
Bolen snickered. West wagged his head back and
forth with a grin. Thursta said no, but Emerald
and Lucy ran to the door and looked up at Clyde.

"We'll go!" they said importantly. Clyde said he
would pick them up at nine thirty, and left amid
hoots of laughter comin' from inside the house.

"I'll hafta' straighten up all the pitchurs' and
paint the porch steps, and start prayin' once in
while!" Bolen laughed.

West said dryly, "Yeah, and don't fergit' ta' put
out the purty' potted plants, and git' a fancy new
rug fer' the floor!"

Thursta turned and narrowed her eyes at
them. She placed her hands on her hips and
tapped her foot. She didn't hear their words.

"The girls'll have to have nice dresses to wear
to chuch," she said out loud to herself. "Hmmm."

She washed and pressed their best school
dresses and washed their hair for them on
Saturday nights. Clyde drove them to and from to
chuch Sunday mornings. Emerald and Lucy
loved listening to the singing, the stained glass
windows and the smell of fresh flowers on the
altar. After awhile, Lottie and Thursta bought
them each a new church dress.

Marlene rode with her parents to church. She
wouldn't speak to them. Then Marlene's parents
invited them to Marlene's birthday party. They
went, and one of the girls at the party asked

Marlene why they were there. Marlene said her family made her invite them because they were poor, and they gave them rides to church on Sundays so they could learn the difference between right and wrong. Emerald and Lucy looked at each other and walked out the door. When they got home, Thursta was waitin' for them with a smile.

"Yer' back sa' soon! Did ya' have a good time?"

They nodded and smiled at her. After the party, every time Clyde stopped by to pick them up for church, they were nowhere to be found.

Bolen kept on doin' odd stuff. He brought a television set home. West and him watched the television at night. They made anyone around set down and watch Red Skelton and Art Linkletter and westerns with them. The television entertained Bolen, and he didn't run them out of the house and make 'em stay out as often. The television was turned off when Bolen and West wasn't home. Emerald nicknamed it Tubby, and thanked it like it was a real person.

Then Lester and Lottie moved a long ways away. Lester wasn't workin' and Lottie couldn't, so they moved into the abandoned chicken house down the hill from Lester's folks, and started attending a new church.

They left Neil with Thursta when they moved, for Lottie was sick all the time from havin' babies. They didn't come over much after they moved, for it was far away, and Lottie got car sick.

The former chicken house they lived in was an ugly, long, gray concrete building, but Lottie had a knack for makin' a place a home. She partitioned it off into six rooms leading from one into the next. She put down rugs on the concrete floors and hung up home made curtains over the tiny windows.

Mustard, Eggs, Grease, and Rat Poison

Bolen's friend Willis from back in the hills, moved north and spent a few weeks with them before he found a place to work and live. Willis stayed upstairs in the attic. Before he moved out, Neil went upstairs and got into his suit case. When Thursta found him, Neil had Willis's heart pills scattered across the floor. Thursta screamed. "Did ya' eat any of the pills?" Neil nodded happily. Thursta thought rapidly. Bolen was gone. There was no phone or car to take Neil to the hospital. She rushed him down the stairs, into the kitchen, and frantically started mixin' up things to make him throw up the pills.

Emerald, Lucy, and Hank watched her mix raw eggs with mustard. She made Neil drink it. Nothing happened. She made him eat lard mixed with flour and water. Then bakin' powder and vinegar. Nothing. He just rubbed his belly and said, "More!"

She kept askin' him how many of the pills he'd eat, and he kept sayin' he didn't know. A long time passed. Thursta finally gave up. She put her hands on her hips and studied him. He looked fine and happy. She shook her head.

Enough time had passed, and she'd run out of food to give him. If he was goin' to get sick or die, it would a' already happened.

Thursta doted on Neil. She wouldn't let anybody touch the thick, frizzled head of blond hair stickin' out around his craggy, rough lookin' little troll face. She set him on the edge of the kitchen table and spent hours tamin' it. His hair grew fast. It got so long she smoothed and combed and curled it into gold ringlets that hung down past his waist. While she worked, he turned the air blue with the few cuss words he knew. She ignored them.

Flint explained to him that he needed to perfect his cussin', and that havin' his hair curled was the best way to get the job done, so he had best put up with it. Neil had a tough, wiry little man's body and rugged face and deep voice. Nobody could stop from laughin' when they saw him swaggerin' around with long, golden curls. It made him mad, but he bore with it, his wide mouth, big teeth and challenging green eyes makin' him look like a Shirley Temple from Hell.

Their cousin Von came to visit. He'd just moved north with his family. He was thirteen years old and a bully. They went outside, and he went to bossin' Emerald, Lucy, Hank and Neil around. But Neil wouldn't take orders from him. Von was afraid to punch Neil because Lottie and Lester was in the house, so he grabbed his golden locks and pulled him up on his tiptoes.

"You coward, you damn bully, you low down yellow bellied, sap suckin' son of a bitch!" Neil yelled. Von held on to his hair and started slappin' Neil to make him shut up. Emerald, Lucy and Hank pitched into the fray, hitting Von and stompin' on his toes. Von let go and danced in a circle while Neil hollered names at him.

"You shit faced, pecker headed, ugly, fat faced, blue bearded dinkle ball," he yelled. Von's face turned bright red, and he began huffin' and puffin'.

"You red faced, yellow bellied pole cat, chicken shit varmint, shittin', low down, stinkin, lyin', polecat, cheatin' snake in the grass'... uh... let's see--"

Neil stopped and studied the ground. Then he said, "I ain't old a' nuff' to go ta' school yit', but when I do, you'll hear plinty' more!"

Emerald, Lucy and Hank started laughin' and quit hittin' Von. Von took the opportunity to swagger off.

"I ain't never seen sich' a bunch of damn kids before!" he yelled hastily back over his shoulder.

Neil shouted, "You go ta' hell!" at his back. Von broke into a shamblin' run while they thowed rocks at his back.

The Green Cathedral

The woods in back of the house were haunted. Nobody went back there, not even to hunt. Emerald remembered Thursta warnin' her.

"There's somethin' bad wrong in them woods, Emerald. Somethin' lives in there we don't want ta' know one thing about. You best mind me and stay outta' there, 'cause I cain't save ye', if it gets ye'."

But the woods called out to Emerald, and one day when nobody was around, she slipped across the field and into the trees. She shivered as she made her way along the edge of the trees, keepin' the red barn in sight.

She started going to the woods. Nobody noticed. After a few days, she sneaked Neil into the woods with her and showed him the tree house she'd found. They climbed the tree and stood on the small square of rotted boards, peerin' through the leafy tops of the trees around them.

"Nobody else knows about this! If ya' tell, we'll lose this place!"

"I'll never tell."

Neil solemnly crossed his heart. The next morning they stole the few fried taters left in the skillet, wrapped them in one of Thursta's clean dish towels, and headed fer' the woods.

Emerald kept goin' and Neil went with her once in awhile. She explored shade and shadows, felt the quiet peace. She smelled damp, soft earth and learned how far it would sink in from her footsteps. She dug hidin' places in the soft ground underneath bushes and picked out trees she could climb easy and hide in their branches.

After awhile, she went to Thursta.

"Do ye' know what plants in the woods are safe ta' eat?"

She was always hungry. Thursta turned and give her a long look.

"I know somethin' about em."

"Would you show me when nobody's around, and don't tell?"

"We'll go early in the mornin'."

Emerald watched the worry lines fall from her mother's face as she moved gracefully through the woods. Thursta stood tall and stately and sauntered along like she was among old friends. She didn't break twigs or disturb leaves. Emerald realized that she already knew what she herself was tryin' so hard to learn. She saw that bein' in nature come natural to Thursta. It strengthened her. Thursta was at a disadvantage in a house. She lost her power there, whereas out in Nature, she gained it back.

Emerald stared at the beautiful, powerful woman before her. No wonder Bolen never quarreled at her in the onion fields. He waited til' he had her trapped in a car or a house. What a different life they could lead if it was all outdoors! But they had ta' live inside a house. She sighed. With Bolen. If it wasn't him, it would be somebody else. Now she understood somethin' to take with her to new places someday.

The blood they shared through their mountain generations stirred and came alive in the woods. Thursta instructed her in a low voice that didn't disturb any thing. She showed her which berries were good to eat, which ones to avoid, and the order the berries, tree fruits, and ground plants ripened in. She dug up blood root and yellow dock and showed Emerald what it looked like. She found the snow white trillium that dwelt in shade. She said the green apples hangin' under the round, umbrella leaves of the May Apple was good ta' eat when they got soft. She said the Jack in the Pulpits was fer' prayin' beside of, for they held the answers to life's secrets inside of their closed over tops. There were tiny God pulpits in there where things only Nature conceived of preached. Purple and white violets grew on the shady edges of the woods.

Thursta's face grew stern. "There is one rule ye' must foller, or the woods will turn on ye'. Ye' only take what ye' need, and leave the rest alone."

She spoke of the different kinds of winds and rocks and dirt and smells in the woods. She showed Emerald animal signs and tracks and paths she hadn't noticed. All of a sudden Thursta stood still as stone and listened and looked around for a long time. Then she shivered.

"There's somethin' that comes through here that's bad! It ain't human! And it's big!"

She pointed her first finger at Emerald. Grandma Drusa once told her when someone pointed that finger, it was the fire finger, attached ta' their soul, so they meant business.

"You NEVER come in here in the dark, or when it's even gittin' close ta' dark! Only in the broad daylight will you be safe from it, and you be damned careful even then!"

Emerald stared at the scared look on her face and nodded. She felt the wind sigh, and the brush of Drusa, Mercy, and Fallon's hands around her. She closed her eyes until the sighs and sad love went runnin' back home to where it lived in constant sorrow. When she opened her eyes, she looked at her mother's face with a knowin' sadness fer' her. Thursta acknowledged the look with a learned, keen indifference before she put her arm around Emerald in a rare display of affection.

"Let's go home. Cain't do nothin' about it now."

They'd shared a place without anyone else in it and Emerald wanted more. She tried to talk to Thursta about the woods, but Thursta turned away with a sour look. Emerald dogged her tracks, looking at her with mournful eyes, silently asking her to go back to the woods again, but Thursta was done with it. The reason she wouldn't finally dawned on Emerald.

"Oh! It's 'cause of that man ye' loved before Bolen tricked ye'."

Thursta slapped her, somethin' she'd never done before.

"Don't you name it ever agin'!" she shouted. Emerald stared at her. Then she turned and run out the door. The screen slammed behind her. After a little bit, she crept back to the screen door and spoke to Thursta's back through it as she turned the potatoes in the skillet.

"I won't. I promise ye."

Thursta nodded without turnin' around.

Eve's Sons and Daughters

The lilies of the valley
sway high up in the hills
white bells that ring in night and day
while blue birds sound their trill
Ere' many roads and far away
Eve's daughters walk the woods
ever since the dawn of time
they've always known they would.

The stately Son lies weeping still
beneath the hollow vines
where ivy creeps a' windingly
across the wounds of time
the wild flare's bloomin' merrily
larkspur and tree branch deep
call to the Son when life is done
they'll keep the perfect peace.

So listen to the children
dancin' cross the creeks
sweeping times away with them
they think they'll always keep
the blessings of a latter day
will come again in time
to keep them happy on their way
when the sun comes back to shine

Chapter 19. Sticks and Stones and Haircuts

Hank was tryin' to learn to be mean. He picked up little rocks and thowed 'em halfheartedly at Emerald, Lucy and Neil. They dodged the little rocks and ignored him. They knew he was good inside, but he'd watched Bolen too much. He'd picked up a few of his ways, that was all, and he would git' over it.

One mornin' they wandered over to the gravel pit. Hank started throwin' rocks at 'em. They were tired of him actin' like Bolen, so they picked up rocks and thowed 'em back at him.

"Hey!" he yelled. He stood there, lookin' surprised.

"Don't like gittin' back what you're a' dishin' out, huh, Roy Towhead?" they yelled. Hank reached down and picked up a little bitty rock and thowed it straight up in the air with all his might. They stood there, looking up, mouths open, watching Hank's tiny rock fly high in the air, then hurtle back down. They watched the little rock hit Neil square in the middle of his forehead. Blood gushed out of the tiny cut. Neil's rugged face and long blond curls were quickly covered in blood. Most of the time, nobody thought about Neil being a free bleeder like Lottie was.

Emerald and Lucy grabbed his arms, intending to carry him to the house. But Hank grabbed Neil's legs and pulled him the other way. None of them would let go of him. They hollered and argued and pulled him back and forth until Neil shouted, "What the hell are ya' doin'? Tryin' ta' tare' me in two? I cain't see a damn thing! And here you assholes are a' fightin' over me! I'll bleed to death 'fore you git' me ta' the house!"

Emerald and Lucy jerked him away from Hank. They ran with him to the house, with Hank followin' behind. Thursta grabbed him and set him on the edge of the kitchen table. She grabbed a washcloth and got the bleeding stopped. Then she placed a small square of clean sheet over the tiny cut, wrapped a strip of torn white sheet around Neil's head to hold it in place, and tied it in a knot.

"What happened?" She stood Neil down on the floor.

"Hit' was an accident of some kind."

They all looked at each other innocently and nodded.

"A rock fell out of the sky!"

Lucy announced. The others looked at her, then hollered.

"Yeah! That's what happened!"

Thursta rolled her eyes at them.

"So, a rock just happened to fall out a' the sky, huh?"

They all nodded solemnly up at her.

"That rock better not fall outta' that sky agin'!" she scolded them.

"It won't, it won't!" they promised earnestly and glared at Hank, who stuck his hands in his jean pockets and scuffed his bare feet on the worn lineoleum.

"What do I look like?" Neil demanded. Thursta owned a small hand mirror enclosed in blue plastic. She'd won it at the carnival. She took it from its hiding place and held it up in front of Neil. He examined his face in the mirror and felt of the white bandage around his head. One of his eyes was turnin' black, and the other one was already puffy, with green lookin' skin circlin' it. His clothes were bloody, and he had a white knot tied on the side of his head. He liked the way he looked, long curls and all. He grabbed a long handled wood spoon and swaggered around the kitchen, pretending the spoon was a sword, and he was a pirate, while Emerald, Hank, Lucy and Thursta watched him.

Just then, Bolen staggered through the kitchen door, stone blind drunk, primed to whip somebody. He stood there swayin' with rage, blinkin' at Neil's bandage, at his black and green mottled eyes, the long handled spoon in his hand, at the thick, blond, bloody, Shirley Temple curls hangin' around his face and down to his knees.

"Damn! I never seen sich' a sight! I gotta' be in the wrong house," he said, and staggered back out the door.

Pretty soon, West come in. He stared at Neil and snickered. "Pon my honor!" he said, shakin' his head. He turned and went back out the door.

Thursta stared at Neil. Then she bent over and went to slappin' her knees and laughin'. They all laughed while Neil swaggered happily around the kitchen.

The next afternoon, a couple hours before dark, Bolen strolled in the kitchen. Thursta was at the stove. Neil was swaggerin' around with a short stick, still pretendin' he was a pirate. Bolen put his mild face on and talked nice to Neil, who he generally ignored, and they went out the kitchen door together. A couple of minutes later, Bolen slipped back in the kitchen and plugged the old, black extension cord in. Thursta stopped cookin' and looked at him.

"Gonna' give West a haircut," he explained mildly to her, layin' it off with his hands. She went back to stirrin' milk gravy while he slipped back out the door.

West and a bunch of the men had Neil settin' on a chair with a white towel wrapped around his shoulders. They was a' holdin' him down. West plugged the clippers into the extension cord and handed them to Bolen. Bolen went to work on Neil. "ZZZZ" went the clippers over Neil's head, leavin' big gaps.

"Quit a' mashin' me down, ya' sons a bitches! You're a' causin' Bolen to cut it wrong!" Neil yelled at the men, rollin' his puffy black and green eyes up at them. "Let go a' me! I kin' take it like a man, you assholes! I seen enough haircuts give around here, I reckon I know how it's done!"

The men let go of him and stood back, laughin' so hard some of 'em set down on the ground.

"Go on, Bolen. Lets git' this over with," Neil ordered. "And it better look right when yer' done!"

Bolen laughed and shook his head. "ZZZZZZZZ" The long golden curls fell to the ground. After awhile, Bolen stepped back in satisfaction. Neil jumped to the ground. He shook himself like a dog shakin' off water, and rubbed his hands over his new butch haircut.

"Damn, that feels better!" he said, and swaggered towards the kitchen door. They watched the door slam behind him, then listened to Thursta screaming and Neil shouting. All the men laughed and run to their cars and took off, while Bolen calmly unplugged the clippers and wrapped the cord around them. Bolen and West stood there, listenin' to the big commotion goin' on in the kitchen. Before long, Neil shot back out the door, slammin' it hard behind him.

"Women!" he said disgustedly. Bolen doubled over a' laughin', and handed him a bottle of beer.

Chapter 20. Home, Sweet Home

The farmer who owned their house sold it without warning and Bolen and Thursta were forced to move. They sold Bessie and Bossy and sent Neil home with Lottie. Other people kept their furniture for them. They stayed a few days at a time here and there. but they ended up livin' out of Bolen's old black car. Each day, they drove a little further away from Grant, searchin' for a home.

They'd been livin' out of the car for more than a month when Bolen drove into the small town of Chesney to buy a fan belt. He swaggered into the hardware store while Thursta and the kids got out and leaned up against the car.

A local farmer noticed them. Thursta knew he couldn't miss seein' what their plight was. He told her his name, she told him hers, then she told him what he already knew. Bolen swaggered out of the store with the new fan belt in his hand and saw her talkin' to a strange man and bristled right up. His actions gave the large, slow speaking farmer the rest of the picture.

The farmer offered to let Thursta move into an empty farm house he owned a few miles out of Chesney. He said his grandparents built it, and lived there 'til they passed away. The rent would start a month after she got settled in. He shook his finger at her and said.

"I'll put the rent contract in your name only."

He gave her directions to the house, not looking at Bolen. Bolen grudgingly followed the directions. About five miles out of Chesney, they turned off the highway onto a gravel road with fields on both sides. The first house on the road was supposed to be the rent house.

They topped a small hill and Bolen slowed down. They all sucked in their breath. A tall, thin white house with gingerbread trim stood on a little rise in the middle of a big green yard, surrounded on both sides by fields of wheat. The driveway to the house curved between two tall pine trees and stopped at one side of the house. The house was made of the thin boards used for building a hundred years ago. Long, skinny windows and doors were ever where. The roof sloped up into two sharp peaks. A newer attached garage was on the side of the house.

They looked at each other in astonishment. Bolen ordered them to stay in the car until he checked the address on the mailbox. He swaggered back a' whistlin', and drove between the two tall pine trees and up the gravel driveway. He ordered them out of the car.

"Looks like this fancy place is 'aars!"

He swaggered to the front door and opened it. Thursta followed him inside. Emerald, Lucy, and Hank wandered around the back to see if the whole thing was a trick. They examined the big back porch and the double doors slanted over the cellar. An outhouse stood at the back of the yard. A water pump stood a few feet from the back porch. Behind the back fence was a pasture with a big red barn and a corral beside it. A dirt path leading to the barn and fields ran to the side of the lawn.

They circled the house, counting doors, window and small porches.

"Why, that's four front doors, one back door, a cellar door, and God knows how many winda's..." Emerald puffed, runnin' around the house.

There was a large library room at the front of the house. Behind it were double living rooms. Behind those was a large kitchen-dining room. One door in the kitchen led down into a cool, clean, dirt basement. One small bedroom lay to the side of the upstairs door. The upstairs held a open bedroom leading into a central room, with two smaller bedrooms off to each side.

Bolen checked the wiring and said it was old and frayed, but still safe. Thursta rolled her eys at him and scoffed.

"What you know about electricity could fill a thimble." He laughed.

Emerald kept an eye on West. She listened to Thursta and West talkin' about the old fashioned pantry in the kitchen. Thursta said she wanted to change out the wallpaper in the pantry.

"That's the same wallpaper as Grandma Drusa has," Emerald said.

"Why do ya' think I'm a' gittin' rid of it?" Thursta answered sharply. Emerald stared at her in surprise. Thursta turned away.

They settled in and spread out. The migrant worker farm, that bad, ugly place, was many miles away now. Thursta never went back to work there and their new place was too far away for easy driving for the drunks. They liked to stay local for many reasons. But Bolen still left the house each mornin' to make the long drive back to the farm to work and drink.

Thursta turned the library into a bedroom for her and Bolen. She shook her head in wonder at the big room.

"This is the busiest room I've ever seen! Three doors and six winda's!" she counted. She put her hands on her hips. "Now what am I supposed to with this set up?"

The six windows let natural light into the room for reading during the day. The library had three doors. One door opened to the front of the house, the other two doors opened into each of the living rooms. Thursta locked the front door, covered the windows on each side of it with heavy curtains, and put their bed up against the front wall.

The double living rooms were missing the double doors that once separated them. Each living room had two long, thin, small paned windows and three doors. One door led out to a small porch on the side of the house, another into the library. The third door led to the stairwell, and the dining room-kitchen.

Emerald, Lucy, and Hank got the upstairs bedrooms. Emerald settled into the middle room while Lucy and Hank chose the side rooms. Someone gave Thursta a rusty bed frame and springs. Thursta sandpapered it and painted it white. Emerald, Lucy and Hank finally had a bed to sleep on. They didn't have sleep on the floor any more.

Mabel

Lottie dropped Neil off a few days after they moved in. Neil wanted the girls to go outside and play with him, but they were too busy fixing up their new bedrooms. He complained.

"Ain't nothin' in them rooms. Jist' floors and walls. There's a whole bunch of stuff outside we ain't looked at yit'!"

Thursta had given Emerald and Lucy two old dresses and a cardboard box.

"Go play by yerself'!" they commanded. He tried exploring by himself, but it wasn't much fun. He went back and asked them again. They wanted him to stay so they could dress him up. They already had Hank a' settin' on a box, waitin' for a dress to be put on him. Hank yelled in his big, deep voice.

"Save me, Neil!" Emerald pinched his arm. "Owww!" Hank howled. Neil clattered back down the stairs.

"What's the matter? Afraid to go around this BIG old place by yer'self?" they jeered after him.

Emerald and Lucy kept Hank upstairs all day. Just before dark, Hank escaped. He left Emerald and Lucy sittin' on the bed in the middle room, laughing, chattering like magpies. Neil crept to the bottom of the stairs and listened. Then he grinned to himself, slipped out the back door and climbed the roof.

Neil had put in a busy day. He'd hunted up some old fishin' line, then stole Lucy's doll, Mabel. Mabel had a cheap plastic head and a stuffed rag body. He'd tied the clear fishin' line around Mabel's neck, then knotted Thursta's good white blouse over her body. He held her up, and the white blouse hung down perfect, makin' Mabel look jist' like a ghost.

He hid Mabel in the garage and waited until it was almost dark before he climbed over the roof until he was right above the middle bedroom window. He listened to Emerald and Lucy laughin' and talkin' a mile a minute. Then he slowly lowered Mabel down in front of the window.

He snickered to himself. He hoped Lucy saw Mabel first. She got scared the easiest. When she got scared, her mind left her, and she screamed on and on in a high voice until somebody shook her or slapped her ta' get her to come out of it.

Neil heard her scream. Shore' enough, luck was with him. He couldn't see her, but he could imagine her eyes poppin' out of her head. He laughed and jerked the doll back up out of sight.

He listened to Emerald scoldin' her. "There wadn't nothin' in the winda'! It's all in yer' head!"

Lucy flowed whichever way the water run, and she could be talked in and out of anything. Emerald convinced her nothin' was out there. "Nothin' kin' git' up two stories high ta' scare ye', ya' fool," Emerald said scornfully.

"Downstairs, maybe, but not up here!"

He heard Lucy reluctantly agree. Then they went back to talking. He edged Mabel down in front of the window again, and pulled her back up when Lucy screamed. He knew Lucy would be pointin' at the window. He heard Emerald jump off the bed and run to the window.

"I told ye'! Ain't nothin' out there, ya' fraidy' cat!"

Right then he lowered the doll again and listened to both of them screamin' before they run out of the room. He pulled Mabel back up and hid and waited. It took a little while before they stopped runnin' around the outside of the house a' lookin' up. He climbed down and hid Mabel. He strolled into the kitchen like nothin' happened. Thursta was standin' at the stove when he set down at the table. Pretty soon, Emerald and Lucy skidded to a stop in front of him.

"There's a giant monster outside the upstairs winda'," Lucy moaned.

"No!" Emerald said "It was a moanin' ghost!" Lucy shook her head sadly, her eyes big as saucers.

"No! It was the bloody dead body of a person who once lived here, with long hair and they walked in the night!"

They both agreed that the thing had appeared out of no where right outside of the winda' while they was a' settin' on the bed talkin'.

Thursta looked at them and shook her head. Emerald and Lucy grabbed Neil's arms and pulled him up the stairs, both talkin' at once. He swaggered over to the window they'd seen the apparition in, and looked outside. They waited for his verdict. He grinned at himself in the panes of glass and silently admired his ability to fool them before he turned around.

"Why, there ain't nothin' out there. It's all in yer' heads."

He pointed at his head, and run his finger in circles in the air. He scoffed.

"Looks like you've scared yerselves' haf' ta' death over nothin!"

Emerald and Lucy looked at the floor, and didn't speak.

"You should be ashamed of yerselves'!"

They turned around, dropped their heads and crept downstairs. That night, Neil took a blanket and slept on the floor in the front bedroom at the top of the stairs. He listened to Emerald and Lucy whisperin' in the other room, and turned over with a grin and fell asleep.

He slept good until Lucy woke him, screamin' fer' Mabel. She wasn't able ta' find Mabel anywhere, and she always slept with her. Neil had decided to leave the doll in the garage. He might want to scare 'em again. But after puttin' up with Emerald and Lucy's fearful whisperin' all night, and Lucy's bawlin' and whimpin' for her lost doll all day and another night, he was gittin' fed up.

Then Emerald and Lucy decided they were not gonna' sleep upstairs any more, and commenced to drag the mattress down the steps. Neil didn't want to sleep up there by himself, so he ran down the stairs and grabbed Mabel from her hidin' place in the garage, He ran back upstairs and thowed her at Lucy. Lucy screamed and dropped Mabel. Mabel had dirt and grease from the garage all over her. Neil hollered.

"Damn it! I did it! I fixed Mabel up, and climbed up on the roof, and dangled her down in front of the damn winda'! Now are ye' satisfied?"

Thursta climbed the stairs, picked up the dirty doll.

"Let's go clean Mabel up."

Her lips twitched with laughter as Lucy clattered down the stairs behind her. Emerald and Neil pulled the mattress back into the middle bedroom.

Lester and Lottie and their boys came over Sundays to visit Neil and eat dinner. Bolen carried a chair outside on Sundays in the summer. He held court, smoking and sipping coffee and talking with the men while they watched the kids playin' baseball in the yard Thursta and the women cooked in the kitchen.

Flint rarely came got there before Sunday dinner was ready because him and West wasn't getting along. Then West married Jan, and moved into a house down the road from them. Jan was a good housekeeper and a good cook, and she worked and paid the bills. West didn't beat her so much she couldn't work.

It wasn't long before West was at the house every mornin', drinking coffee with Bolen before Bolen left for the onion farm. After Bolen left, West went out to his car and drank. When the car got too hot, he spent his time drinking or passed out in the shade under the big pine tree in the front yard. The pine tree was crammed full of bird nests. Emerald, Lucy, Hank, and Neil liked to stroll past when he was passed out under the tree. When they got far enough away, they laughed at the sight of West, a long, thin skeleton, a' layin' on his back with his mouth wide open, snorin' away while the birds chirped and carried on in their nests and pooped on him.

When West wasn't drinkin' at their house, he was parked in his car, drinkin' at the little cemetery over on the next gravel road. He found it right after they moved in. Wildflowers grew in the fields around the cemetery. Big shade trees stood all through it. It was cool and quiet. West said he would end up buried there, so he may as well git' used to it.

Emerald heard him say it and knew he was right. Him being gone was okay with her. Bolen and Thursta gave him all the time he wanted with them. Bolen set with him and talked mild in his high, clear voice. Thursta fixed him food, but he never could eat much of it. Emerald figured some mistakes couldn't be mended.

Main Street in Chesney ran straight as an arrow right through the middle of town. One red light blinked solemnly above each of the two intersections crossing Main Street. All the stores were neatly sandwiched against each other in tall, faded red brick buildings. Their owners carried their welcome mats outside to the sidewalk each day, nodded and smiled at each other, shook the mats out, and opened their stores.

The streets in Chesney were clean with wide sidewalks and huge trees shading fine old houses and nice neighborhoods. Ever thing was planned. It was a small town where everyone knew ever body.

Emerald and Lucy stood out by the road, waiting for the school bus. It was the day after Labor Day. The first day of school. The big yellow bus topped the hill, a cloud of dust behind it. The bus stopped. Lucy followed Emerald up the wide metal steps with their black rubber matting. They looked for back seats to set in, for they were shy with people other than family. They dropped their eyes and blushed in front of the young strangers starin' solemnly at them. They found an empty seat and set down. The bus moved forward to pick up more children.

The buses dropped the children off at the old three story, red brick schoolhouse in the middle of town. All the grades had gone there back when Chesney was a smaller town. Now the seventh through twelfth grade went there. The elementary students attended one of the two schools on each end of town. The country kids boarded the bus to Bass Elementary school on the north end of town. The town kids walked to Rogers Elementary on the south end of town.

Bass Elementary was a new school, built in the latest architectural design of open classrooms. Each room was divided by two walls, front and back. The wall at the front of the room was mostly blackboard. The wall at the back was brown corkboard. A side wall of windows faced the outdoors. Instead of the fourth wall enclosing each classroom with a door, a wide hall ran the length of all the classrooms. The boys and girls bathrooms, coat hooks, and an outside door was on the other side of the wide hall.

The school was a one story brick Ushaped building surrounding a central courtyard yard on three sides. The two long classroom corridors connected at the bottom of the U, merging into offices, a gym, and the cafeteria. None of the classes were noisy, for they didn't have a fourth wall or doors to close to contain sounds.

Emerald watched Mrs. Clancy applying powder. Mrs. Clancy opened the thing she called a compact and delicately removed a little round sponge. She tapped it over her face while she stared at the round mirror inside the compact. The whole class watched in rapt silence while she reapplied bright red lipstick to her mouth and fluffed up her short brown hair. When she finished, she snapped the compact shut and carefully placed it in the large red purse resting on a corner of her desk. Then she smiled a red, freshly lipsticked smile at the children sitting in front of her. Class began.

Emerald helped Lucy get ready for school each morning. Most of the kids in school made fun of the way they talked, and labeled them "Hillbillies." They expected to be scoffed at in this new place, where everybody spoke their words funny, and nothin' they said made any sense. A few others in school sounded like them. They spoke the mountain language Bolen and Thursta spoke. They were poor, and it showed. The other kids laughed at them when they said "Wawsper" instead of "Wasp", and "flare" instead of "Flower", and "Pon my honor!" when somethin' surprised them.

The New Place

Poverty, hardship, ain't no place to go
Here, the people's guns are the words they say
They hunt each other with 'em night and day
They clack and chop their words off sharp,
and wait quick and mad, fer' us to ketch' up.

The farm work ended in the fall, and Bolen couldn't find work. There was no money and barely enough to eat. When winter set in, they went to school without coats.

"Where's your coat?" the teachers and other kids asked.

"Hit' ain't cold enough ta' ware' 'em yet!" they retorted. They'd been taught that only people with bad manners would ast' sich' a question! They tried their best not to tremble and shake from the cold in front of anyone, but it wasn't long 'til they caught bad colds, making their noses run all the time.

Mrs. Clancy embarrassed Emerald ever day in front of the class by scolding her for wiping her nose on her sleeves and bare arms.

"Buy some Kleenex, and wear your coat to school!" she ordered, glaring at Emerald with disgust. Emerald went home and asked Thursta what Kleenex was. Thursta got mad and rummaged around and found Lucy and Emerald each an old white handkerchief of Bolen's to carry to blow their noses on.

There was hardly any food at home, so they couldn't take lunch to school. It had always been that way, so they were used to it. Mrs. Clancy and Lucy's teacher scolded them again and again. They answered, as they always had.

"I ain't hungry."

One night Emerald, Lucy, and Hank were sitting at the empty kitchen table with Thursta. They were complaining about being hungry and cold, and about being called "hillbillies" at school. Thursta stared at them, ruminating. They knew that look, so they settled back and waited. They knew she liked to tell them stories, but not in front of anybody else, especially Bolen.

The Story of Handsome and Beautiful

"Let me tell ye' a story," she spoke sadly and formally. They nodded solemnly.

"Back home, there was a young man, and his people named him Handsome fer' some reason. I guess his folks thought they'd made the purtiest youngin' alive!"

She shook her head like they should a' knowed better.

"Now Handsome, he growed up ta' be a regular feller, jist' like ever body else. He wadn't no better lookin' nor worse lookin', but he had that name, and so people expected all kinds a' different things from him, and they all added up, fer' good or bad, to a whole lot more than he could provide.

People either laughed at him or talked down ta' him after they heard his name. He was purty' nerved up all the time, a' waitin' ta' see what the next person might make of him 'cause of his odd name. That name caused him no end of trouble," she said, shakin' her head sadly.

"Now there was girl lived down there, had close ta' the same kind of trouble. Her people named her Beautiful."

Thursta shook her head solemnly and frowned.

"I don't know what comes over some people that makes 'em do sich' things. I guess we'll never know what made 'em name her sich' a thing."

She sighed a big, sorrowful, sigh.

"Beautiful was a well enough lookin' young woman, jist' like anybody else, but people expected somethin' more or different out of her, 'cause of her name. And she didn't have it ta' give 'em."

She grinned at Emerald and Lucy, while Hank leaned against Emerald and played with her hair.

"Well, they was both good people, and their names made 'em turn out a whole lot better than they would've, had they been named Jack or Robin or Sadie or June."

She shook her finger at them and grinned.

"Now tomarra', if anybody calls you "hillbillie" you girls jist' call yourself "Beautiful" and Hank over there, you kin' jist' call yer'self "Handsome" startin' right now!"

Christmas Coats

The day before school let out for Christmas vacation, Mrs. Clancy called Emerald to the front of the room. She handed her a brown grocery bag. Then Mrs. Clancy made a speech to the class about helping people in need. Inside of the bag was a new coat and a barrette to keep her hair out of her face. Mrs. Clancy handed Emerald a box of Kleenex to keep in her desk.

Emerald stared at the floor, red faced. She needed the coat and the Kleenex, but Mrs. Clancy didn't have to give them to her in front of ever body! Mrs. Clancy kept talkin', while Emerald weighed it out. She'd stood all she could of the cold weather. The winters here was a lot colder than home. She settled it in her mind, thanked Mrs. Clancy, and put the coat on. It felt so good to be warm! The coat was tan with polished wood pegs for buttons, a red plaid flannel lining and hood.

Lucy's teacher give her a short gray coat, a warm cap with earflaps, 'cause she was always gettin' earaches, and a pair of black rubber boots to wear over her shoes.

Emerald saw a look of shame cross Thursta's face when they ran in the door wearing new coats. She glared at Thursta. She wasn't giving up her coat to Thursta's pride, and it showed on her face. Thursta didn't say anything.

Thursta made baked beans out of pintos, and corn cakes with onions and a can of corn for Christmas dinner. There was a blizzard. Nobody could reach their house. West couldn't get there. Lottie and Lester and the rest of their boys couldn't get there. Nobody.

That was Emerald, Lucy, Hank and Neil's Christmas gift! They ate the food they didn't have to give up. They played in the snow in their warm, new coats while the snow poured down. It snowed Christmas Eve, and all day Christmas day. They made snow forts, snow men, snow angels, and threw snowballs at each other. They ran in and out of the house for four days, with Thursta and Bolen a' smilin' at them, before the snow ended, and the rest of the bunch come back.

Bolen couldn't find a job he could work at and drink too. Bolen and West set together in front of the stove in the livin' room. Emerald glanced at them when she went by, and thought they looked liked two run down watches with not much innards' left in 'em. Jist' a bunch a' silence. Sometime in the afternoon, West started his car and let it warm up for his wandering drive home.

Then Bolen's luck changed. He got a job workin' the night shift at the big car parts factory in Chesney. He was to run the furnaces that tempered the parts the workers made durin' the day. He carried his whiskey to work in a thermos in his black metal lunch pail. He made a few drinkin' buddies among the other men workin' at the factory. They rode up and down the gravel roads, drinkin' with each other on their time off from work. He was makin' more money than he'd ever made in his life. Now he had a steady, year round job, if he could manage to keep it.

He used his money to buy whiskey, and kept what was left in his pocket. He give Thursta money to buy survival groceries for the family and Maxwell House coffee for him.

Thursta found Twinkie wrappers and other wrappers from vending machines in his lunch pail.

They didn't own a clock, and they ran out of toilet paper for days on end. They warshed their hair in Tide when they had it. Other than that, it went greasy. Emerald and Lucy wore their clothes and shoes long after they were too small. They patched up the big holes in their shoe bottoms with folded up paper, rags, or cut up pieces of old tires. Ever body slept downstairs. There was no insulation in the old house. The upstairs was too cold to sleep in durin' the winter, and too hot in the summer.

The little pot bellied stove in one of the living rooms gave off a small circle of heat in the winter, keepin' them as warm as they were going to get. They used the outhouse, primed the kitchen pump, and heated pans of water to clean up.

Winter passed, spring came, school ended. It was warm again. Emerald, Hank, Lucy and Neil ran up and down the roads and through the woods behind the fields. They explored the barn, discovered a creek in the woods, and scooped up baby tadpoles in their hands. Spring water was everywhere. They found ladybugs and an old dump in the woods in a far back field.

In the dump lay an old, ornate clock at an odd angle. It had numbers on it. When Emerald saw it, an odd feelin' that things were going to change came over her.

In her mind, she saw Bolen and West settin' together, starin' out at somethin', not needin' to say a word. Then she saw West stand up and walk away from Bolen. He never looked back. Somethin' was over between them. She felt an infinite sadness comin' from him. Then Neil found something else, and the moment passed from her mind.

Chapter 21. Bolen Quits Drinking

Emerald remembered the clock when Bolen quit drinking. One day he was the drunken, mean, loud, threatening man they feared and suffered with. The next day, he set down in his green chair in the living room, pulled a long face, and shut up. It took ever body by surprise. Bolen was damn proud of his drinking. He'd never once named quitting. Emerald guessed that's what he'd been thinkin' about, settin' there with West in front of the stove all winter. From then on, they measured time as before Bolen quit drinkin', and after Bolen quit drinkin'.

He quit drinkin' in May. He spent the summer settin' in the old green arm chair in the livin' room. He gripped the arms and set there. He poured stinkin' sweat all the time and his face stayed white and scared. His voice was light and mild, and he didn't say much to anybody, only what he had to.

Thursta carried plates of food to him and West. In spite of his troubles, Bolen got out of the chair and went to work ever night. Once a week he made the long drive to Grant to get a shot from the doctor to help him through the quittin' of the drink.

His drinkin' buddies came around for a while, but he stayed steady agin' the drink. He had nothin' ta' say, and he had nothin' to drink, so they took up with West.

West drank a little in the kitchen, then went in and set by Bolen in the livin' room. In a few minutes, he'd go drink a little more, and then go back and set by Bolen again. Neither one of them said much to each other.

Bolen never went back to drinkin. Some things changed for better, some for worse.

His boasting stopped. The big commotion he'd made for years was over. He didn't run any body out of the house, and he quit hittin' Thursta.

In the fall, when he was feelin' better, somebody gave him a bunch of concord grapes. Thursta made jelly out of a few. He carried the rest to the basement and made wine for West and whoever else wanted it.

He kept his job at the factory, made good money, and got good benefits. He had a lot more money left each week, 'cause it didn't go to whiskey, but he still kept it, like he had when he was drinkin'.

He paid the rent and the utility bills and bought what little groceries they had to have, and put the rest in his pocket to save for his boys. He was already in the habit of payin' the way for West.

Every now and then, he swaggered around and pulled the big roll of bills out of his pocket. He showed it to Thursta and the kids, braggin' about how much money he had. They just looked at him and walked off, takin' their hunger for meat, and their worn out shoes and clothes with them. Emerald thought of the money in Bolen's pockets as tiny green whiskey bottles, rolled out flat and pressed out on paper.

"Well," they told each other, "it's still better than it was before.At least we git' ta' eat." They could be satisfied with it.

Every Saturday afternoon Bolen drove Thursta to the Piggly Wiggly grocery store on the outskirts of Chesney to buy groceries. Everyone in town shopped there. Thursta had never learned to drive. She was home all of the time without any friends to talk to. She wanted time to get dressed up and fix her hair before going, but he wanted her to be ready to leave whenever he took a notion to. Since he never went in any store unless he absolutely had to, he didn't need to clean up, and he complained about the time she took to get ready.

On the way to the store, he lectured her about spendin' too much money on food.

"Now woman, don't go spendin' too much money. You're purty' bad for that if you git' a chaince'. Don't buy anything we don't hafta' have. I'm not made of money, ya' know."

After he parked the car at the store, he made a big show of takin' his wallet out and countin' out two or three one dollar bills, or a five, and handin' them over to her. He knew it wasn't enough. She knew he wanted her to ask for more, so he could shame her. Sometimes she asked, but most of the time, she shut up and took what he handed her.

Depending on how mad he gauged her to be when she came back out of the store, he complained that she shore' took her time in there. Then he laughed.

None of the kids would ride to the store with them. Emerald went a couple times, and by the time they got there, she was furious with Bolen. She saw Thursta barely had the heart to go in the store, but she would so's they could eat and not starve.

Bolen looked at her in the rear view mirror, back seat, expectin' her to admire what he did to Thursta. Emerald glared back at him. When he saw the look on her face, he averted his eyes. She knew by the set of his head and the back of his neck he knew he was bein' mean, that he liked it, and he was ashamed 'cause he knowed better.

When Thursta hurried back out of the store, he asked, "What, no change?"

She flushed red and handed him a few coins. He looked them over before he put them in his pocket.

"You're still a' spendin' too much."

She turned her head, clamped her jaw shut, and stared out the window.

The next time Emerald rode with them, she chattered all the way to keep him from beatin' Thursta up with his words. Then she jumped out and went in the store with Thursta. She watched her look at all the good things, saw how much she wanted them. She watched her mother smile, and speak to people proper, dressed up as good as she could. She saw that people liked her mother and she liked them back, but she couldn't stop and talk. Bolen was waiting. She hurried through the store with Emerald trailing her. When she stopped, Emerald said, "Let's take our time. Let the old son of a bitch set out there and wait!"

Thursta looked down at her for a minute. Then she sauntered off with Emerald following. When they came out of the store, Emerald looked at Bolen's red face and started chatterin' again. After that, he wouldn't let her ride to the store with them.

When Thursta had to go to town to buy what the kids needed to start school, he complained, handing her just enough money to buy a couple pair of underwear, a pair of shoes, and one pair of socks for each of them. Sometimes West drove Thursta to town and waited in the car. Sometimes she borrowed money from West. He always said, "Jist' keep it." They both knew his money come from Bolen or Jan.

Lottie gave Thursta a nice big purse and two fancy scarves she got from the Salvation Army store. Thursta tied one of the scarves around her neck and carried her new purse when Bolen drove her to the store the next Saturday.

Bolen came back from the store red faced. He swaggered around the house, jinglin' the change in his pockets. The next day, he complained to Thursta about the rent bein' too high, that he might not have enough to pay it.

The rent contract called for the rent to be paid on the first of the month. He started keepin' her upset and mad at him by waitin' 'til the third day of the month to pay it. He ordered her to get his name put on the rent contract instead of hers. He said he would pay it on time if she did.

He kept his money from them, and it kept him thin and mean in new ways his drinkin' never had. His money poured out of his pockets to West and to the drink for West and his friends. He handed West money ever week to help him feed his growin' family. He bought his whiskey, gas and cigarettes for him.

He never offered a dime to help the kids at home, or Thursta. They needed him, but he knew they didn't like him, and none of them would give him the satisfaction of askin' for anything.

He hated losin' the fearful power he once held over them when he drank. He couldn't make them hide in terror and wait while he decided whether he was gonna' kill 'em or not. That part wasn't in him any more, and they knew it.

Those bad old days were gone, like leaves flying before a hot, hurtful wind. Sometimes they felt the love a' hidin' in him somewhere, but there was no way to make it come out of him in a good way.

Summer came. School let out. They hid under the lilac bush across the road and tallied it off on their fingers. Bolen quit drinkin' the past summer. West, Lottie, Flint and their bunches weren't around. They looked at each other and laughed in glee. They ticked more things off on their fingers. Thursta was home and she always kept a pot of pinto beans on the back of the stove.

"Yay!" they shouted, joinin' hands and runnin' down the dusty road together. Freedom and a bunch of summer days ahead! They'd watch for trouble, for they didn't know when it would come back, but for now, they were on their own. All of them had nicknames. Hank was Roy Towhead, Neil was Pissy Frog, Emerald was Spider, and Lucy was Miss Priss.

"The world is our oyster," Emerald solemnly announced, flinging her arms wide, spinnin' in a circle.

"What's an oyster?" Neil asked.

Emerald answered, "Hell if know. I heard it somewhere."

The days flew by. They walked and ran up and down the dusty roads. "Boo!" they hollered, jumpin' out at each other and laughin'. They crossed fenced fields and run though forbidden wheat fields. They roamed further and further away from the house, slippin' into shady woods behind fields, climbin' trees. One day they found a small creek, dug up yellow flowers and carried them home to Thursta.

When it rained, they packed tight together in the big wood swing on the back porch. They sang songs an' made up new ones. Lucy's voice was high and sweet. Emerald's voice was low, and they sang harmony together.

Sometimes Thursta stopped her work and came out on the back porch while they were singin and waved her hands back and forth like a opera conductor.

Ever week Thursta put back a little somethin' from the groceries so she could make sweets for 'em. While they sung songs and told stories on the back porch, they smelled sugar cookies or scotch cake a' bakin'. They slept good, eat good, and traveled to wherever their interest took 'em.

They sneaked upstairs and jumped up and down on the beds. Then they hid under the covers and giggled when Thursta stomped upstairs, pulled the covers off, and made faces at 'em. Sometimes she left the covers on 'em, and made half hearted whacks with her hand at where she thought their rumps was located.

Chapter 22. Thursta, the Storyteller

Once in awhile, Thursta came upstairs and made moanin' ghosty or wind noises. That meant she was in the mood to tell a story. They'd pulled the covers off their heads and she'd grin at them, and start the story. She always started out the same way.

"Once upon a time, there was a..."

She'd say it, and wait, like she couldn't remember what come next. After a long silence, they'd yell. "Tell us the tale!"

She'd jump like she'd been shot. They'd giggle. Then she'd pace back and forth.

"This is the story of *How the Bear Lost His Looooong Tail!*"

She'd clear her throat to make it formal, then begin.

"Once't upon a time, there was a grouchy old bear, who's tail was as looong' as a fence rail," she'd say, lumbering around the room like a bear, pawing the air and scratchin' herself.

"How long's a fence rail?" they'd ask. She'd spread out her hands, moving them as far apart as they'd go.

"Used ta' be this long and more back in the olden days!" she'd answer.

"That bear went ever where a' huntin' for food."

"What does the bear like to eat?" they'd ask timidly, and cover their heads.

"Mmm Meat?"

"Naw," Thursta would answer. "They can kill ye' with their big paws and teeth, but they ain't likely to eat ye'. They like berries and fruits, and nuts and fish and ants a lot better than people."

They always shivered and hollered, "OOH!" from under the covers.

"Well, that grouchy ole' bear was a' goin' through the woods one day, and he got his tail caught on a briar. He roared and hollered and pulled, and finally, he tore his tail loose from the briar. But a little piece of it got stuck on the briar and stayed behind."

She looked behind herself in surprise, and clapped her hands over her hind end.

"Ouch!" she roared and rubbed her rump. The kids laughed at the look on her face. When they got quiet agin', she went on with her tale.

"Then that there bear come to a fence and tried ta' cross it to git' ta' the ripe berries on the other side. His tail got caught agin', and he pulled and pulled on it. He was scared to death some farmer might come along and shoot him. He couldn't run or hide, a' bein' stuck like he was on that damn fence."

Breathlessly with awe in their voices, the kids hollered.

"That damn fence!"

Thursta acted like she might whup' them fer' cussin' for a minute, and they laid there with big eyes, acting terrified.

"Well, that bear's tail come loose after a long time, and he saw that another piece of it was left in the crack of the fence."

She acted out the parts, roarin' and frownin' and clawin' the air.

"The next day, that grouchy ole' bear had another piece of his tail pulled off when he tried to cross another fence. Then the NEXT day, another piece tore off when he tried to climb a honey tree, and his tail got caught in a branch."

She muttered and walked up and down, rubbing her sore butt in exasperation before she grinned at their wide eyes.

"Well, that bear kept on a' gittin' his tail caught in thaings'. He got so's' he dreaded a' leavin' his den 'neath the roots of the big holler tree. He got afraid to hunt food or play. But bears are curious, and he wanted to know what was a' goin' on in the woods, so he kept a' comin' out when he could bear it, and a' comin' home at night, grouchy, with a sore tail.

Ever day, he lost a little bit of his tail, and it growed shorter and shorter 'til one day, he was out in the woods, and he saw some ripe pears in a tree across a fence. Now, he wanted them purty' yeller pears real bad, but he didn't want the hurt of his tail a' gittin' caught in the fence railin'. so he run back and forth, a' cryin' and a' takin' on, and a' roarin' some.

Finally the wind blowed the smell of them ripe pears across the fence to him, and he knowed he had ta' do it. He had ta' cross that fence. Well, he climbed across real slow, waitin' for his tail to git' caught, but it never did!"

She grabbed her butt and acted surprised, while they giggled.

"When he got on the other side of the fence, he looked down at his tail. Why, it wadn't no longer than that!"

She measured out her thumb.

"So that old grouchy bear eat all the pears he wanted, and crossed back over the fence without his tail a' gittin' caught. His tail didn't hurt no more, and he got so he wadn't near as grouchy as he had been. He liked his tail a' bein' short. But bein' a bear, he still stayed fairly grouchy and short tempered, and couldn't stand anyone to come near him, or play jokes on him. Sooooo, if ye' ever come across a bear, git' away from that place as quick as you can!"

She put up her hands like claws and roared at them, and acted like she was a' bear and gonna' git' 'em. They hid under the covers and pretended they was scared to death, while she pawed the covers and slapped their rumps. The story was done.

Another story Thursta told them was "The Black "Painter" Story".

Emerald told her once that it was spelled "p-a-n-t-h-e-r", and Thursta just said, "Oh," and laughed at her. She told it different than she did any of her other stories. She told it the exact same way ever time, for it was a memorized piece, a part of her family heritage. The story was about Thursta's great, great grandmaw and grandpaw.

She had to get ready to tell that story. She'd set down on the bed, put her hands in her lap, start swayin' sideways, tappin' her foot 'til she got the right rhythm. Then she'd sway back and forth and sing-song the story to them.

"They was my mother's people," she said. "Biblical Sarse. The Angel of the Lord encamps round about them that fear Him.

They come from Virginnie' to settle up in Plum Holler in Kentucky. Nobody else lived up there. Vinegar and Holly. God is the First Doctor.

They went ta' buildin' a log house up on the side of a hill in the deep, dark woods. Greens and a' tarryin'. God is the Great Healer.

No one else lived near that place, jist' the two of 'em startin' out, and all they had was some lard and a bag a' salt fer' seasonin', and flare and bakin' powder fer' bread, and a piece of honeycomb in a jar for sweetenin'. Pines and Oaks a' standin'. The Robin pulled the thorn from His crown.

They built and they worked hard, and their pride kept a' growin' with ever piece of wood they split, 'til they had a fine log house with one room with a sleepin' loft above it. Lightenin' time come. The load that was sa' heavy, was a' liftin' off a' them. They had a home, waitin' fer chilern, and a field open and seeded with new crop. Poor man's weatherglass and Cardinals. The Lord is our Help, ever present in time of trouble.

It come time to go back out, and git' leavenin' so's they could make bread and salt ta' season their wild meat. They went to rest the night before in their bed up high in the loft. They'd trade for what they needed. Corn meal, flare', fat back, salt. Maybe a little bite of horehound candy. And in their peaceful sleep that night, the cabin fire faded down into ashes. Elder and vervain. All is sane. Our Lord giveth and He taketh away. Blessed be His name.

All of a sudden, the night was rent with the scream of a big cat. They jumped out a' the bed. He grabbed his gun and run ta' the door, opened it jist' a crack, and looked out. Under the full moon and the pine trees, stood the biggest painter' he'd ever seen. It was a' standin' in the yard a' lookin' straight at him. It was as black as midnight, and it opened it's mouth big and screamed, and run at him. Mint leaves and moss marbled rock. The Lord is our stronghold in times of sorrow.

He slammed the door shut, and they both run back up the ladder and pulled it up behind 'em. The painter hit the door and broke it open. Hit' pranced in a' screamin'. The man drawed a bead on it with his loaded gun in what little moonlight was a' comin' through the open door. Bladder Campion and mountain pulpits. Be not frightened nor dismayed for the Lord stands with us.

The painter' paced and screamed, and tore the place up. The man follered it with his gun, but he couldn't tell it from the black shadders'. The horses screamed in fear in their little lean to outside, but the painter' didn't pay them any attention. Hit' wanted people ta' kill. Sage and quince. I shall fear no evil, for He is with me.

The painter' tried hard to git' up to 'em but couldn't make it. Finally, hit' run back outside, and they heard hit' a' walkin' on the roof above 'em, clawin' and tearin', tryin' ta' find it's way down to em. Liverwort and red clover. The name of the Lord is a strong power.

The long night passed, and it was breakin' dawn when the painter' left from the house. Hit's screams rung in their years', and in their bellies, and never stopped. Yarrow and mustard seeds. The Lord is faithful to protect you from the evil one.

The house stunk from the cat. They put the ladder down after the sun had been up awhile. The man stood in the doorway with his gun, and looked out at the fenced horses. They was fine. The man and the woman looked at each other, and didn't need ta' speak nary' a word. That thaing had already killed people and liked it, or hit' wouldn't ha' been after them instead of the livestock. Milkweed and violets. Rock of ages, cleft for me.

He went out and got the wagon ready. They packed up ever thaing' they owned, loaded it in the wagon, and left that place 'fore evenin' ever come agin'. They called their names out as bein' gone from that place fer' good when they left so's the painter' would hear 'em. Jemimah Stone and Journey Webb. He will put his angels in charge of you to protect you in all ways.

Without any pride, and without wantin' to be alone ever agin', they moved over to Singin' Branch, where a bunch of their kin lived. The people there helped them build a new house, after they see'd they was all tuckered out from a' bein' up on Plum Holler. Mugwort and divination. Let us thank the Lord who has not let our enemies destroy us. The end. They had only one child, her a' bein' my great grandmaw."

Thursta stopped swayin' and wavin' her hands through the air and a' countin' on her fingers.

"Ye' tell the story the same way ever time," they said admiringly.

"That's cause' I learned it that way. I keep the parts straight with my hands and my fingers. That's the way our people used to learn stories. I tell it the same ever time in memory of my grandmothers Mercy Music and Fallon Quick."

Time flew by, and before they knew it, it was almost time to go back to school. They spent the last few days walkin' up and down the road together, and helpin' Thursta string green beans.

"Make a hole in between the the beans. Then pull the twine through real easy, so the bean don't break. Then jist' stack the beans up, one on top of each other, until the twine is full, and leave a long enough string ta' hang 'em up with." She measured off the length with her hands.

Yep. School was startin', and they would hafta' take up that habit agin', but not yet. They'd walked halfway out to the highway before Neil spoke.

"Does your stomach hurt ye' when ye' hafta' go ta' school?"

Lucy stuck her thumb in her mouth and then pulled it back out. They all nodded.

"Even if you've et'?" he asked.

"Yeah!" Hank shouted and run over to the side of the road and pretended to puke. He made loud, retching noises. The rest of them rushed over and pretended to puke, too.

"I hate that damn hell hole of a school!"

They shouted, "I hate that damn hell hole of a school!"

"I hate ever damn teacher in that damn hell hole!" Hank shouted.

"I hate ever damn teacher in that hell hole!" they shouted back. He went to pacin' back and forth like a Baptist preacher on fire.

"I'm not gonna' go to school! Nobody's a' gonna' make me!"

They shouted the words after him.

"We're a' gonna run away! That's what we'll do!" he shouted.

Lucy ran off to the side of the road and started cryin' while they shouted the words back to Hank.

Emerald added, "Amen!"

"I don't wanna' leave home!" Lucy wailed at the top of her lungs. Emerald went to her and started singin' the "Amen" song, and a' rubbin' her back. Hank and Neil looked at each other. They shook their heads in disgust, picked up rocks and threw them at the telephone pole by the edge of the field.

Lottie came over the next Sunday for dinner and took Neil home so he could get ready for school. Bolen drove Thursta into town to buy shoes, underwear, and new socks for Emerald, Lucy and Hank. Thursta had their measurements written down on a piece of paper. Bolen shook his head sadly, jingled the change in his pockets, and complained that they was about to break the bank. They all turned away from him, carefully blank looks pasted on their faces.

School started, and the three of them boarded the bus. Emerald was shy and stuttered when the attention was focused on her. She believed the answers to fixing things lay in books, and she planned to read them all until she found the answers she wanted.

She won the district spelling bee and wrote a play that was put on for the whole school. The play was about a rocket ship that went to Mars. It had a lot of facts in it that the principal thought would be good for the students to know. She made it into a script, then she had to pick people to play the parts, and those she didn't choose wouldn't speak to her. Next, they were excused to go to the auditorium to practice the parts while she watched. Other students made props for the play. It turned into a huge ordeal she nevert expected.

When the play was over, she stood up while the whole school applauded her. She was trembling with tension at so much attention being focused on her for so long a time. Her stomach started hurtin' from the attention that began with the spelling bee, and it got worse with the play.

Emerald liked to read and do her homework. She didn't like making what people called "conversation". But words on paper, she thought, "You could take 'em anywhere. You could go and be what you wanted to be, and you didn't have to say a word out loud to anybody to do it."

The teachers and other kids in school wanted to talk to her. They seemed to think she wanted to talk, too. The teachers praised her, and the other students cast admirin' glances at her. Only when she lost herself in a book, did her stomach stop hurtin', only when she could go off to another place and be somebody else.

Drunk Drivers

School let out. Summer came, and West started makin' Hank ride around with him. Bolen wouldn't stop West forcing Hank to get in the car with him and his drunken friends. He turned his head the other way and acted like he didn't see a thing. Emerald heard Hank beggin' Bolen to not let West take him in the car any more.

"Bolen, I wanna' stay home, what did I do that was sa' bad ye' won't let me stay here?"

None of the kids were allowed to call Bolen dad or father. Just Bolen, as though he wasn't kin to them.

Bolen wouldn't stand up for Hank. Emerald, Lucy, and Neil figured out a plan to help him. They watched for West's car. He was a slow driver, which gave them time to warn Hank so he could hide from him. West couldn't ever find Hank, so he got out of the habit of takin' him with him.

Bolen got a man from his work place to come out and till up a big garden spot for him in the side yard. Then he refined the soil with a rototiller and planted neat rows of tomatoes, corn, beans and other vegetables. When he was done, he planted blue and red mornin' glories in different spots through the garden, and sweet peas along the edge. He liked his garden and tended it every day.

Bolen had changed about trouble. Before he quit drinkin', he either made the trouble, or was right slap in the middle of it. Now he avoided it like the plague whether he should've or not. He fled to the garden, or set in his car, listenin' to baseball games on the radio. He went to the basement, mowed the lawn, or chopped wood when there was trouble. Emerald figured he'd used up his courage a' givin' up the drink. He left Thursta to handle the trouble, after he give her strict instructions about what he wanted done.

Maggie

Emerald was lonesome. Neil, Lucy, and Hank were spending all their time together in and out of the house. She went to the road and fields and waded in the creek, watched the sandpiper's, and teased the little red crabs livin' in the clear bottom water. She stayed bored and lonesome until she met Maggie.

Hank and Lucy didn't like to go to church. Neil and Emerald went without them. The church bus picked them up Sunday mornin' and dropped them back off after church.

One Sunday mornin', a new girl set down by Emerald. She looked like a short, chubby angel. She shook out thick blond hair that cascaded past her waist, glanced over at Emerald and shrugged. The preacher ranted on and on about sin. Finally he held out his hands and rolled his tear filled eyes up to heaven. The girl snorted and said under her breath, "Jist' git' it over with!"

Emerald sucked in her breath and surveyed the new girl's angelic button nose, soft pink skin and gray eyes. The stared back at her, waiting. She grinned at her. From that minute on, they were best friends.

Church let out. They stood outside and talked. The girl said her name was Maggie. She was two years younger than Emerald. She said she was from Missouri, and too old for her age, and always would be, 'cause she'd been raised by her grandmother until her parents come back and took her away from her granny. She said she was rock solid and opinionated, 'cause that's the way her grandmother raised her ta' be.

She said she was the oldest of four girls, and that her hare-brained sisters, Ginny, Maude and Clara, had always lived with her mother. But she hadn't had to put up with the torture of being raised with the petted "Twits", because her mother had her before she got married, and give her ta' her grandmother ta' raise. Emerald sucked in her breath in admiration at her forbidden revelation.

"Then I turned eight," she said to Emerald, "and damned if ever thing didn't fall apart! My grandmother," she rolled her eyes heavenward, "God rest her weary, and I do mean tired and wore out soul, mostly from a' havin' to deal' with fools like my mother, fell sick, and didn't tell me she couldn't take care of me any more. So my mother come and got me. My grandmother died not long after I left. I've been livin' with them since last winter," she said, "and I can tell you, it's a trial and a tribulation!"

Maggie and her family lived in a cheap, tiny summer cottage beside a small lake outside Chesney. The next Sunday, Emerald went home with Maggie when church let out. The tiny, two room cottage was too small for Maggie and Emerald to stay in. They set outside on the tiny front porch and looked at the other tiny, empty wood cottages clustered around them. After a long time, Maggie's mother called them in the house to eat. There was one bowl of pinto beans and a small cake of cornbread on the table.

The next Sunday, Maggie went home with Emerald after church. Thursta called ever body in to eat. A punch bowl full of green jello set in the center of the table, surrounded by a huge pan of baked beans, two platters heaped high with chunks of cornbread, a big meatloaf, and a huge bowl of mashed taters drippin' with butter.

Maggie eyes lit up. She looked around the table at all the people, and grabbed her plate.

"Fill er' up fast, or I'm afraid I won't git' any!" she ordered in her deep, booming voice.

Bolen was walkin' to his chair, and he missed a step at the sound of the deep, rumbling voice coming out of the small, dainty girl. He stared at her and reached out his hand and touched her hair as he passed by her, a thing they'd never seen him do with anybody before. Maggie set still and let him touch her hair. His hand moved briefly over her thick, golden hair like a butterfly, then moved on.

"Ever body likes to do that. But if I let 'em all do it, I'd be bald!" She explained to all of them and shrugged.

"It is the bane of my existence."

They all laughed. Then one of West's drinking buddies walked by Maggie's chair and touched her hair. She jerked her head away.

"Don't you ever touch me agin', er' I'll slice your balls off and stuff 'em down yer' throat!"

Maggie ordered in her deep rough voice.

"I already told ye' I only let who I want touch my hair."

Ever body stopped eatin,' and gaped at the flushed, angry, angelic little face and snub nose. Then they started laughin' and poundin' the table, while West's friend slipped out the back door.

"Y'all have yer' fun, I'll jist' go on eatin'!" She declared.

Maggie fell in love with Hank the minute she met him. She started comin' home with Emerald Sundays after church. She had never played with other kids.

"My grandmother never saw any use for more than one youngin' bein' around at a time," she explained to them. Ever one liked her. She made them laugh, and she liked to run up and down the roads with them. They played in the forbidden fields. They hid 'til the neighbors drove out of sight, then climbed their cherry trees and ate the forbidden cherries.

One Sunday afternoon, the farmer that owned their house caught them jumpin' in a big pile of grain in the middle of the barn floor. He shouted at them. They scrambled to their feet and ran. They jumped the fence into the cornfield by the barn, split through the rows of tall green corn and hid.

They watched the farmer get in his truck and stop at the house to tell Thursta on them. After he left, Thursta stood outside, shieldin' her eyes with her hands, studying the cornfield. They didn't make a move or a sound 'til she went back in the house. They were afraid to go back to the house. They just knew she'd be waitin' on 'em with a switch. The switch grew bigger and bigger in their minds. They got busy tellin' Maggie what all Thursta might do to 'em if they ever went home again.

Maggie declared "I ain't never comin' here no more!"

They stayed in the cornfield for a long time, makin' the stories of punishment bigger and bigger. They got so caught up in their stories, none of 'em noticed the dark clouds gatherin' overhead. All of a sudden, the skies opened up and rain pounded down, surprising them. They was soaked to the skin in a minute.

They huddled together and watched the rain streamin' off each other. They'd been caught and hollered at. Thursta was a' waitin' with a giant switch to beat 'em half to death. They was starvin' and would probably never git' ta' eat agin, and now they was rained on an' all wet, stuck in a damned muddy ol' corn field.

With shoulders bowed in defeat, they slogged across the muddy field, climbed the fence, snuck across the back yard, and down into the basement. They were hungry. They stole two bags of frozen cherries from the old white freezer on the back porch so they wouldn't starve to death. After they ate, they were tired and sleepy. The sound of the rain made them sleepier. They slipped up the basement stairs and into the kitchen. No one was around. The house was quiet, so they slipped up the stairs and crawled into one bed.

They were gigglin' and hidin' under the covers when Thursta came stompin' up the stairs with a big switch. They covered their heads. She whacked the covers a few times with the switch, then Hank hollered.

"Don't hit me agin', Mom! I got the 'pew moany fever!" from under the covers.

Thursta tossed the switch down and laughed. In her big, deep voice, from under the covers, Maggie hollered, "Hank, you'll always be the love of my life!"

Handsome and Beautiful Get Married

Flint married and moved away. Lottie and Lester stood up with them. Vanessa, Flint's new wife, was short and thin, with red hair and brown eyes, and one of the best smiles Emerald ever saw.

Emerald, Lucy, Neil, and Hank watched as tall, lanky, ornery, bitchy skinFlint bent over with a rare grin to awkwardly pin flowers on the shoulder of Vanessa's lacy green dress. She was a' starin' up at him like she'd jist' seen Jesus and got saved. The four a' them squinted up at the sky above 'em to see if Jesus was up there, but they didn't see nothin' but a blue, cloudless sky. Then Flint,Vanessa, Leste and Lottie got in his old car and drove off to meet the justice of the peace.

They stood in the yard, watching Flint's car roll down the dusty road. Lottie had told them that Vanessa said she'd fell in love with Flint at first sight. Lottie said Vanessa told her that Flint Plant was "handsome, brave, true, easy going, kind, generous, tall, humorous, happy, mild, gentle, without a bad word for anybody, ever!"

They rolled their eyes at each other at the romantic words describing grouchy, lanky, ornery, rigid, frowny, tight, gripy, itchy, bitchy skinflint Flint, and ran back in the house a' laughin, where Thursta was cryin' 'cause Flint was movin' sa' far away.

Bolen's garden came in. Thursta sliced big plates of cucumbers and tomatoes and boiled big bowls of corn to go with the pinto beans and taters. She picked dandelion, mustard greens, and poke, warshed them and wilted them by sizzlin' hot bacon grease over them. Sometimes she boiled them and made cornbread. Bolen favored the applesauce cake she made from her mother's recipe. It was made of four thin layers of what Thursta called shortbread. The shortbread was heavier than a regular cake. In between the layers, she spread home made apple butter, leavin' the top and sides plain.

Bolen liked food, and he liked Thursta's cookin', even though he was a picky eater. When he filled his plate, he took very small amounts and put ever thing to itself, for he didn't like his foods to touch each other.

Chapter 23. Bolen, the Storyteller, Quarters and Teachers

Bolen and Thursta were natural born storytellers. Bolen told a different kind of story than Thursta did. Her stories were loose and big. They were about clankin' chains scarin' lonesome people in the night up in the hollers. She told how bears lost their tails, and about a little girl who carried a honey cake across the hill to her grandmaw, but eat it up 'fore she got there. She told about Goldilocks and The Three Bears. She was partial to stories about someone who died and were ready to be buried, then got up out of their coffins, and asked what was the matter when people got scared.

Bolen told his stories when he and Thursta and the young "gang", as he called them, were eating. When none of the older ones were around.

He'd shake his head and grin down the table at Emerald, Hank, Lucy, and Neil. He'd pass the bowls of food on down to them and say, "Boys, I never saw sich' eatin' in my life!" Then he'd laugh in a pleased way. When he got that attitude, they knew he was gonna' tell them a story while they ate.

The Hobo Stories

Before I met you, we fashed away,
where'd you go them times ya' left,
a' runnin' wild through night and day,
a' leavin' our hearts all cleft?...
nobody's ever known...

Bolen's stories were mostly from his real life experiences back in his hobo days. He told stories about the odd characters he met, and of the jobs he worked at. He had a few favorites he liked to tell.

"One time," he'd say, clearin' his throat, scootin' his chair back, lightin' a Camel cigarette, "Back in my hobo'in' days, when nobody in the country had a thing, there was an ol' woman I done some work fer'. I'd got off the train in a little ol' town somewhere ta' try to find some work before I starved to death."

He'd shake his back and forth at the gravity of the situation he'd been in.

"I walked through the little town, a' lookin' around to see if there was anybody needed any thing done. Purty' soon I come up on this little house, where the weeds was higher than my knees, and the screen door was a' hangin' loose. I pushed the broke down gate open, and it squalled like a wild cat.

I waded though' the weeds, and knocked on the door. Purty soon, an ol' woman answered it. I listed out the work I seen ta' be done, and asked her a quarter to do it. She said she couldn't do that, but she'd feed me all I could hold, if I'd fix it up fer' her. I told her that was all right.

Then I sharpened the rusty old sith' she had, and cut the tall grass down. Then I chopped wood fer' her, and fixed the gate and the screen door."

He nodded to himself with approval, and took a long, slow drag off his cigarette.

"After awhile, the ol' woman called me in the house and fed me. Fried taters, a big piece a' crisp fatback, half a dozen fried eggs, and biscuits. It was the best meal I'd jist' about ever et' and I kept eatin' til' I was full as a tick. I couldn't a' eat another bite if I'd a' had to."

At this point in his story, he'd grab a' hold of his skinny little belly, shake it and grin.

"Then the ol' woman set a dried apple pie on the table. She couldn't see good, and the pie was covered with ants. I told her I didn't want any, that I was too full to eat another bite. But she kept right on, so I cut myself a big wedge of that dried apple pie, and eat it, ants and all."

"UUUUW! What'd them ants taste like?" somebody always asked.

"Couldn't even taste 'em, that pie was sa' good!"

He'd grin before he crossed his legs, and looked away from them with the start of an inscrutable look on his face. They understood his action. He was a' sayin' without words, that he was rememberin' somethin' else back in that story time, and that was as much as he cared to say right then. They fell silent, watchin' the stories they'd never hear, the words he'd never say about his life, cross his face like shadders' and fall back down into him. Ever body at the table knowed where he went to, fer' ever one of 'em had the same place in their selves that worked the same way.

In a couple minutes, they'd go back to eatin', and after a minute, he'd clear his throat, get some more coffee, and maybe tell another story. Sometimes he told "Johnny's Story." He met Johnny when he was working as a cook in a lumber camp in the northwest.

"I would a' worked on the trees, but I was too little, and they wouldn't let me, so they put me ta' cookin' fer' the men instead."

He'd grin and thow' his eyes over on Thursta.

"I didn't know a thing about cookin' back in them days, like I do now."

Thursta rolled her eyes at him.

"The lumberjacks shot deer and rabbits and squirrels in the woods, and I figured out how to cook 'em tender, and I made big pans of biscuits and gravy ta' go with the meat. Me and few of the other men made friends, and set around together and talked and drunk a little bit in the evenin's."

"Well--"

At this point Bolen scooted his chair so it set sideways to the table, so he wasn't lookin' direct at them.

"Johnny brought me a letter, and ast' me to read it to him. It was from his girlfriend, and he couldn't read. I started readin' it ta' him, and he jumped behind me, and stuck his fingers in my years. I pulled his fingers out a' my years', and ast' him what the hell he was doin!'

He said he didn't want anybody else ta' know what was in the letter, so he had ta' put his fingers in my years', so's I wouldn't know what the letter said when I read it out loud to him."

His favorite story was about how him and a friend traveled to the Columbia River Gorge in the state of Washington. They camped on the river for awhile, and before they left, they each put a note with their address on it in an empty whiskey bottle, and thowed' it in the river. The notes asked whoever found it, to write back to 'em. Time went on, and they forgot all about the bottles.

Bolen's friend never heard back from anybody. But Bolen did. A young woman in California found his bottle, and rode the train up to see him. She was the daughter of a rich man who owned a big orange soda pop company down in California. She liked him and wanted to marry him. He said she didn't quite suit him, but he was gonna' go ahead and marry her anyway. "But when I come back to the mountains to git' my stuff so's I could go back and marry her, I saw Thursta, and it was all over right then!"

Thursta always glared at him with a mixture of many things in her eyes when he finished that story.

Thursta and Bolen went to bed at ten on the nights he didn't work, but the kids stayed up 'til they got sleepy. They'd wait til' they heard them start snorin', then they'd slip the bedroom door open a crack and watch them layin' in the bed, side by side on their backs, their mouths wide open, takin' turns snorin' like thunder. Thursta's chest rose up, and she'd let out a loud snore. While her chest was going back down, Bolen's chest rose up, and he'd let out a loud snore. Up and down. Up and down.

"It's like watchin' snorin' music bein' made," they whispered, easin' the door shut, and runnin' out of earshot ta' laugh.

Emerald went home with Lottie and Lester at the end of summer so she could be with Neil and the rest of Lottie's boys before school started again. They still lived in the chicken house down the hill from his mother's, and went to the holyroller church all of the time. Emerald loved settin' on a bench with Lottie's boys, singin' at the top of their lungs and clappin' their hands. Lottie still got slain in the spirit regular, and the church held a healin' meetin' ever night, so Emerald and others practicin' the healers ways could lay hands on the sick people.

Lester was still on disability for his bad back. He walked around the house carryin' his Bible, rollin' his eyes up to heaven, preachin' to anybody that would listen. They got government commodities from bein' on welfare. Lottie's was the only place Emerald got enough of the meat she craved.

Lester liked to cook, and he kept a big iron skillet on the stove all the time. He fried bread in it, and they eat all the eggs, cheese, and meat from the round commodity tins they wanted. After the last Sunday church meetin', Emerald went home without complaint. By that time, she didn't feel too good from all of the attention the church gave her, and the rich food she'd eat.

School started again. She knew most of the kids in her class now. That helped her stomach not hurt so much. Thursta baked pans of biscuits and fried eggs and made milk gravy and there was sometimes jelly to go on the biscuits in the mornin's.

Lottie and Thursta canned up Bolen's garden. Emerald helped pick elderberries and currants and the last of the wild strawberries ta' make into jellies and jams for winter. Huntin' season came in, and Bolen and the boys went huntin', and brought home plenty of game to eat and put in the freezer.
Thursta taught Emerald how ta' clean and cook the game, but Lucy couldn't do it. Emerald knew Thursta could cook anything. She was the best hand at cooking turtle, squirrel, pheasants, and deer, than anybody.

Quarters

Bolen got home from work at seven thirty each mornin', five days a week. He set at the kitchen table for a few minutes, then he went off to bed. Before he went to sleep, he took his pants off and placed the top of them neatly under his pillow with the pant legs draped down the side of the bed. He said that was to keep 'em pressed, so Thursta wouldn't have to iron 'em, and laughed.

The bus picked up Emerald, Lucy, and Hank at eight fifteen. Bolen was asleep by then. Sometimes they needed money for library fees or other things. Thursta asked him for the money, and he refused, so she got in the habit of sneakin' into his pant's pockets, getting change out to give them after he fell asleep.

One mornin' he woke up and caught her.

"What the hell's a' goin' on?" he demanded.

"Lucy owes twenty five cents on an overdue library book!"

She waited while he laid there and thought. He ruminated for awhile. Then he said, "Go ahead and get it. But don't make it a habit."

The next time she needed change, she woke him up and asked him for it, but he said no because it wasn't for Hank. She quarreled at him and wouldn't let him go back to sleep until he gave in. He got tired of her wakin' him up and quarrelin' with him, so he ordered her to go ahead and get out what she needed, but only when she had to, and to put his pants back exactly the way they were.

Still Goin' to the School of the Crazies

Emerald didn't like Mr. Shaw. He was her first male teacher. Both he and his wife were teachers at Bass Elementary. He was the tallest man she'd ever seen, with a fringe of white hair circling the bottom half of his shiny, bald head. His lips were tiny and thin, and he wore perfectly pressed gray suits with blue ties ever day. His eyes were small and icy blue, and his right eye twitched violently each time Mrs. Shaw strolled past his classroom.

Mrs. Shaw's brown hair stuck out like straw. Her clothes were crooked and mismatched, like a witches, and her eyes bugged out of her head. They made her look crazy, or like somethin' bad had scared her for life. Mr. Shaw stopped what he was doing and stared at her when she clacked by on the high heels she always wore. She stared back at him without speaking.

Mr. Shaw didn't like hillbillies. After awhile, Emerald noticed that he didn't like much of anything. His frown was permanent, and he had a habit of bouncin' the white stick of chalk he wrote on the board with up and down in his hand when he was agitated.

Hank's teacher, Mrs. Haze, was a crazy old lady. She hit her students with rulers and threw books at their heads. Emerald and everybody else could hear her yelling at her students. The sounds rolled down the open halls between the classrooms all day long.

Hank was so scared of her he couldn't think straight or do his homework. Mrs. Haze got so crazy and out of control with her tiny students that they moved her into an empty room with a door down at the end of one of the open halls. What little bit of control she had exercised before with the little ones, left after she got 'em cooped up in a room all to herself. A couple of her students were sent to the school nurse for injuries she caused. Their parents came in and complained to the principal. But nobody stopped her. One day Hank came home from school with a cut on his head.

"What's it from?" questioned Thursta. Thursta had heard all about Hank's teacher.

"Mrs. Haze thowed' a book at my head and hit me," Hank answered calmly. The next morning when Bolen came in from work, Thursta ordered him to take her to school. She told him what happened to Hank, but Bolen refused.

"I'm all tuckered out from work!" he whined. "I gotta' sleep, or I cain't' keep my job and keep you in food!"

Just then, West drove into the yard. Bolen had his back to the window and didn't see West's car.

"Go on to bed! I'll figure somethin' out!"

Bolen turned and headed for the bedroom. Thursta waited 'til he closed the door before she turned and hurried out and intercepted West.

"Emerald! You ain't none goin' ta' school today'! You git' Lucy and Hank and set in that corner!"

She pointed at a corner of the kitchen.

"Ya' all better be quiet as mouses, so Bolen don't wake up! You stay put 'til I git' back! I won't be gone long!" she said, with purpose in her voice. Emerald grabbed Lucy and Hank and got in the corner. Thursta left with West. A big silence followed. They could hear Bolen snorin' off in the distance.

"Reckin' ya' kin' eat quiet?" she whispered to Hank and Lucy after awhile. They nodded. Emerald went "Shhh!" with her finger over her lips, and stood up. She tiptoed to the pan of biscuits and carried it back to them. Then she tiptoed to the cupboard and brought back a jar of honey and a spoon.

"Naaa! I want some of that meat in the 'frigerator!" Hank whispered. They wanted meat in the morning, but Thursta always saved it for Bolen and West. This was their big chance, for there were a few left over pork chops in the frig'. Hank smacked his lips and chomped on the pork chops while Lucy and Emerald raided the rest of the kitchen.

Thursta came home too soon. Emerald had planned to put everything away and clean up before she got back. But they were still sittin' among the pans and bowls when Thursta and West walked in. Thursta put her hands on her hips and glared at them. West hung back and grinned the beautiful, wide smile that hid his craziness.

"I'm gone no time, and this is what I come home to!" Thursta whispered loudly. She pointed her finger towards the upstairs.

"You all git' up them stairs and in the bed, and you better be quiet, or I'll come up there and whup' ya'!"

"Kin' I take this pork chop bone with me?"

Hank asked plaintively.

"Git' up them stairs! Right now!"

Thursta answered in a furious whisper as they scampered for the door leadin' upstairs.

The next day they went to school as usual. But Hank got sent to a different teacher's room. During recess, Emerald saw Mrs. Haze standin' near the swings with a scarf wrapped around her head. None of the teachers ever wore hats or scarves, and Emerald wondered what was going on. She watched intently as a couple of Mrs. Haze's students acted like they was a' grabbin' each other's hair and dancin' them down an aisle. Then they mimed slappin' a hand with a ruler and shouted with a hillbilly accent, "Thare! Now let's see ya' hurt a pore' little child agin'! Ya' do, and I'll be back fer' ye', an' whup' yor'e sorry whore's ass all over this sorry assed place!"

Freezing weather set in early and Bolen complained to Thursta. "Yore' a' usin' too much wood while I'm gone, Woman."
They argued for awhile, and then he said, "Order coal for the stove... but keep it down, and order only as much as ye' got to."

Chapter 24. Turkey Time and Christmas Presents

Thanksgiving was near. Thursta made a new, ambitious plan. She argued with Bolen while he hitched up his pants and rocked on the balls of his feet. She won. He hitched up his pants one last time, drove her to town, and paid for a big, cheap tom turkey for her to cook.

On Thanksgiving mornin' Thursta put the turkey in the oven. It was the first tame turkey she'd ever baked, and it was huge. She didn't know tom turkeys were famous for stayin' tough. That's why it was so cheap at the store.

The smoke billowed out the doors from the clean, white squares of cloth she smeared thick with butter and laid over the top of the turkey to brown it. While the turkey roasted, Thursta went through the jars of canned goods settin' on their shelves in the basement. She carried the ones she wanted upstairs along with strings of dried fall beans.

Emerald watched her run around the kitchen, busy as could be, a satisfied smile on her face. She put Emerald to makin' green jello and Hank and Lucy to unstringin' the fall beans and puttin' 'em in water to soak.

Pretty soon, Lottie and Lester, West and Jan, and Flint and Vanessa and their families drove into the yard. Every body was a' laughin' and havin' a good time. The men stayed outside or in the living room while the women gathered in the kitchen. The women laughed with each other and carried the mens dirty coffee cups to the sink. Lottie emptied ash trays and grabbed a dish rag to wash the careless coffee stains off the plastic table cloth. Thursta and the women looked at each other with knowing eyes. "Men!" they all said together.

It was six o' clock when the tom turkey finally got done. The sun was setting. The older kids were gone, full of the hastily improvised meatloaf Thursta had made. The younger kids cheered. The older kids didn't git' ta' eat all the meat up this time! They had a whole turkey to themselves.

It was almost Christmas. Bolen hitched up his pants again and drove Thursta to the Piggly Wiggly.

"This is gittin' ta' be a habit, woman," he said sternly. Thursta ignored him. Having learned from the turkey, she baked a giant ham, made a huge, juicy meatloaf, and fixed all of the trimmin's, and ever body come over for dinner on Christmas day.

Bolen was the only one who got Christmas presents. It had always been that way. Nobody had ever questioned it. Bolen got flannel plaid shirts, bright new Zippo or Bic lighters, and cartons of Camel cigarettes from West, Lottie, and Flint's families. He set like a king on his throne in his green chair in the livin' room while they lined up to give him his presents. Thursta and the younger ones stood in the doorway watching.

It wasn't in the way of things where they came from, that people said, "thank you" or "please," so Bolen jist' smiled and nodded, and said, "That's a good un'," or, "that's all right," about each present they give him. When they was done, he stacked his presents neatly beside of his chair, lit up a Camel, and looked across the room at Thursta.

"Woman, I'd shore' like a cup a' coffee."

Emerald looked up at Thursta and saw the same look she knew she wore on her own face when Bolen got presents and nobody else did. It felt like it would take a million miles of walkin' to carry a cup of coffee across the livin' room floor to where the damn "King" set on his throne. And then they'd wanna' thow it on him.

Bolen's Christmas Box

Bolen received a yearly Christmas box from his mother.

Marthy's Lament   "Desolate"

My son has plowed the corn field down,
He's took' the mule and gone to town,
He'll catch the train right out of here,
and leave his home behind.

His mother's desolate with tears,
for her son she always fears,
that he'll git' hurt or like a place,
and never come home no more.

He went to Wabash Ohio,
He rode the train as an ol' hobo,
He's rode the freight trains, one and all,
answerin' to their lonesome call.

every night when the whistle blows,
his mother prays fer' her only son,
he left her fer' the open road,
and never comes home no more

Now I can hear his words to me,
the corn is high again,
mother, you speak of what might have been,
but I'll just go on down the road,
I'm comin' home no more

I watch Mommy set the corn pone down,
wipe her hands and look around,
the table's empty in my place,
waiting for the sayin' of grace,

Child, she says, to sister Maise,
just wash yore' face, and say the grace,
My boy is lost for ever more,
let's pull the shade and close the door.

Now winter's come and summer's gone,
the hills are bare, there's no more song,
so I'll just keep on down the road,
cause I'm goin' home no more...

Bolen's mother wrote to him twice a year. In her letters, she begged him to come home to live or at least write her back, but he wouldn't do it. And every year, she sent him a Christmas box.

The Christmas box was for him only, like the other Christmas presents were. The box always had the same things in it. A huge pair of short legged pants too wide for a really fat man, a bag of old fashioned chocolate creme drops, and a short letter. The letter always said the same thing. That Thursta should take better care of him, cook more for him, and to come home, she'd take care of him.

Ever year, Thursta ranted and raved for two or three days after his Christmas box arrived. Bolen watched and laughed. He said Marthy was right, she should take better care of him.

"I should be fatter than I am, but I'll git' by somehow."

Emerald watched the huge new pants come out of Marthy's Christmas box ever year. They were wide enough to make a set of curtains out of. She felt sorry for Thursta and watched with sympathy while she held the pants up and cussed Marthy out.

Bolen's Christmas box came right on time, and Thursta pulled the pants out of the box and held them up like she always did. She was frownin' and workin' herself up to cussin' and throwin' her yearly fit about Marthy, when Emerald looked at the pants and burst out laughing.

She was picturin' little bitty slim Bolen in them, all puffed up like a blowfish she'd seen in a picture book. The puffed up part was his arrogance and pride. Thursta stopped and glared at her. Emerald threw herself on the couch.

"Woman!" Emerald ordered in a voice as much like Bolen's as she could manage. She stuck out her little sharp chin that was so much like his. "Braing' me some hot coffee! I'm a big shot smart ass who git's it all while nobody else gits' anythaing', and that's what we like ta' draink'!"

Thursta stared at her.

"And here's West's buddy, Eddie Hager."

She set up and pulled a pious look across her face. She reached around like she was blind, a' gropin' for a coffee cup.

"Did I jist; git' a' hold a' the coffee cup, or was it the women's asses agin'? Damn! I guess I'll just have ta' settle fer' either one...."

She spoke in a voice humble and accepting of its fate. Thursta's tight mouth started to tremble with laughter.

"And here's Lester!"

Emerald jumped up and thowed her hand on her hip and scowled at Thursta.

"Praise God and pass the meat, halleluah!"

She slapped a fake Bible and tapped her foot.

"Well, I believe I'll jist' go git' me some more meat and cake and pussy, and you all better be dressed for church when I git' back!"

Thursta burst out laughin'. Just then, Hank strolled into the living room. Emerald grabbed the huge pants out of Thursta's hands and put them on him. He grinned and waddled around in circles. Thursta grabbed him up and stuck him in the chair Bolen set in when he was a' holdin'

Christmas court, and a' gittin' all the presents.
She pretended she was kissin' his feet, then she
turned him around and pretended like she was
kickin' his ass. Hank giggled. He didn't know
what was goin' on, but he liked to make ever
body laugh.

Then Thursta pretended to be Marthy. She
put her hands over her face and pretended she
was cryin'.

"Boo hoo! Boo Hoo! Come home, my precious
little son, my precious!.. pure!..perfect! Boo hoo!
Boo Hoo!..That bad woman's took ye' away from
me! .. Boo hoo! Boo hoo! my .... poor little ...ass
hole son!!"

They laughed. Thursta pulled the pants off
Hank. The pants had just landed in the box when
Bolen strolled into the livin' room, jinglin' the
change in his pockets, ready to watch Thursta
throw her yearly fit over his Christmas box. But
they was all laughin' instead.

"What the hell's a' goin' on?" he asked. They
shook their heads and ran past him into the
kitchen, laughin'. Bolen's Christmas box kept on
a' comin' ever year' but it never made Thursta
mad agin'.

Snow on the Winda' sills

It's cold agin' and I still ain't got no friends
in this place
Jist' the snow fallin' like it did back home
soft and slow
keepin me company.

Early Christmas mornin', Thursta slipped out of bed and fed the stove some wood. Ever body was still asleep. She pulled on her coat and stepped out the back door. In her hand she carried the skimpy bunch of leftover scraps to feed to the dogs. Lottie's bunch had spent the night. The rest of them had gone home. A light skiff of pure white snow sparkled like diamonds on the ground and across the windows. It was her yearly Christmas present. "Nature"s sa' beautiful, it makes up fer' a lot of misery in life," she thought.

She stopped and studied the patterns on the windows. Emerald, Hank and Lucy didn't think a thing about not gettin' Christmas presents. They were used to it. They'd been happy to get some meat.

Lottie had brought over rolls and a pumpkin pie, handing them to her like they were gifts. Flint's wife brought blanched corn her mother had made, and a pound cake.

She stared out across the frozen fields. They all seemed to think that a Christmas dinner was enough for her and the little ones. A few dishes of food for them, and for her, the usual small package of two cheap handkerchiefs from her mother, along with a skimpy letter. She bent over, made a snowball, and thowed it at the house. It hit without a sound, and broke apart.

"Well, I got the Christmas dinner out a' him fer' the first time!" she reasoned to herself.

"And the little uns' had a good time. It didn't cross their minds, and I'm not gonna' say a word

about presents, or the one gift I can never have –
my dearest Robert!"

All of sudden, she felt as blue and lonesome
as the winter wind a' blowin' bitter back up in the
hollers above home. She would forever remain
homeless, her true love far away. She did the
best she could, but she ached ta' see her mother,
her father and her beloved brothers and sisters.
She hadn't seen any of them since they left the
hills sa' long ago.

Mostly she missed the beautiful man who
once looked down at her with flashing brown
eyes carryin' ever color of the little pebbles in the
creek bottom, whose hands had tried to give her
a warm hearth to set at.

She stood in the snowy silence and held her
chest, remembering the creek above her
childhood home and how it had healed a long ago
heartbreak. She knew now that her heart would
never heal from the second loss she had taken,
nor the first. Not completely. She silently wished
the first, her mother, and the second, Robert and
his family a Merry Christmas. She blew a kiss of
love ta' him on the winter wind, askin' it to carry
her love to him, wherever he was now. Her
mother and Robert. She loved them, always
would, and they'd always love her too. One bad
mistake had ruined her chainces ta' stay with
those two great loves.

Fate's plan had give her a forked road ta'
choose from, and she was the one who made the
bad choice. At least she had beautiful children
and finally, a good house ta' live in. Those were
good gifts.

After a long time, she took her hand away from her heart. A new year was startin'. This spring, she'd go to the creek back of the house and make it safe once more for the kids. She'd walk it and clean it and kill any snakes, and do what needed to be done. None of them would know she was a' lookin' out for 'em.

A long, lonesome, day stretched out before her. She would have to act like ever thing was all right, but it was almost too hard to think about. She crossed the back yard and headed across the snow covered fields to walk her mood off. After awhile, she returned and slipped into the house.

Spring

Spring came. Thursta and Lottie gave Emerald a birthday party. They told her she could invite five girls. She chose five girls from her class that were poor like her. They were told not to bring a gift. But the rich girls got mad. They wanted to come to the party. The five girls rode the bus home with Emerald. They laughed and ate hot dogs in soft, fresh buns, and drank orange pop from the big punch bowl Lottie borrowed from somebody. The birthday cake was home made white cake with white frosting.

While they were eatin' the birthday cake, a young mouse, drunk on D-Con, staggered across the kitchen floor. The girls asked if it was a pet mouse, and Thursta said yes, swept it up in the dust pan, and carried it outside. The girls wanted to pet the mouse, but she told them it needed ta'

240

rest fer' now, it had been played with too much already today.

Emerald said to Thursta after the party.

"Wasn't that the best color, the orange soda fizzin' in the punch bowl, with the sun a' shinin' through the door on it?....And the way the hot dogs tasted on the fresh, soft buns..and the sounds of the girls laughin'?.. Oh!...what gifts!"

She stood in the doorway, starin' across the road at the lilac bushes. Soon they would bloom dark purple, and she and Thursta would pick bunches of them for the house. She imagined the sweet, dark smell of them spreadin' through the house before she laughed and ran outside.

Next fall, she'd be goin' to the junior high-high school in the center of town. The idea scared her. She left the house early each day and stayed away. She roamed the fields and roads, countin' ladybugs piled up in bunches around tree roots. She studied the way the new leaves were a pale, crunched up green, wrinkled up like they was in pain. Ruefully she nodded to herself. Nature made them grow up too, jist' like she was havin' to, like it or not.

Bolen let Hank set in his car and listen to the baseball games on the radio with him. Sometimes she saw Bolen settin' in the car with one arm around Hank's shoulder. Seein' Bolen touch anybody in a kindly way was a new thing to behold. He never ruffled their hair or patted them on the back or anything like that. They'd never seen him and Thursta smooch, either.

Then he started bringin' Twinkies and Snowball cupcakes home in his lunch pail from the vending machine at work.

"Don't bother my lunch pail," he ordered Thursta. "I've got a little somethin' in there for Hank ta' snack on when we listen ta' the ball games."

He bought his own rototiller and made his large garden even bigger. He worked the garden dirt until it was soft, velvet brown dust, with not a weed in it. Emerald watched him sift the dirt through his fingers and study it.

Thursta come outside, dryin' her hands on a dish towel and went to him. "Bolen", she bragged, "A weed would be scared to death ta' try and grow in yore' garden!"

He worked on the garden in between getting his sleep for the night shift and huntin' up places to cut wood for the comin' winter with his new chain saw. The woodpile he started against the fence behind the house grew higher and higher in neat, orderly rows.

The smells of constant drunkeness almost left the house. They could smell the good food a' cookin' now. The sounds in the house changed. They heard silence, and Thursta and Bolen talkin' and arguin' now and then, instead of crashes and mouthy, threatenin' people hurtin' somebody. They still went to the outhouse, but Bolen was talkin' about makin' the little bedroom downstairs into a bathroom. Hank set in the car with Bolen or followed him around, and Lucy stayed glued to Thursta's side.

Emerald and Neil strolled down the road, scuffin' their bare feet through the warm dust, tryin' to find out who was moving in next door. They were almost past the house when a girl about Emerald's size and a smaller boy Neil's size ran out in the front yard. The stocky girl wore boy's jeans and a white tee shirt. Her short, straight brown hair was slicked down over her ears, and her eyes were blue. The boy wore a plaid shirt and tan shorts. His hair was dark brown and wavy. His eyes were blue, and he was as handsome as the girl was plain.

Emerald and Neil looked at each other. They'd never seen a girl wearin' boy's clothes, or a boy in a pair of shorts. All of them stopped and stared at each other. Now was the time they would either become friends or enemies. They waited for each other to show some sign of how they wanted it to be from now on. Suddenly the girl whooped with laughter.

"Neighbors! We got kids to play with, Russel!" She pointed to the boy.

"He's Russel, and I'm Annie!"

Emerald and Neil grinned back at them. Lucy and Neil became best friends with Russell. They spent most of their time at his house, playing tag and card games, jumpin' rope and talkin'.

Emerald and Annie hit it off right away. Annie had a gift of gab, and she liked to manage ever thing. Her smile beamed on all of them and made them feel good. Annie was awkward. She bumped into things and tripped over her own feet. But she laughed at herself and sung a little piece of a song each time it happened. Best of all for

Emerald, Annie and her family loved books. Their livin' room was filled with bookshelves.

Their mother worked every day at the Foster Miles factory. Their father was a lot older than their mother. He was a handyman, and did odd jobs and painted houses for people. He stayed home with them in between jobs.

They were left to take care of themselves when both their parents were working. They had strict rules to follow, and a phone number for them to call if there was an emergency. Annie's mother called them every few hours from work to check on them. Emerald and the rest were amazed. Nobody they personally knew ever checked on kids. Only on television shows.

Emerald, Lucy, Hank and Neil left the house early each mornin' to roam endless miles up and down the dusty roads. They visited Annie and Russell when their parents weren't home, explored the woods, and played in the fields.

Emerald recited poems to them from the books she read. She was Robin Hood and Neil became Little John for the summer. Lucy was Friar Tuck. Hank was the rest of the Merry Men. They were all quick studies, their roles changing with each story they made up. They were characters in books, roamin' forests and roads, little nomads usin' sticks and leaves and nature's things as props for their play.

Then Hank started stayin' at home with Bolen. They set in the car listening to Walter Winchell and baseball games on the radio. Then Bolen started callin' Hank in to watch television with him. Hank set up agin' him, and Bolen put his arm around him. He never taught Hank to drink like he had with West. Emerald thought maybe he'd learned his lesson.

It didn't take long before Hank started getting uppity with them. His birthday was in the middle of summer. Bolen had never bought anyone a present in his life. But that mornin' he went to town and went all out. Thursta wouildn't go with him, so West went. Bolen bought Hank a new cowboy outfit with fringed gloves, a double holster with cap guns, and a shiny red bicycle. Thursta frowned at him but didn't say nothin'. Instead, she baked a big cake for Hank, and they ate cake and drank soda pop.

Hank put on his cowboy outfit and rode his bicycle around and shot at Emerald and Lucy and Neil with his new cap guns. They ignored him until he wanted to play with them. He had to let them take turns ridin' his new bicycle before they would play with him agin'.

Next, Bolen started giving Hank a little pocket change. He drove Hank to town and waited in the car while Hank swaggered in the store and bought candy and small toys with the money.

"Boys need a little money to feel good about their selves," Bolen told Thursta.

When the girls asked him for change, he scoffed at them.

"Girls don't need no money, 'cause they're foolish with it. Their men'll take care of what they need."

Chapter 25. Mabel, a Tooth and a Phone

Lucy always wanted to sleep with Emerald, but Emerald wouldn't let her, for she was trouble with a capital T. She talked in her sleep, traveled all over the mattress, threw her arms and smacked Emerald, Hank and Neil across the face like Joe Louis, the famous boxer.

But the worst thing was, Lucy wet the bed ever night. Pissed. Peed. She never failed. In the winter when it was freezin' upstairs, Thursta made 'em let Lucy sleep with 'em ta' keep her warm. Emerald and Hank never slept in the middle, 'cause both Neil and Lucy wet the bed. The only chance they had was to sleep on the outside. Then Neil quit wetting the bed, and nobody wanted Lucy to sleep with them any more.

About that time, some body give Thursta two old rusty twin bed frames and mattresses. She painted the frames and found sheets somewhere ta' put on 'em. She put one bed in Hank's room and one in Lucy's. But Lucy was afraid to sleep by herself.

"Kin Mabel sleep with ya'?" Lucy asked hopefully to Emerald, Hank and Neill.

"She don't pee the bed."

"Naw!" Emerald said. "You keep her with you." Lucy dropped her head and walked away, draggin' her doll Mabel by the arm. She looked so pitiful. They looked at each other and nodded.

That night she peed on both of them. Real good. A lot. A Soaker.

The next night, she asked if Mabel could sleep with 'em agin'. They said no, and she turned sadly away from them. They took pity on her and let her in the bed with them again. She peed on them again. Another Soaker.

The next night come around. Emerald and Hank were ready. Lucy walked up to them, draggin' Mabel by her arm.

"Mom said Mabel could sleep with her tonight," they told her before she asked.

"Jist' go put her in Mom's bed, so she kin' git' warm, and go to sleep right away."

Lucy nodded and left. The next morning, Thursta cocked her head, put her hands on her hips, and gave Emerald, Neill, and Hank long looks that said they better not try that again.

Lassoing the Tooth

Emerald felt real mean towards Thursta. She didn't like the way she kept house, and she didn't want to eat her cookin' much. She picked over the food, mad 'cause she was the only one warshin' huge piles of dishes ever night. Thursta had put her to work, and her free evening time was over. It wasn't fair!

"Now I have to work to live in this house!" she thought, crossly. There were mountains of dishes to do, even though Thursta washed them at least once a day herself. Everbody ate whenever they wanted to. They helped themselves from the pot of pinto beans on the back of the stove, and they left their dishes wherever they pleased. Then there were the endless coffee cups left sitting all over the house.

Thursta had built a fire pit in the backyard right after they moved in. The firepit was close to the pump. She used it for lots of things. She set the big tin washtub over the firepit and boiled clothes in it. She scalded the canning jars in it and she scalded the chickens for Sunday dinner in it so's their feathers would pull out easy.

Emerald watched Thursta start a fire in the firepit one Sunday morning. Then she went back in the house and came out carrying the old blue enamel pot. She filled it with water from the pump and set it on the fire pit to heat.

Bolen had built a new chicken house in the corner of the back yard and they were raising chickens now.

Thursta was teaching Emerald to clean and cut up chickens and how to cook them different ways. Thursta instructed her.

"The old layin' hens are suitable fer' boilin' and makin' into dumplin's. The extry meat can be chopped up and used ta' make a chicken pot pie. The middle size chickens are fer' roastin', and the young chickens are fer' fryin'."

But nobody else would kill the chickens; they called it murder until dinner time came so Thursta had to do it. She tried different methods. At first, she chased them down, grabbed them up, wrung their necks, and thowed 'em under the tin wash tub to die. But they flopped all over and got dirty. Now she caught 'em and tied their legs together with a piece of clothes line. Then she laid them across a stump, chopped their heads off with an axe, and hung their tied feet over a long nail hammered inta' a post so their blood could drain out.

Emerald frowned when Thursta stepped on to back porch with a short length of thin clothesline in her hand. She didn't want ta' help clean chickens! This was Sunday. The dusty road out front called out to her. Her bare feet itched to take off around the side of the house and disappear. She was damn tired of all this work! Thursta should make some of the damn men git' off their dead asses and clean up after their selves! Then they wouldn't be sa' quick to leave big messes ever where!

She watched Thursta stick out her chin with purpose, stride across the backyard and enter the chicken pen. She watched Thursta place the piece of rope between her teeth like a lasso, run down a chicken and grab it up by its feet. She watched Thursta jerk the rope out of her mouth, but instead of tyin' the chicken's legs together with the rope, she dropped the chicken and clapped both hands over her mouth.

Emerald watched, puzzled. Blood started runnin' out between Thursta's fingers. Emerald screamed.

"Mom!"

She ran down the porch steps, across the grass, jerked the gate to the chicken pen open and rushed in. Chickens flew around her and raced out the open gate.

Thursta grabbed the tail of her workshirt. She dobbed the blood off her mouth with it before she lifted up her upper lip with a finger. She poked a finger of her other hand in her mouth. One of her large, beautiful white front teeth was gone! She dropped on the ground and went to huntin' around for her missin' tooth. Emerald dropped to her knees beside of her, and started riflin' her fingers through the dirt and chicken poop. Then she happened to look over at Thursta. Her mouth had stopped bleedin'. She was holdin' it open, her lips curled in a funny sneer. Emerald snickered. Thursta slapped her. She snickered again.

Thursta found her tooth and put it in her shirt pocket. She slapped Emerald again, but Emerald kept on laughin'. Thursta set down in the dirt and chicken poop and yanked Emerald across her lap. She whacked her across her rump again and again, until Emerald finally got to her knees and then staggered to her feet. Thursta stood up and pointed her finger at her.

"S'at wudn't sas sery damn 'sunny," she scolded. Emerald started snickerin' agin' at the way Thursta was holding her mouth, tryin' ta' talk. Thursta grabbed Emerald's arm and danced her in a circle, whackin' half heartedly at her rump while Emerald laughed at her. Then she shoved her away, and hurried to the house. After that, Emerald quit complainin' sa' much about work, and Thursta got a new peg tooth put in.

Just a Phone Call Away

Thursta slammed the door and wrung her hands. She watched the car back out a' the driveway.

"Bolen, we got ta' git' a phone put in! Somebody might be a dyin', and we'd never know in time to git' there!"

She paced the floor, her face red with worry and frustration.

"What if West's friends hadn't come by ta' tell us he needed us? What if one of the others needed somethin'? We need a phone!"

Bolen kept on shaking his head no, but Thursta kept on talkin' about gettin' a phone.

"It's a' gonna' be too late to help somebody someday, and you'll be sorry fer' it! All it'd take is one phone. You don't have to talk on it, I'll do that."

She kept on until a black wall phone with a round dial got put up by the kitchen door. It was a party line, which meant when the phone was picked up to make a call, somebody else might be talkin' on it, and ya' had ta' wait 'til they hung up. People could listen in on your calls, and did. Bolen and West wouldn't have anything to do with it, so it was left to Thursta or the kids to handle it.

Not long after the phone got put in, Thursta's brother Samuel called. He said their mother Drusa was a' dyin', and if Thursta was ever gonna' see her alive agin', she best be on her way. Flint drove Thursta and Emerald back home. He drove straight through without stopping except for gas. He said he was used to driving long distances. When they got close, they started passin' under railroad trestles and on curvin' roads with creeks runnin' beside them.

Emerald set in the back, not mindin' the silence between Thursta and Flint. She stared out at the little houses perched on the sides of hills and squattin' down in valleys among trees. They went around a bunch of curves and into a small town. Men set or stood in little groups outside of the stores, talkin' to each other. They stopped talkin' and watched their car move down Main Street.

The car moved like it was goin' through heavy molasses all the way through town. Abruptly, the town ended. The narrow, black topped road squeezed between two high, gray rock cliffs before it widened back out into two lanes. Small farms and tobacco barns dotted the sloping hills. Emerald watched a man workin' a field with mules and a drag.

Flint turned onto a little dirt road beside a small, white general store next to a church. The little path led up a steep hill, crossed railroad tracks and ended in front of two little white houses perched on the side of the hill.

Flint coasted to a stop in front of the little houses and looked at Thursta. They sighed real big and climbed out of the car. Thursta's brothers and sisters came out on the porch, stared at them like they didn't know them, then they started laughin' and hurryin' down the steps. Emerald got out and pressed up against Flint. She looked at him, that at the tall, slim people gathered around them. Ever one looked like Thursta, Flint, and herself. Nobody else in their family looked like them. So that was why Thursta brought her. Not 'cause she was a Healer, but 'cause she belonged to these people. She let out a sigh of relief. Her eyes traveled over their tall, lean figures, their dark hair and high cheekbones. They were handsome people. Moreover, they felt right. Her heart lifted with delight. They were her kin. She was home.

Drusa lay in a double bed in the hot little livin' room. She moaned with pain and tossed around like Lucy did when she had nightmares. Thursta went right to her, set down in the chair by the bed and took her hand in hers. Emerald went and stood beside the bed. The long black hair she remembered was white and thin. Her grandmother's face was gray, her cheekbones standing up like sharp blades. Her nose curved like a hawk's beak.

Emerald looked around the tiny room. The walls were covered with the cabbage rose wallpaper she remembered, but it was yellow and faded now. The two narrow windows overlooking the front porch were covered with thin, sheer, patched curtains. On the other side of the room was a couch covered with a sheet, sagging in the middle. A kitchen chair set by her grandmother's bed.

Thursta rubbed Drusa's hands and spoke in a low voice. Emerald looked at their hands. For an instant, she saw Thursta's hands back when she was a little girl.

Drusa opened her eyes and recognized Thursta. They looked at each other. Emerald watched her grandmother hold on to knowin' Thursta was there as long as she could before she went back to where she had been.

Stanford paced in and out of the livin' room. He didn't want Drusa to die. They were married past seventy years, and part of their children had gone on before them. Emerald looked at him and remembered him raising his eyebrows and wigglin' his big ears at her.

Two days passed. Thursta took turns settin' with Drusa. She spent the rest of her time with family in her brothers little house next door. On the afternoon of the third day, they left Emerald to set with Drusa while they went next door to eat a bite.

Emerald didn't want to be left alone with her grandmother, but they all, without direct words, in one way or another, had let her knew they accepted her as one of the ones their healing lineage had been passed on to. She was one of their Healers, so she could stand up to anything. If they knowed she was afraid, they wouldn't admire her, and she wanted to keep their admiration.

She climbed up on the bed and tried to smooth her grandmother's hair back, so she'd look like she used to, but Drusa knocked her hands away. She climbed back down, set in the chair and watched Drusa mumblin' and turnin' her head from side to side like she was sayin' no.

Suddenly Emerald felt the air in the room change. It grew cold as ice. She knew somethin' big was about to happen. She watched the air thicken above her grandmothers head. Drusa's mouth gaped open like a fish tryin' to get air. Then a loud rattlin' noise come up out of her chest. Her head fell forward, and she lay still.

Then somethin' white and wavy slowly floated up from Drusa and hovered above her head. It looked like thick, white smoke. Then she heard somethin' that sounded like a balloon poppin', and felt her grandmother let go of somethin'.

She'd had enough. She jumped up and ran next door. Thursta ordered her to stay there. She was glad to be out of the little white house.

A short time later, Thursta came back. She stood in the middle of the floor looking at Emerald like she didn't know what to do. Then she clapped her hands over her face and broke into a high, keening wail.

A woman with a heavy black mustache and dark skin strode over to Thursta and slapped her. Thursta slapped her back, and sent her reeling. There was big silence, then ever body filed out the door, leavin' Thursta and Flint and Emerald starin' at each other.

The three of 'em went back north before the funeral. Emerald wanted to stay and see where her grandma would rest in peace. She wanted to put wildflowers on her grave and know where to find her, but Thursta wouldn't stay.

Stanford didn't want to live without his beloved Drusa. He took to his bed and quit eating. Thursta's brothers and sisters took turns settin' with him so he wouldn't be alone. He died

a month later. Thursta didn't go back south for
the funeral.

Ćhapter 26. Moon Days and Other Ways

Emerald's friend Elizabeth started her "moon." She told Emerald all about it in school. Emerald went home and told Lottie about it.

"Hell fire and damnation!" she shouted, pacing the floor. "Why'd that happen to her?"

Lottie laughed and said, "Emerald, you're a girl too, and all girls start 'em, sooner or later. Men don't. That's why they don't have babies or get big titties to feed the babies from!"

Emerald froze in shock. "Feedin' a baby from a titty?"

"Ya' gotta' start behavin' like a woman instead of a tomboy when it happens. And ya' cain't' let anybody know when you're a' havin' your period."

Lottie rattled on while Emerald stared at her in horror.

"I won't do it!" Emerald shouted.

"I didn't want to, either. But we don't git' a choice," Lottie answered calmly.

Emerald paced the floor. She didn't want periods or breasts or babies. She didn't want whatever men and women did together to make babies. All of the women she knew were owned by their men. She prayed to stay as she was, but deep down, she knew there was no way out.

She fell into a deep grief and fear, for she surmised that the coming change would put her on an even more dangerous ground with boys and men. They would be able to take advantage of her in a way they couldn't before.

It was time to say goodbye to her childhood. Everything became bittersweet. The new problem would separate her from Lucy and Hank and Neil. They traveled with her while she roamed roads, climbed the trees and crossed fields. She started in at daybreak, and kept it up until dark. She talked constantly about her coming trouble, but none of them understood it.

"Shoot it!" Hank declared.

"Is Mabel gonna' git' sick too?" Lucy whimpered.

"Put a damn bandage over it!" Neil shouted.

After awhile, their eyes glazed over, and though they loved Emerald, they started hidin' from her.

"We cain't keep up with ya', so's yer' better go on alone," they solemnly declared to her one mornin'.

Emerald did all the things she'd put off doin'. She walked down the road to a creek she'd never explored. She crossed the fields and talked to a giant oak she never got acquainted with. She carried cardboard up to the hill and slid down on it, and followed the ditch clear across to the other road to see where it went. She stopped searchin' out more hidin' places. Instead, she set on a rock in the back field and watched the sandpipers.

One mornin' she woke up, filled with new purpose. She sent Lucy and Hank and Neil to steal scraps of material from Thursta's sewin' box, while she slipped upstairs and got the coins she kept hid behind the wall. Nobody saw them cross the field in back of the house. The little parade stopped under an old, gnarled tree standin' in the fence row. That tree had endured a hard life. She knew, 'cause it was all twisted up like she would be soon. They'd never played under the tree or climbed it, 'cause it was out in the open, and could be seen from the house. They had run by the old tree countless times in the summer. The old tree had watched her grow up.

They wrapped the coins in some of Thursta's scraps and buried them in the ground beneath the tree roots. Then they made a pact. She made them swear to love each other forever while Neil and Hank snickered and rolled their eyes. They pledged that if any of 'em ever needed to, they could come back to the tree and dig up the "gold coins" and use 'em. "Amen!" Neil hollered after they all took turns prayin' over the stash beneath the tree. "Damn right!" Hank echoed.

Emerald started two months later. Lottie tried to get her to be happy and excited over it, but Emerald gave her such a look of disgust, Lottie threw up her hands and walked away. But the monthlies weren't as bad as she thought they would be. She had mild cramps. She was still able to play with Lucy and Hank and Neil and Annie, and run and climb trees. Thursta and Lottie scolded her for actin' like a tomboy. They told her she was to start actin' like a grown up woman, now that she was one.

"Go to hell! I'm not givin' up a damn thing I like so's I can be like you two! The men ain't gonna' run me!"

In a way, the words estranged her from them, for she instinctively knew she was different, that no matter what happened to her, she was a Healer first. Something more was driving her. She would overcome what they couldn't, but wanted to.

She went home with Neil before school started. She went to church with Lottie, Lester and the boys. They set on the benches and clapped hands and sang. Lottie's boy's were like stair steps, only there were more of them. With their clean, shiny faces, and their hair slicked back, they hoped and loved and planned big futures for themselves. They were going to be firemen or doctors, and all of 'em damn good preachers.

The people in the little Pentecostal church were glad to have her back. They led her around ta' the sick people, fer' they knowed her linage from back in the hills, and she laid her hands on folks and spoke to them from the place she carried in her that held Mercy, Fallon, and Drusa's Healer ways.

School started. Emerald went to the junior high-high school in Chesney. School made her nervous, as did all things to do with bein' social. She liked books and learnin', but nothing else about school.

Junior high was harder than she expected. She was ordered to buy things for school. She had to buy books, a combination padlock for her locker, gym clothes, and pencils and paper.

Thursta got the pencils and paper out of Bolen, and some used books, and eventually got him to part with the money for a padlock.

She was not good at opening a combination lock. She had seven classes, and only five minutes between each class to get to the next one. She ran to the locker to pick up the books for the next class in between classes.

Then there was the physical education class. Mrs. Flinch, the P.E. teacher, was slim, tough and mean. She shouted and blew her whistle a lot. She saw how easy the exercises and games were for Emerald, who had spent her life outside, walking and running and climbing, while most girls stayed in the house.

At first, Emerald liked Mrs. Flinch's interest in her, but it took Thursta weeks to talk Bolen into parting with the money for her gym uniform. Mrs. Flinch humiliated Emerald every day in front of the other girls in the class for not having her gym suit. Emerald's joy in getting exercise in school faded. She turned grim and silent, obeying Mrs. Flinch's orders without any vitality. When she got her uniform, Mrs. Flinch started treating her nice again, but she didn't give a damn by then.

Then there were the mandatory showers after gym class. When she undressed, the other girls whispered about Lottie's bras Thursta had cut down and sewed for her. They snickered in disgust at her ragged underwear. She'd never taken a shower in her life, and she had trouble figuring out how to do it. They all wore shower caps. She'd never seen one, or used any deodorant. Her towel was old and ragged.

The worst time was when she was on her moon. The stress of the new things she was learnin' made her have hard cramps and a strong flow. The pieces of rag she pinned to her underwear were not acceptable to the other girls, who had used Kotex pads from the time they started. She'd never seen a kotex pad before, and didn't know what they were until she sneaked looks at the other girls.

She needed a purse to carry pads in, but Bolen wouldn't pay for one. Lottie gave her an old one of hers. She despised carrying a purse around. Lottie said she'd get a nicer one later, then she could carry lots of other things in it, too, like lipstick and makeup and combs. Emerald turned away from Lottie's encouragement. As far as she knew, the only reason girls and women wore makeup was to impress men and boys, and she didn't intend to ever dance to any man's tune. She would do what she had to. That was all.

Girls were not allowed to wear pants to school. Very few girls wore pants at any time. She experimented with her homemade pads and made them thicker, and changed them over lunch hour at school. Most of the time it worked, but she had a few "accidents" when the blood came through and spotted the back of her skirt. Some of the other girls had "accidents" from time to time too, and the other kids whispered and pointed at them.

Lucy was having trouble in school, too. Trouble with Mary Fields. Mary was in Lucy's class and rode the bus with them. Mary's family was well off, and Mary said mean things to Lucy about her homemade clothes on the bus ride home.

Lucy had a quick temper, but she quickly learned to keep her mouth shut in school and on the bus. She bottled it up, and as quick as she got off the bus, she ran in the house and told Thursta the latest mean thing Mary said.

Thursta heard her out day after day without sayin' anything. She watched Lucy's growin' dread of getting on the bus, and of bein' in school all day long with Mary.

A month after school started, Thursta started making Lucy a new coat. She'd never before made anything as challenging. She set the old treadle sewing machine up in a corner of the dining room. When Emerald, Hank and Lucy ran in the door after school, she was settin' in front of the sewing machine. They were used to her rushin' her way through any sewin' she did. And, she only sewed simple, easy things. They stopped.

"What's goin' on?"

Thursta ignored them.

"What ya' makin'?"

"I'm makin' Lucy a coat."

She took her time sewin' Lucy's coat, tryin' each and ever little piece of it on Lucy as she went along. She'd never measured much of anything before. Usually she made her own patterns, and didn't try 'em on anybody before she sewed it. Lucy had to stay close ever night, and be measured constantly. She complained that Thursta didn't listen to her stories about Mary any more.

No one asked where Thursta got the expensive plaid material and a real pattern to make the coat. Thursta calmly attended to every detail of the coat. She took her time sewing the pretty purple and gray plaid material. Ever body wanted somethin' from her, but she never went a day without sewin' on some part of Lucy's new coat after school when Lucy was home.

Lucy stopped complainin' and laughed and clapped her hands when Bolen had to put the pinto beans on ta' cook, and Hank had to wash his clothes 'cause Thursta was workin' on her coat and didn't have time for them. Bolen made a big show of complainin', but ever body knowed his heart wasn't in it. He was jist' puttin' on a show for Lucy.

Thursta finished the coat, and they thought she was through. But she wasn't. She started a bonnet to go with the coat. She lined the bonnet in a rich, dark blue silk matchin' the coat lining. Then she made a muff for Lucy's hands.

"Like the fancy ladies wore in the olden days," breathed Emerald in awe.

When the coat set was finished, Thursta laid the pieces out on the table one evenin', and called Bolen, Emerald, Hank and Lucy into the dinin' room.

She tried the coat and bonnet on Lucy. They watched her twirl around in it. It fit her like a glove. The pleat in the center of the back flared out when she twirled. The three big buttons down the front of the coat were a dark, shiny purple with silky black piping around their edges. They set like ripe grapes in the soft gray and light purple plaid fabric.

The piped bonnet rim framed Lucy's pointed little face and wide mouth, giving a deep luster to her large gray eyes. To them, she looked like a storybook princess. Thursta picked up the muff and put Lucy's hands in it, and the picture was complete.

All of them fell silent and stared at the miracle Thursta had wrought. There was never enough soap in the house, and no wire hangers for their homemade clothes. Bolen wouldn't let her buy enough food or toilet paper, so they each kept their own little stashes of what they needed hid away here and there. People had fought and cried and suffered in the old house. The thin, old windows let the heat in or out, dependin' on the season.

But Thursta's jars of canned food from Bolen's big garden was a' settin' in purty rows in the cellar. There were crates of taters stored for the winter, each one wrapped in paper to keep it from touchin' the others and rotting. Piles of butternut squash lay by the tater crates, and strings of dried beans hung from the nails in the shelf edges. Bolen's woodpile was stacked high and neat against the back fence, and there was a fresh cooker of warm pinto beans settin' on the back of the stove. He just' forgot to salt 'em, was all.

They sighed with warmth and pleasure at the beauty and security standin' in front of them. A memory tugged at Emeralds mind, a story about a coat. A sharp thrill ran though her. She ran and got the big Bible from the bottom of the closet and carried it to Thursta while Lucy was still twirlin' in her coat.

She pushed the Bible into Thursta's hands. "Look, Mom, its right here! The same thing you did! You made Lucy Joseph's coat of many colors!"

Thursta looked at her and started cryin'. Emerald was dumfounded.

"What's wrong, Mom?" Bolen cleared his throat and wagged his head.

"She's right, woman. You done the best job on that coat I ever seed'!"

Lucy and Emerald crowded close to Thursta. They'd never heard Bolen give her a good word before. She grabbed all of them in a hug while Bolen watched, grinnin' and daincin' from foot to foot, hikin' up his pants.

The next mornin', Thursta dressed Lucy in her new coat and bonnet and handed her the muff. She walked her out to the bus and watched her get on. She was waitin' in the kitchen when Lucy come runnin' in the door after school. Lucy's eyes were shining. She wore a great big smile. She was beautiful in her new coat and she knew it.

"Mom! Ever body wants a coat jist' like mine! Mary was sa' jealous, she couldn't speak!"

Then there was Emerald to look to next. All her life, when Emerald went to Thursta for help, Thursta pushed her away with words.

"Yer' smart, ye' kin' take care of yerself'. Ye' don't need me like the others do."

There was Bolen, Hank, Lucy, Lottie, West and Flint, and behind them, a long line of others waitin' for Thursta's attention. But after Thursta finished Lucy's coat, she paid attention to somethin' she already knew. Emerald was having a hard time in school, too.

Thursta pondered on what to do. Finally she saw a way. She had held on to her antique black library table through thick and thin. She offered it to Emerald to use as a desk, and they carried it upstairs and set it in a corner of her room. Thursta set her black panther figurine on it, so Emerald could gain strength from their family heritage and what they'd overcome.

It was cold but quiet upstairs. Emerald loved sitting at the old black table, spreading her books and papers out on it. She desperately needed some kind of emotional help, and this had come just at the right time. She felt like Thursta had wrapped a good, warm blanket around her.

But Bolen, Hank and Lucy nagged at Thursta about the library table. They wanted it back downstairs so they could use it, too. But they had to wait until Emerald was through her rough patch, then they carried the desk back downstairs together.

Next was Hank. He was a' havin' trouble, too. Thursta studied on him, then went ta' Bolen and told him he had ta' find a way ta' help Hank. She said she couldn't, 'cause it was men's stuff an' she didn't understand it.

Bolen asked Hank about his troubles. Hank told him he kept a' havin' the same bad dream. In his dream, a monster he couldn't quite make out kept a' comin' out of a hole and comin' after him and scarin' him to death.

Huntin' season come in. Bolen taught his boys how to shoot, hunt, and clean game at an early age. West usually went huntin' with Bolen, but Bolen took him aside and talked to him, and he nodded and left.

Bolen took Hank huntin' with him instead of West. One day they was a' huntin' in the woods behind the house. Bolen shot a squirrel and wounded it. He stood watched the squirrel crawl into a hole high up in the tree. Bolen never missed. All he ever needed was one shot. Hank watched him with a puzzled look on his face. He'd taught the boys to never leave a hurt animal. They was ta' foller' it up and kill it quick, so it wouldn't die a slow, painful death. He'd learnt' them ta' be good shots, so they could kill the game with one shot, and he took 'em huntin' with him 'til they could kill an animal clean and quick.

Bolen lowered his gun and looked at Hank.

"Kin' ye' climb that tree?" Bolen pointed to the tree the squirrel hid in.Hank studied the tall tree.

"Yeah," he nodded, a dismal look on his face. He was afraid of heights.

"Do ye' think ye' could climb up there and wrap this here rag over yer' hand, and pull that damn squirrel out of that hole, and thow' it down ta' me?"

Hank nodded dismally and started up the tree. He was scared of how tall the tree was, but he kept a' goin'. He reached the hole the hurt squirrel was hidin' in, and looked down at Bolen. Bolen nodded, and Hank wrapped his hand in the rag. He reached in the hole and grabbed the squirrel. The squirrel bit and clawed Hank's hand and arm, but he held on tight, jerked it out, and thowed' it ta' the ground.

He watched Bolen shoot it dead, and then look up at him. He swayed in the tree top while they stared at each other. Bolen nodded his approval. Suddenly Hank felt his blood start singin' high. He barely remembered climbin' back down the tree. It was over! He'd done it! He didn't know what, but he'd done it!

Bolen looked at the bites and scratches on Hanks arm in approval.

"By God, that's how a man does it! That's the way a man handles a damned monster!"

Bolen studied the dead squirrel layin' on the ground. He didn't look at Hank.

"By God, that damn dark thaing' ain't a' gonna' hurt nobody's insides agin'!"

He knelt down and started diggin' a hole beside the squirrel.

"What are ye' doin?" Hank asked in surprise. "I thought ya' was takin' it home ta' eat!"

"Not this 'un," Bolen answered. "This' 'uns a' goin' in the ground fer' good!"

Hank went to help him, but Bolen stopped him.

"It's my job ta' do it," he said.

Hank watched him lay the squirrel gently down in it's grave. He covered it with dirt and put rocks on it to weigh it down. When he was done, he stood up and dusted his hands off.

"By God, it'll never git' outta' there, will it?"

He nodded his head in satisfaction.

"Hit' was awful little ta' only be a squirrel!"

"Whadda' mean, Bolen?"

"I mean that ever thaing' has ta' folla' the rules of the Great Hunter in the Sky. No exceptions!"

Hank swaggered beside of Bolen on the way home. He felt like he was on top of the world. Something bad had been taken care of. Something ugly and loud that had been trying to beat him to death, something that had been after his soul and body ever since he could remember, was gone!

Something that had been tryin' to tare' a hole in him and make a place to live in. He'd climbed high to git' it outta' there. He'd climbed to the place where it hid in it's dark hole, and he'd tore it out of it's hidin' place, and thowed' it ta' the ground. And Bolen had killed it. They swaggered in the back door, grinnin' at each other.

Thursta took one look at the blood and cuts on Hank's arm and hand and went ta' scoldin'. She rushed to heat water to warsh the cuts and bites the squirrel give Hank.

Hank's heart started to fall. The wounds didn't matter. She was takin' his victory away from him! The good feelin' was drainin' from him, her

scoldin' words dryin' up his courage, replacin' it
with fear again.

He shouted "Shut up, Mom!". Bolen grinned at
her and said, "Hit's been took care of."

She quit scoldin' right then. She warshed and
dressed the cuts and bites on his hand and arm
with hot, soapy water without another word.

A Sweetheart Comes Calling

Emerald through she'd worked out her shool problems, but ever morning when she got to the girl's locker room, a handful of seventh grade boys was waitin' outside. She didn't want them to think she didn't know what they were doing there. They might think she was an ignorant hillbilly. She listened close to their talk to find a clue. They was a' waitin' ta' carry her or osme other girls books for them. Why, when they could carry them for themselves?

Lottie cut and permed her hair before she started school. Thursta made her new skirts, and Lottie cut down blouses and resewed them for her. She liked her homemade clothes, but she didn't know she was lovely.

She handed her books to one of the boys and waited to see what happened. He smiled at her while the some of the other boys joked about how they wished she'd chosen them. Then ever body hurried off to their classes. The boy asked where her first class was. He walked beside of her, carryin' her books. At the classroom door, he handed them back to her. She thought, "Well, that's simple."

After a few days of handin' her books to which ever boy was closest, she figured out that the whole thing meant she was choosin' one of them for a boy friend. She thought about them wantin' her to be their girl friend. Maybe they heard how good she was in school. Maybe they knew her name from the spellin' bees.

She stared at herself in the mirror at home before she ran outside to play. The other girls in school knew things she didn't. They wore nice clothes from good stores and owned more than one pair of shoes. She guessed they owned more'n two pair of underwear, too. She didn't know she was tan and clean, and small and quick, with humor and a zest for livin' from all the time she spent outside. Her eyes were bright, her hair shiny and clean. Her smile was pagan, rich with Irish and Native American heritage, and all the places her charming mountain families sprang from. And more than one of them had jumped the fence, so who knew?

She was interested in learning. She loved books. She had read encyclopedias from cover to cover, puzzled over Shakespeare, and she loved poetry. She could talk about those things, but she'd never eaten in a restaurant, and never been to a movie.

She scoffed at makeup and junk jewelry. She wouldn't wear them if she could afford them! She never wanted ta' know the first thing about finger nail polish or fashion. Liking any of them things would signal her willingness to be dominated by men and boys. And, like her mountain ancestors, she didn't have the art of makin' front porch conversation, she either went straight to the heart of the matter, or shut up.

She couldn't imagine assessing herself in terms of what to do to attract a boy friend. She liked baseball and basketball, rock and roll and country music. She listened to music on the old radio Lottie give them. She loved to dance and go to Pentecostal chuches and watch the preacher get all worked up to get everybody saved.

She decided to get rid of the things she didn't have to do, one by one. She started with the boys. They were not allowed inside the girl's locker room, so she hid at the end of the rows of lockers until the first class of the day was almost ready to start. The boys waitin' for her left so they wouldn't be late for their classes. But that made her almost late. The boys stared at her in the halls and in between classes. They asked where she'd been, and would she let them walk with her. She made a habit of ducking her head and ignorin' 'em. Then she started carryin' her books with her all the time. They were heavy, but she didn't care. She carried them home and back to school in the morning. That way, she didn't have to go to her locker at all.

When the boys and books problem was solved, she settled on knowing that Mrs. Flinch, the P.E. teacher, was a mean person. She wouldn't try to please her again. She threw herself into learnin' basketball and other games because she liked them. But she kept her reserve with Mrs. Flinch, who alternated between frustration and fawnin' over Emerald, who was a fine natural athlete.

She concentrated on her schoolwork, and kept quiet and out of sight as much as she could. Sometimes she heard the town girls whisperin' when she walked by. Some of them tried to be friendly, but she was painfully shy and hurried off. She didn't know that some of the girls

admired her and thought she was smart and
pretty.

Chapter 27. Rituals

Coffee

Bolen made rituals out of certain things after he quit drinkin'. His pocket watch, his coffee, and the way he placed his pants under his pillow when he went to sleep were a few. His rituals were the way he kept himself and made every day right, and they had to be just so.

His coffee was important to him. He liked it strong. He packed the metal basket in the small, cheap aluminum coffee pot to the brim with Maxwell House coffee for each pot he made. Then he filled the pot with a few cups of water and put the lid back on. He set it on the burner to percolate until it reached the right color in the clear glass bubble on top of it.

West declared that Bolen's coffee was so strong it made his hair stand up straight and kept him awake for three days at a time. Everybody else that sampled it agreed. It was thick like mud. But Bolen was well satisfied with it. He wouldn't drink any body else's coffee. He said they made it way too weak.

"May as well not even drink it." He scoffed happily. He liked the stories goin' round about his coffee.

The Clock

It was Thursta's job to get Bolen up for work at night. He came home in the mornin' when his shift ended, went to bed, and slept 'til noon. He got up and worked at whatever needed doing. Then he went back to bed at seven at night, and slept 'til ten. That give him the eight hours of sleep he needed.

They didn't own a clock. Never had. Bolen used his pocket watch to keep time. He bought it when he quit drinkin'. His watch cover had a fancy snap lid with deers running through a forest engraved on it, and he admired it very often.

Bolen handed Thursta his fancy pocket watch in the morning and prepared his coffee pot. He wouldn't let anyone fix his coffee pot for him. Only he could do it right. She perked it for him just before she woke him at noon. At seven at night, he handed his pocket watch to her again, fixed up his coffee pot, and went to bed.

She packed his lunch pail, perked his coffee, then woke him up at ten o'clock sharp. She handed his watch back to him, and set up with him until he left for work shortly before eleven.

The television was turned off when he went to bed at seven. Ever body in the house had to be quiet so he could get his sleep. The kids were asleep by the time she got him up at ten for work. There was nothing for her to do between seven and ten at night, except wait the long hours out. When he got up, he liked to drink coffee, smoke, reminisce, and tell her what to do about things.

Thursta rose at daybreak each mornin' and did the work of three people each day. She had to cater to his smug importance early in the morning and late at night and in between, three times a day, as though he was the only working. The last hour before she woke him up at ten was the hardest for her. She started dozin' off, and waking him at the last minute, so he didn't get his usual forty five minutes to run the show. He was forced to run out to the car and go without his coffee or dinner pail a couple times.

He told her she was lazy, but she still kept dozin' off instead of starin' at his watch for hours, waitin' to wake him up. Shaming her didn't do any good. He bought a second coffee pot and left it at work so he could make coffee there if he had to. Pretty soon, he started tellin' anybody that would listen that he couldn't depend on his woman to get him up for work any more. That was the least he expected from her, 'cause he was the one making the livin'. He made it sound like she laid around all day with nothin' to do except wait on him. He kept on until she got over feelin' guilty, and got mad.

"I'm sick and tarred' of yer' damn whinin' ta' ever' body about me! I git' damn tared' of havin' ta' stay up late ever' night to git' ya' up for work! Three times a day I put up with your bad mouthin!

I work hard around here all day, and I git' tarred, too! And I don't sleep durin' the the day like you do! Then I git' you up, and have ta' set and listen to ya' brag to me about what a big shot ya' are, 'cause yer' the only one a' makin' a dime!"

She stopped. An idea had come to her. "Why don't we git' us a wall clock, so's we kin' all tell what time it is? I'm tarred' a' gittin' the kids up way too early, or almost too late to catch the bus! I'm always worried about what time it is!"

She paced back and forth, liking the idea of a wall clock better and better. Bolen shook his head at her and snickered. "If'n ya' fall asleep, ya' won't know what time it is, whether it's my pocket watch or a clock on the wall!"

She looked puzzled. She didn't know what to say to that, and he turned away, satisfied he'd won the argument. She worried the problem out loud every day until one day Emerald snapped at her.

"He needs ta' git' hisself' an alarm clock so's he kin' git' his own sorry ass out of bed ta' go ta' work." and huffed off.

Thursta stared after Emerald. Then she went straight to Bolen and ordered him to get hisself an alarm clock. But he wouldn't do it.

"It's yore' job ta' perk my coffee and pack my lunch pail, and set up with me til' I go ta' work!"

Emerald coached Thursta.

"Set a day ta' tell him ye' ain't gonna' git' him up that night. Tell him early in the mornin' so he has the whole day ta' drive ta' town and buy hisself' an alarm clock. If he don't do it, jist' tell him yore' a' gonna' go on ta' bed and git yer' rest."

In a few days, Thursta announced that she was goin' ta' bed at nine o'clock that night, and he best go ta' town and get hissself an alarm clock. He turned his back and acted like he didn't hear her. That night, Thursta got in the bed.

Bolen stayed up a couple of nights instead of goin' to bed at seven, and sleepin' 'til ten. He wasn't gittin' his sleep, and he could hear Thursta in the bed a' snorin'. He had to have his sleep, so he decided that Thursta was lazy, and there was nothin' a man could do about havin' a lazy woman. He drove her to town, and grudgingly sent her in the store to buy him a Big Ben alarm clock.

He set the clock by the bed. He set the alarm for nine, so she could git' up and fix his coffee and fill his lunch pail. After he left for work, she reset the alarm for mornin' ta' git' the kids ready fer' school.

She slept peaceful fer' the first time in years, knowin' the alarm clock was set, and ever thing would happen when it was supposed to. She carried the alarm clock to the kitchen so she could watch the time for them to catch the bus, but she kept forgettin' to put it back by the bed for Bolen.

Then the kids borrowed it, and they had to hunt it up. Bolen complained to her, and she got mad at him all over again.

"I need a clock on the wall out here! Then ya' kin' jist' keep yer' damn ol' alarm clock! Yer' not the only one that needs ta' keep track a' time!"

He drove her to town again, and grudgingly gave her money ta' buy a wall clock. The new clock was a cheap, small circle made of shiny red and white plastic. She hung it up on a nail on the kitchen wall, and plugged it in. She set it to match his alarm clock, and it worked perfect.

Thursta hummed to herself and cooked him a special breakfast ever mornin' after he got her the wall clock. She got up without complaint ever night to fix his coffee and pack his lunch pail after the alarm went off.

She knew she'd pushed him far enough. He liked his sweet tooth fed, and his pride needed savin' fer' givin' in to a woman, so she baked his favorite cakes and other things, and packed big pieces of 'em in his lunch pail. Sometimes she packed him so much she had to pack the extry' in a paper sack. Bolen groaned and acted like he couldn't carry it all. It was her way of sayin' thanks to him, and he knew it. He wouldn't say he liked it, but she could tell he did.

Along with feedin' his sweet tooth, she bragged on him and how hard he worked. Along with the coffee stories, his work history become epic in their family, a story to be passed down through their hard workin' generations. He made it to work no matter what. The winter wind blew all the time, and it was common for them to have a few feet of snow a' standin' on the ground all through the long winters.

But Bolen Hawks the Worker, drove to work in the dark of night, summer and winter. He drove through hot nights, and lightnin' and thunder and heavy rains, and through blizzards and ice storms that caused other men to give up and stay at the house, even them that lived in town

near the factory. He never missed but five days of
work in all of his years at the factory.

Chapter 28. Finishin' Love and Heartbreak

Emerald's gym class was just before lunch, so time was on her side for at least one class. She didn't bring a lunch to school, never had. Her gym locker was downstairs, and she kept what she needed in it for gym class. She tried to be the last one to shower and dress so they wouldn't see her body or her underwear.

One day, when she was leaving the locker room, she heard music. She crept up the stairs and into the gym. Kids circled the edge of the gym floor three deep, watching other kids dance. A student deejay played forty fives of the latest popular songs over the loudspeaker. The kids looked like they belonged on American Bandstand. She hid behind them and listened. They said the school had decided to put on a noon dance every day in the gym to get the bad boys that rode motorcycles to school off of their bikes and into the gym, where they would interact with the good kids, who would eventually influence them to change their ways.

Emerald laughed to herself. She admired the angry, moody looking guys that wouldn't cut their hair short like the good boys did. They wore their hair long and combed it up into oiled rolls that hung forward into their eyes. She liked their blue jeans and their tight, snow white tee shirts with the cigarette packs rolled up in their short sleeves, and how their black leather motorcycle jackets fit them.

A lot of other girls must have felt the same way. When she slipped down the stairs to the parking lot to watch them, there were always a bunch of the "nice" girls hanging out, pretending they weren't watching the motorcycle guys. The guys called their motorcycles "chick magnets". They weren't about to hang out in the gym and dance with girls in pony tails and poodle skirts.

Lottie had taught her to waltz, rock and roll, and to do the hoedown the people back home did. When Elvis appeared on the Ed Sullivan show, Lottie had pinched her arm black and blue in excitement.

The town kids in her class seemed to take everything in stride. They ran around together, beautiful and sophisticated in their expensive clothes. There was an air about them the country kids didn't have. They went to the noon dances and stood together, and they were not bashful about dancing.

One day Emerald forgot herself, and edged up to the front row of kids. She noticed a tall, thin blond boy watching her from across the gym. He was standing with the girls that wore cashmere, and the boys whose clothes looked carefully fitted and carelessly expensive. She backed up and hid behind the other kids.

He crossed the gym floor to her to dance, but she hid, and he ended up dancing with whoever was standing near her before she disappeared.

Some of the girls in his group were in her gym class. They gathered around her one day and told her Curtis liked her, and asked why she was avoiding him She didn't know his name until then. She said she didn't know him and didn't want to, that she wasn't avoiding him. The girls left. She knew they were taking what she said back to him. It didn't make her feel very good. She wondered if it would hurt him.

She kept thinking about Curtis. She was fighting her liking of a boy, for boys turned into men. They were the doorway to the kind of prison Thursta and the other women she knew lived in.

Also, he was one of the rich, good looking town boys, and she was plain and poor as a church mouse, and a hillbilly to boot.

He watched her from across the gym every day while she studied his face and the goodness in it. His movements were slow and well thought out. They were gentle and intelligent, and didn't seem to hide any bad intentions.

One day when she was staring at him, she realized he knew what she was doing. He was putting himself out where she could see all of what he was, so she could take or leave him.

She thought about the boys in school from back home. If one of them asked her to dance, she would turn them down in fear and disgust.

Maybe some of the boys here had learned different values about women. She'd been watching how the young guys were in school. Some of them were respectful and nice to the girls. Others were just what she expected.

The next day, she edged up to the front of the dance floor and waited. He came to her like a moth to a flame. The noon dance was almost over. The few songs left would be slow ones, so the kids wouldn't go back to their classes all excited and wound up.

He held out his hand. She placed her hand in his. This was her first dance with a boy. He held her carefully while they danced. She wondered why he was shaking. She laid her head lightly against his chest for a second to see what it felt like. He smelled of goodness, like the moss on the bark at the bottom of Elmer the tree when she pulled a piece off. She felt his health and clean warmth surround her.

When the song ended, he introduced himself. His voice was changing, and he said his last name on a high note. He was embarrassed, but she didn't laugh at him. She told him her name and he said, "I know."

He didn't leave when the dance ended. He stayed with her like the kids that went steady. Another song began playing. He took her hand in his again. They moved onto the dance floor. They held each other in in a delighted daze. Just as the song ended, he looked down at her and said, "I'm going to marry you when we grow up."

She smiled up at him and said, "Yes."

She didn't tell anyone at home about Curtis. Curtis was funny and smart, and he admired her. He carried her books and stood with her while she waited for the bus after school. They weren't in any classes together, but they met at the noon dances, and soon everyone knew they were a couple.

Curtis was an only child. Both his parents were teachers. He lived a few blocks from the school. She was too young to see the sadness in his eyes when he spoke of his parents. She was too busy dreading his questions about her family and how they lived.

Bolen had declared many times that rich folks thought they was big shots, and to stay away from them. He didn't like the farmer who rented the house to them. He wouldn't go see Flint, 'cause Flint owned a big, fine home now, and made plenty a' money.

Most teachers set the mountain kids in the last rows in school. They assumed their capacity for learning was limited, caused partly by being poor. The northerners made fun of their accents, how they thought things out, and how they talked slower than northern people did. They made fun of the words they used, the food they ate, and the clothes they wore.

The practice of being close mouthed didn't change when they moved away from their mountains. It was the strongest habit they carried away with them.

Emerald was a mountain girl with a Healer's heart. She had learned well to keep her home life away from school. She had been forced to lie about her clothes and being hungry since the day she started school.

The other kids wanted to get to know her. She was asked questions every day. She didn't like questions. They felt invasive, regardless of their intent. She met most of the questions with silence or surliness, but answered one ever now and then. She had to, if she wanted to be Curtis's girlfriend.

The girls in his crowd knew she didn't have their kind of social skills. Some of them were in gym class with her and they'd seen her ragged underwear and cut down bras. They'd watched her go through the embarassment of learning how to take a shower, and learning what Kotex was.

Because of Curtis, they invited her to go to the dairy bar after school. She turned them down because she had to ride the bus home. They invited her to a pajama party, and said their parents would drive her home the next day. She lied, and told them she had to take care of her little sister ever night.

She listened to them talkin' to each other. They owned clothes she'd never heard of. Day clothes and night clothes. Allowances and pajamas. They lived like the families on "Leave it To Beaver" and "The Donna Reed Show". She'd never slept in pajamas in her life. She would of been laughed out a' the house if she said she wanted a pair of "pajamas". They slept in whatever was handy. Bolen give his boys money. That was as close as anybody got to an allowance in her house. Her secret agony grew and her stomach started hurting again. She was getting too much attention, and it was ceaseless.

She couldn't tell the girls or Curtis about herself, even though she knew some of the girls liked her. They were city people, how could they understand her ways, when she didn't understand theirs?

She couldn't tell them, or Curtis, that she loved the land and the smell of wet earth, and dancin' in the rain. There was no place she could find that would let her tell them about the sandpipers and the little red crabs livin" in the gray, clay banked ditch. She couldn't tell about the stately, tall tree she slept in sometimes, or about corn bread fried real crisp and gold, mashed up with pinto beans. She couldn't tell them her mother had stayed up late last night ta' finish the bright turquoise home made skirt she wore today.

There was no place they could meet. She felt backed into a corner. She started avoiding everyone except Curtis. The girls quit choosing her to be on their teams in gym class. Finally they just ignored her. She was a hopeless case.

School days dragged slowly by. At last December came. Time for semester exams. Curtis said he was looking forward to spending the two hours between exams with her. They never had much time to talk, because she got on the bus right after school. He said that now they would have a whole week of extra time to spend together.

It was too much. She couldn't stand the tension any more, so she broke up with him. But Curtis wouldn't stay away from her. He tried to talk to her, to get her to tell him what was wrong but she turned away from him. She could not break the bond of silence she had inherited, and tell him any of the truth.

Christmas vacation ended. School started again. Emerald stopped going to the noon dances. Spelling bee time came around, and she deliberately spelled a word wrong so she wouldn't have to be in it.

She started hangin' around with the plain girls nobody gave the time of day to. Some of the girls weren't very smart in school. Most of them were fat. A couple of them wore thick glasses, and didn't wash their hair very often. But they all had soft, mournful edges she could lean into and get some relief. The days went by. She settled into a routine of isolation with her new friends. At home, nobody knew she'd almost broke their taboos about lettin' other people in. She hurt alone, and it caused her to separate farther from them.

One day she was sittin' on the bus, staring out the window, thinking sad thoughts of Curtis and what might have been. She had adjusted to the school routines, she worked hard, and was an excellent student. But every time she climbed on the bus to go home, she relived being with Curtis, and the way it ended.

Bus ride after bus ride passed by before she noticed what was goin' on with Hank. One day she found herself watchin' him. For some reason, he was becoming truly beautiful. He was sittin' beside the new girl whose family had just moved into a big farm house on their bus route. They were talkin' soft with each other, both of them in their own little world. She stared at them in wonder, at the sweet innocent glow surrounding them.

She glanced at Lucy sitting beside her. Lucy was watching them with a look of contented happiness on her face. Emerald leaned over and whispered.

"What's her name?"

Lucy jerked her eyes away from them and glared at her.

"Karen," she said. "It ain't none a' yer' business!"

They rode for a few minutes without speaking. Emerald studied the pale, pretty little blond girl with the lovely oval face sittin' next to Hank. Her eyes were light blue and her straight hair was cut neatly to her shoulders.

She leaned over to Lucy again.

"Hank's got a girlfriend and I'm glad."

Lucy bristled at her.

"Mind yer' own beeswax and leave 'em alone!"

She whispered.

"I ain't doin' nothin', Lucy. I'm glad somebody git's ta' have it."

Lucy looked up at her, searched her face and shrugged. Then they both turned back to watching the love unfolding before their eyes, afraid of the absolute innocence of it, both willing to protect it any way they could.

Hank and Karen were in the same grade, but in different classrooms. Karen was Hank's first love, and it brought out his goodness. Emerald knew Hank held a large capacity to love. She had seen it come out in him once in awhile.

Hank made the long walk over to Karen's house on the weekends. Karen's father liked him. He let Hank help him with the farm work. Hank came home and talked about the things Karen's father taught him.

Her father made him feel smart, 'cause Hank didn't learn easy out of books. Her father said that was okay, there was plenty to learn that wasn't in books. Hank spent more and more time at Karen's house. He ate dinner with them. He told Thursta they put a tablecloth on the table before they ate. He'd never seen a tablecloth before. He learned to use a spoon and a knife, not just a fork to eat with, and Karen's mother sent him home with pieces of chocolate cake and chocolate chip cookies.

Karen's father taught Hank to drive his tractor, and he drove it all over their farm with Karen perched on the fender. Bolen and Thursta didn't know whether to be happy or insulted, so they left it alone. Bolen said Karen's dad was a smart ass and a bigshot.

Karen wanted to come over and visit, but Hank kept makin' excuses. He needed the love and care he was getting and he didn't want it to end. He glowed with good health and the nourishment love gives. He took on a personal dignity no one had seen in him before. There was strength and generousity in his softness.

He took his bicycle out of the garage and cleaned it up and greased it. He told Emerald, Lucy, and Neil to ride it any time he wasn't usin' it. Then he let them wear his cowboy shirt with the fringes on it and shoot his cap guns.

Next he asked Emerald questions about his homework. He wanted to do better in school, and he set up straight at the table and ate careful, and didn't take more than he could eat. He rode his bicycle over to Karen's house on Sunday mornings and spent the day there.

He missed out on the Sunday dinners at home. All of them protected him from West, Lottie, and the older kids questions. They gave vague answers when any of the older ones asked where he was.

"Ah, he's got a little job helpin' a farmer over on the other road. He's a' gittin' paid fer' it."

Then Karen's family moved away. Hank was getting ready to take a final ride on his bicycle over to her house, knowin' it was the last time he would see her. But he cried so much his eyes were all red. He had to wait, so Thursta talked Bolen into goin' to town and givin' her the money to buy a little locket from the dime store for Hank to give Karen.

When they came back, Thursta handed Hank the locket. "Pon' my honor, boy! You better shut up now!'"

Karen and her parents hugged Hank goodbye. Karen cried when they told him not to come back, the house would be empty. In a short time, they were gone. Hank never saw Karen again. He went around grievin', his face white, his eyes filled with pain. He stayed silent and pale.

Bolen joshed him about havin' the lovesick blues, but Hank didn't smile. He didn't care if he did his homework any more. He set around and got skinny. He didn't want to set with Bolen and watch television, or eat the special treats Thursta made him. Nobody knew what to do with him. Emerald wondered if he would ever smile again.

Then one day Emerald boarded the school bus for the ride home. Her eyes searched the bus for Lucy and Hank so she could set with them. She found them, then blinked her eyes in surprise. Instead of the sad, solemn looks they usually wore, the two of them were setting in the back of the bus. Hank wore a huge smile on his face.

Her eyes traveled down farther as she reached them, and she saw the big cage Hank was holding on his lap. There were two white mice in it. Emerald sank into the seat beside of them and peered at the snow white mice in the cage.

"Where'd ya' git' 'em?"

"Mrs. Smith give 'em ta' me!.. and I'm a' gonna' keep 'em no matter what anybody says!"

Mrs. Smith was Hanks new teacher.

"What about Bolen?"

"Bolen can go straight to Hell!"

He waited a minute and then ventured his plan.

"Mrs. Smith said she knowed I was awful sad, and she didn't want me ta' sink into somethin' called a slough of despond, so she gimme' these mice! They're classroom mice, and ever body else wanted 'em 'cause they're smart, but she give 'em ta' me, because I been such a sad boy!"

He thought for a minute.

"Now, I'll be happy agin'."

He shrugged.

"That's what she said."

Emerald asked.

"What are their names?"

Hank pointed at them.

"This here's Bobby and this one is Buddy."

Lucy chimed in.

"They're both boys!"

Emerald nodded.

Bolen and Thursta were thunderstruck when Hank come in the door carryin' Bobby and Buddy in their cage. They didn't like rats or mice, and they weren't happy. But Hank was smilin' like new mornin' sunshine. Emerald laughed at their expressions, while Lucy frowned at them and tapped her foot.

"Ya's better let Hank keep 'em cause' look, he's a' smilin'!"

Hank obliged by smiling hugely at them.

Bolen staggered over to a chair and fell into it.

"Boys, I'm bad got over this! A keepin' damn rats in the house on purpose!"

"They're white mice, not rats!" Hank objected.

Thursta rolled her eyes at Bolen and tapped the spatula in her hand like it was a ruler. Bolen sneaked a grin at her as if to say, "Hank is smilin' agin'!"

Hank kept the cage by his bed. Before he went to sleep each night, he held a long conversation with Bobby and Buddy. Their little pink eyes were bright as they sniffed the fingers he stuck through the bars of the cage. Sometimes Emerald had to sleep with Lucy mumblin' and flingin' her arms around on one side, and Hank's long winded conversations with Bobby and Buddy on the other side.

Then one morning, Emerald heard Hank shoutin'.

"Come here quick and look!"

Hank sounded so excited, they all ran to him. He was dancin' 'round Bobby and Buddy's cage, pointin' at some small, pink, wigglin' things.

"Bobby and Buddy's had babies!"

Hank shouted, grinning from ear to ear. Bolen stopped dead in his tracks.

"I'll be damned!" he said in disgust. He shook his head mournfully at Thursta and turned to leave.

"I won't never buy no more lockets for you to give some girl agin', boy!"

Bolen threw the words righteously back over his shoulder and left. Thursta started laughin'. "Ha ha ha ha ha!" she roared, leanin' over and slappin' her knees. Emerald, Lucy and Hank started laughin' and dancin' around and slappin' their knees because Thursta was.

"Ha ha ha ha ha haha !!"

Finally Thursta stopped laughin' and wiped her wet eyes.

"What r' ya' gonna' name the girl one, Hank?"

Hank looked and the floor and scuffed his feet.

"I doan' no'."

"Well ya' better think of somethin' right quick!"

Thursta said.

"How about Betty to go with Bobby?"

Thursta prompted.

"Sure, we'll call her Betty!"

Hank shouted

"Well, how many babies does Betty and Bobby have?"

Thursta asked.

Hank rushed to the cage and peered in.

"Ya' gotta' stick yore' hand in and count em," Emerald said. Hank looked at Thursta with big round eyes.

"Will Betty bite me if I stick my hand in the cage?"

"Let me do it first and and find out."

She stuck her hand in the cage. She moved her hand around the mice gentle as a feather.

"Seems to be five of 'em," she said at last, and pulled her hand out of the cage.

"Now remember ta' name ever one of 'em a name that starts with B for good luck." She laughed all the way down the stairs.

Hank had no end of good luck. West started takin' him to the store and buyin' him orange sodas and Crackerjacks. Pretty soon, Hank started hangin' out again with Bolen and West.

The War of the Petunias

Bolen oversaw everything that got planted. He had a green thumb, he loved the place, and ruled everything that went on outside. Except, Thursta and Bolen shared the flower bed in front of the house.

Every year in the spring, they went to town to choose two flats of petunias to plant in the flower bed. And ever spring, they argued over the petunia colors for days before they went and got them.

Thursta favored deep purple and hot pink. Bolen liked white and pale colors, and that's all he wanted to pay for. When they returned from their "Petunia Wars", they'd been gone for hours, they were wore out, and there was always a mix of the two kinds of petunias.

They dragged into the house like two soldiers that had just defeated a hostile army. The kids had a meal and hot coffee waiting on them so they could recuperate. Emerald could tell how much each one had won because of the colors that bloomed all summer.

The Chauffer

Thursta had picked out more colors than Bolen, and that set him off. He seethed around the house for days, a look of self pity on his face. He grumbled all through the planting of the petunias. After the petunias were planted, he took one of his uppity spells. He decided things were getting out of hand in his house, and he'd damn well had enough of it. The petunias were the last straw in a long line of wrongs done to him.

There were white mice living in his house, and his kids wouldn't mind him. Sometimes them or his woman laughed at him. Nobody was afraid of him any more. They owned a damn wall clock now, so nobody needed him to tell them the time. He'd bought a locket for a boy, and he'd shared the colors of flowers he'd paid fer' with a woman.

He paced the floor, shaking his head angrily. After awhile he figured out what to do. He nodded his head in satisfaction. Thursta and the girls would just hafta' ride in the back seat of the car. That'd teach 'em their place agin'. Ever body would see he'd put 'em back in their place. Only men would be allowed to ride in the front seat.

He made his announcement to Thursta.

"So, I git' ta' act like a rich woman who rides in the back of yer' car! Yore' gonna' be my chauffer?"

His temper flared up, and he told her he wouldn't take her to the store unless she minded him. She knew he meant it and she already knew how he was when he stubbed up about somethin', so she shut up.

The next Saturday mornin', Emerald watched Thursta tie her scarf around her head and pick up her big, shiny black pocketbook. She stepped out the door and solemnly climbed into the back seat of Bolen's car.

Bolen drove out of the driveway, looking straight ahead while Emerald hooted with laughter. On the way into town, Bolen passed by his friend Bud's gas station. Bud was outside. He started to raise his hand in his usual greeting when he saw Thursta settin' in the back seat. He dropped his hand and stared at them. Thursta waved and smile at Bud. Bolen hit the gas and speeded up.

When Bolen drove into the big parking lot in front of the store, a couple people he knew from work gawked at the sight of Thursta in the back seat.

"Lord, what is it with those hillbillies?" he heard a stranger say. Thursta had a big pair of oversized black framed, plastic sunglasses Lottie had given her. She wore them when she got embarrassed. She cried easy, and she didn't want people to see her red eyes. She heard their words, pulled the huge, black framed sunglasses out of her purse and hastily put them on.

Bolen looked back at her in the rearview mirror and didn't say a word. His expression was that of a lost soul struggling to figure out how to stay out of Hell. Thursta slid out of the car and walked slowly into the store. She didn't ask him for money.

She spent what she already had on a bouquet of cut flowers, went back to the car and got in the back seat again. She sat there, holding the first bunch of bought flowers she ever owned. Bolen stared at her from the front seat. Finally he started the car and drove home without a word.

Emerald, Hank and Lucy watched Thursta get out of the back seat with her large black sunglasses on, holding a bouquet of cut flowers in her hands. They started laughin'. They laughed until they cried. Emerald watched Bolen's angry red face carefully, and edged up to his window and said, "Don't that woman do some of the funniest things?"

At her words, Bolen's pride quickly seen the way out, as Emerald hoped it would.

"Woman," he ordered. "Yer' a fool! Git' back in the car, and I'll take ye' back ta' the store!"

He scoffed at her.

"Flares! What the hell's the matter with ya'?"

Thursta just stood there until he said, "And git' in the front seat, so's I don't look like a damn fool ta' the people I know!"

Thursta handed Emerald the flowers and meekly got in the front seat. Bolen drove away. Emerald, Lucy and Hank watched the dust roll up behind his car and laughed 'til they had to set down on the ground.

Chapter 29. Where's the Meat?

Thursta didn't cook meat for them during the week. She saved it for Sunday dinner, for West and Lottie and their big families, for Flint and his family and their friends. The list went on and on.

They ate fried taters' and cornbread and pinto beans. They ate the vegetables from the garden, and biscuits, eggs, gravy, and milk. They had plenty of good food, but they still craved meat.

Every Sunday morning, Thursta got up early and cleaned the house. Then she started cookin'. She killed chickens, baked meatloafs and big hams, and fried piles of golden brown chicken or crisp pork chops to go along with the rest of the food. She did it all by herself because Emerald wouldn't help her, 'cause she saved all the meat for the older ones and their families.

Emerald, Lucy, Neil and Hank drooled with hunger from all the good meat smells coming from the kitchen ever Sunday morning. Lottie came over early to help Thursta cook and scolded them for not helpin' out.

They wanted to tell her to go to hell, but they kept their mouths shut. They knew West and Flint and her and the rest thought Sunday dinner was the way they got to eat all week.

Thursta made them wait while the older ones and their kids eat first. Nobody ever left them a bite of meat. Thursta ignored their complaints. She put up with Bolen's miserliness with grocery money ever week, then she had to put up with

him settin' in the kitchen ever Sunday mornin'.
She'd be workin' away, hopin' he'd stay out a' the
kitchen, but the son of a bitch never did. He'd
pour a cup of coffee, set down, light up a Camel
and start in.

"What's all this big fuss about?"

Then he'd laugh.

"Ya' needn't go ta' all this trouble 'cause a'
me."

She ignored him and didn't answer.

"Besides, it's a' costin' me too much anyways."

"Im' a thinkin' that next week, we could git' by
with a little less."

Emerald watched his words beat the joy out of
Thursta and she wanted ta' whip his ass. As soon
as the first carload of the older kids drove in,
Bolen changed his tune. He didn't want them to
find out the mean things he said to Thursta
about the Sunday dinners.

He strolled into the livin' room or went outside
to the picnic table in summer to hold court. He
let on that he was a generous man, glad to put
out the money for a good Sunday dinner for
them. He drank his strong coffee and smoked his
Camels while the men and boys set with him,
askin' his advice about life.

The women went to the kitchen. They helped
Thursta and laughed and talked with each other
while they loaded the table with the good food
she cooked. When dinner was over, ever body
formed baseball teams, or set around and talked.

Bolen was careful to wait until all of the older
kids left before he told Thursta in great detail
what a failure each of them was. Thursta never

answered. She slammed food and dishes around in the kitchen while he talked. She got madder and madder at him. After the food was put up and the dishes were washed, she stalked out of the kitchen.

"I'm not gonna' listen ta' any more of this!"

She left him setting there alone. Emerald knew the big Sunday meal was Thursta's way of making up to the older kids for what they'd suffered because of Bolen's drinking back when they were kids.

Thursta needed to give them somethin' back for what they'd missed out on, what she'd not been able to prevent. She had to fight Bolen at the grocery store ever week to do it, and she did.

Ever week she made a place of atonement for her kids to come home to. Bolen could have stood in that place with her, for it was his fault to begin with. But he wouldn't do it. That would be admitting that he'd done wrong, and he'd never said he was sorry for anything in his life.

Emerald knew what Bolen would do after Thursta left the kitchen, for she'd slipped around and watched him. He'd cross his legs, sip cofee, light up another cigarette, and lean forward. Then he'd drop his head down and stare at the floor for a long time, while he rubbed the first finger of his right hand in circles over his thumbnail, the way he did when he was thinking hard about something.

He'd set there and finally dismiss whatever it was he'd been thinkin' about, with a " aaaahh" sound. Emerald never heard sich' a sound come out of a human bein'. Then he'd git' up and walk off slow, like he was a hundred years old.

The sorrow was deep in him when he was alone, and it showed. But he never let anyone else see it, and Emerald had to sneak to find it. He hid it and hoarded it, the one thing they needed from him most of all, like it was precious gold. The children came and went, never knowing he held any sorrow in him at all for what he'd done to them. All they saw was his pride, and the meaness he inherited from Marthy that still run deep in him.

Feedin' Redemption

Bolen got West a job at the factory where he worked. West made best friends with Eddie Hager, another hard drinker who worked the day shift. Wherever one was, the other one was.

Before long, West found a rent house close to them. Bolen still bought groceries for West and his growin' family. He paid West's rent every month, even though West made more money than he did. When Thursta asked Bolen for money, he always said he was short on it.

West had five kids, and they soon found their way down the road to Thursta and Bolen's house. Emerald, Lucy, Hank, and Neil despised them. They'd been raised on the migrant worker farm and they'd picked up the nasty habits of the people livin' there. It didn't take long for them to get bold. They ate ever thing on the place without askin' anybody if they could have it, and they pilfered through ever body's things and stole whatever they wanted.

Emerald, Lucy, Hank and Neil were miserable. Thursta was forced to cut back on her Sunday dinners. Ever body knew it was West's fault. He was completely irresponsible and liked it that way.

Bolen wouldn't listen to their complaints. He kept right on takin' Jan to the store and buyin' big sacks of groceries for her, while they stood in the yard and watched him drive by with the food they needed.

Emerald, Lucy, Hank and Neil spent their time playing in the fields and going up and down the roads. They left the house and it's constant lack of good rules behind. They laughed and sang church songs. They admired the earth and how busy life was in all seasons. Their spirits lifted when the wind blew, and late one night they stole the sheets off the beds and became ghosts while Bolen and Thursta were sleepin' like stones. Thursta found the eye holes in the sheets when she went to wash them.

"Hmm... I wonder what them holes is?"

She stuck two fingers through the eye holes they'd cut out with her sewing scissors.

"Probly some old ghosts got cold, and wore them sheets' ta' keep warm..."

"...and cut holes out, so's they could see where they was a' goin'!".... she looked at them with raised eyebrows and waited. They hastily embellished their story.

"Them old ghosts like ta' froze ta' death in the night air, but them sheets saved 'em from a sure death!" ..they solemnly explained to her. ...

"Well, if they was already ghosts, then they didn't need no sheets, fer' they was already dead."...she jerked and looked around her.

"I felt somethin'...did you'ns feel it?"

She jerked again.

"Aw.. yer' jist' tryin' ta' scare us!" they chorused.

"Shhhh!" she put her finger across her lips and looked around.

"Yer' jist' tryin' ta' scare the Hell right out of us!" Hank hollered. She reached down to swat him. They all turned and ran. She hollered after their retreating backs.

"Them ghosts I saw said they'd git' ya', if you ever touch them sheets agin'!"

Nate Newman, Paul's kin

Thursta found a job. She decided to take driving lessons so she could get a car and drive herself to work and get away from Bolen and West. She was tired of Bolen's high handedness. When the lady she rode with wasn't on that day at the Chapel Home for the Elderly, she had to ask him to take her to work. She hated askin' Bolen for a ride.

"I might teach ya' myself, if ya' asked me real purty," Bolen said. Thursta scowled at him. "Go ta' hell!"

Flint nicknamed Thursta's driving teacher Nate Newman. He said he called him that because he was short, had sky blue eyes and was very brave.

But Thursta couldn't get the hang of drivin', and on her fourth lesson, she ran herself, Nate Newman and his car, right into the ditch in front of the house. Nate Newman righted the car, and came in the house.

"I'm quittin' this job before I get killed or maimed!" he said. He pointed a finger at Bolen, who was sittin' there, calmly drinkin' a cup of coffee.

"You or somebody else will have to teach her to drive!"

Blessed Be the Refrigerator

Bolen started naggin' Thursta about her weight.

"Yore' a' gittin' fat 'cause we got too much food in the house now!"

Thursta was big boned and capable. Each day she did the work of three women and at least one man. The girls helped out, but they were all smaller than her, and so the heavier work was left to her.

Bolen kept on makin' fun of her until she decided to go on a diet. She barely ate all day and went to bed hungry. But the food in the frig' would be gone or moved around each morning. She didn't think too much about it for a while, because the boys came in and fixed somethin' to eat in the middle of the night. But she kept gaining weight and the food was gone when nobody came in. She couldn't figure it out.

"Yore' a' sleepwalkin' and eatin' at night!"
Bolen declared.
"I don't believe a damn word of it."
Thursta scoffed. She asked Emerald to watch her to find out if it was true. Emerald stayed up and watched Thursta go to the kitchen in her sleep and raid the refrigerator. She was afraid to wake her, so she waited until the next mornin' to break the sad news to her. Thursta was mad at herself, but Emerald thought the whole thing was silly.

"He's jist' littler than you, an' he don't like it. Never did, never will. So go on back ta' eatin'! Ta' hell with what anybody else says about yore' eatin', and ta' hell with him! He's gotta' find somethin' ta' bitch about all the time, anyway. Ya' need ta' eat ta' keep up yore' strength!"

Thursta looked thoughtful, then she grinned and went to the 'frig. She turned to Emerald. "Ya' want some lemon pie?"

Netty

People moved into the empty house at the end of the road. Emerald wanted to see who it was. She strolled past the house like she didn't have a care in the world. A girl about her age ran out on the porch and smiled at her. She smiled back, and the girl came out to the road to get acquainted.

"I'm Netty. I 'spect it's pretty lonesome way out here in the boondocks. Do any cars ever go by?" She stuck out her hand for Emerald to shake.

Emerald started going to Netty's house to visit. One day Netty's mother told her she had to stop comin' over unless she went to church with them. They had an old car and a bunch of kids, and she squeezed in with them when they picked her up for church. They asked her to invite Lucy to go, and Lucy agreed.

Lucy's voice was a fine, clear sophrano, and Emerald sang alto. They sang a church song together, standing on the small stage by the piano with the sunlight streamin' through the church window behind them. Lucy's hair stood out like a blond, thick, curly cloud around her head. Emerald was still thin as a whip, with short auburn hair haloing her head in fine ringlets. Thursta had made them new skirts with little purple flowers running through them. Before they left for church, she pinned a little bunch of violets to the shoulder of each of their snow white blouses.

As soon as church let out, the boys swarmed around Emerald. Most of them attended high school in Birchwood, a small town a few miles from the church. Emerald liked James. He was tall and strong, with flashin' brown eyes and a quick, ready laugh. His straight brown hair hair was neatly cut, and he had an air of humorous ease about him. He talked with his hands, and drove an old black car. He was an average boy who came from a poor family of thirteen. She felt safe with knowin' that. She sat behind him in church so she could stare at the back of his head. She watched his profile when he turned to smile or speak to the crowd of boys he set with.

James gave her his class ring to wear. He picked her up on Wedneday and Friday nights, and they went out for two hours each time. That was all Thursta and Bolen would allow. They set together Sunday mornings in church, and he called her after school every day.

She trusted him completely. He took her to her first restaurant and to her first drive in movie. They went to an amusement park, and she rode the merry go round with him. They talked about school and the things they would do together in the future. She liked to kiss him and she loved the hugs he gave her and the way he smelled.

All of her life, when she was alone, she had done things like smoothing her hands down the green corn stalks. She licked the petals of flowers. She sifted through milk thistle pods and blew their innards into the air. Her hands knew well the sharp round lines and textures of wheat tops without lookin', the tender rounded feel of milk corn, the dented in feel of hardness it got when it was full and dry.

Her feet and legs knew the feel of different grasses and hurtful stickers, and the clay and mud in the creek. She knew the feel and smell of bird wings and their tender down underneaths. She walked through dust, stood in rain, and played in the hot sun. She rested in the shade of trees, and hid under canopies of pine. Her senses were keenly attuned and awake.

Now she had a playmate that smelled and looked just right, and she treated him just as she did the plants and trees and birds she loved. She poured the tenderness out on him that she reserved only for them. When he went on vacation with his sister, she missed him terribly. As soon as he got back, he brought her a silk pillow with fringe around the sides of it. He brought his big heartiness and laughter back into her life again, and she nestled close to him in absolute trust.

James never asked questions about her family, or told her much about his. All she knew was that he lived with his sister, and he was from a large family. He called every night after school, and they talked about what their day was like. He was the center of her life, and she relied on him more and more.

But the sister he lived with didn't like it because he was getting home later and later from his dates with her. She warned both of them in a joking way about messing up their future by starting somethin' too soon. Emerald didn't know what she was talking about.

One Sunday night, they set in a pew together, sharing a songbook, holding hands like always. Fall had set in and the weather was crisp and cool. They'd gone on a chuch hayride and apple bobbin' the night before.

Church ended. Emerald stood up, but James wasn't ready to leave yet. He dawdled around until everybody was gone, then he asked her to go up in the church loft with him. She'd never been up there, but she had heard that some of the boys took the girls up there and kissed them.

She took a deep breath before she nodded yes to him. He didn't notice. Lately, for some reason, she had become afraid of unknown things. The more afraid she became, the more she clung to him in the dark when they were alone in his old car.

She leaned against him when they got up in the church loft, but he stepped back from her. Her heart started pounding. A terrible fear washed over her. The unknown thing her Sight had warned her about was here.

James did it just as easy as anything. He asked for his ring back like it didn't matter. She couldn't speak. She wore his ring on a chain around her neck, day and night. It was the first thing she touched in the morning, the last thing she touched at night.

She looked in his eyes, and recognized where the Shadow that had been haunting her rested. His sister. She had forced him to do this thing. To do it in a safe place, a place where Emerald couldn't turn to him and touch his body. That's where he was told he was weak with her. She felt humiliated, just like the tramp people once called Lottie. She grabbed the railing and almost fainted. She felt like she was trying to swim through thick black water, and she had never learned to swim.

She never remembered taking the ring off or giving it back to him, or what he said to her. She never remembered who drove her home. She only remembered going upstairs, falling across the bed and crying. Great huge sounds comin' from somewhere, hot wet salt water soakin' her face. She remembered it being night, then day. She heard Thursta's scoldin' voice off in the distance, tellin' her it wasn't the end of the world. She never went back to Netty's church again.

The next time she remembered anything, it was spring. She was standin' in Bolen's garden, looking at the ground. She had finally come back into herself. Her soul had returned. She stared down at the blue morning glories bloomin' at her feet. Where had she been? She only remembered that the past winter was cold.

Little pieces of the lost time returned. She remembered reading constantly, not washing her hair, or brushing her teeth. She remembered Thursta complainin' that her teeth were yellow as a punkin', and ta' stop slouchin'.

She remembered sitting in Mr. Bardsons class. He had walked into his classroom, wearin' a World War Two helmet on his head, with the loose straps swinging down by his double chin. He was short and stout, and he was good at knowing what ever one in the class was feelin'. He knew she wasn't present, and he had looked out for her. He taught them well, and with truth. He explained moral dilemas to them, and how doing the right thing always worked out. Most of all, he said over and over, it takes guts to live life. He finally convinced her. She had somehow found her courage again and brought her soul back home. He had saved her. He was her Healer.

She held out her hands and stared at them. She was a Healer, too. She had a Healers lineage. When she was little, her Healer grandmother Drusa had come to her and saved her soul. This time a teacher, who looked like a wise frog wearing an army helmet, had been the Healer who saved her soul.

A kind of knowing flooded her, a mix of serenity, peace and strength. She recalled Bolen's drunken friends orderin' her to put her hands on their heads so their hangovers would go away when she was seven. She remembered being in Lottie's church, and the people wantin' her to lay hands on them.

It had been a long time since she'd gone to church. It was time to go back again.

The next Sunday she went home with Lottie and stayed for two weeks. She slept and ate and rested, and went to church ever night and laid hands on volunteers to find out if the Healer's power was still in her. She stayed in a high and holy place, obeying the voices of Mercy, Fallon, and Drusa. They led her hands to the places they needed to go on the people. She told them her story, and they gave her sacred, healing words from the Bible to speak over herself. The held back love she couldn't give James any more was used up by the people around her in the church. Her heart began healing.

"Thank you, God!" she breathed in relief. "Amen!"

Startin' Over

When Emerald got home from Lottie's, James was in the past and she was herself again. The need to love and touch him was over. She knew her path now.

She started going to church with Annie and Russel. Their church was more formal than Lottie's, but they still held healing sessions. She was cautious, but soon people asked her to lay hands on them in love. It became easy to step into that place where nothin' mattered except the high wind blowin' from the Holy place where the voices of the Healers she sprang from told her ever move to make.

Bill and Joanie were an older married couple with no kids. They were avid churchgoers. They adopted her. She set between them ever Sunday and they smiled and prayed together. They invited her to go home with them whenever she wanted.

She started spending time in town with Joanie and Bill. Their big family came from the same old hills she was from. They joked and had a good time together eating, working and going to church. She helped with babysitting and housekeeping jobs, and Joanie paid her. They talked about herbs from back in the mountains, and about layin' on of hands healin', like it was the most natural thing in the world.

She felt herself changing again. Her gaunt skinniness had fled. She ate and took warmth, and was solitary when she needed to be. She had been given the space she needed to grow up in.

Her brown hair was shiny and bright. It bore coppery redness in the tender little curls layin' at the nape of her neck. Her hair still curled ever which way, but it was soft, and she kept herself clean, and hid her monthlies from all of them.

The journeys with Lucy, Hank, and Neil up and down the roads and across the fields, the books she'd read, the friends she'd made, all of her life had brought her to this place of leavin' her childhood behind, and someday, when it was time, she had already dreamed it true, a fine man would kiss her and call her Emmy instead of Emerald, and her life would change again.

One Sunday morning, she walked out in the front yard and stood waiting under the pine tree for Bill and Joanie. Thursta came outside and stood in front of her. She took Emerald's face in her big hands, looked deep in her eyes. Emerald looked into the eyes that were the same green as her grandmother Drusa's. She remembered her grandmother studyin' her the same way before they left the old hills so long ago.

It was time to speak the Hallowed Words that intentioned and kept their Healers heritage going forward. It was time to claim the intention. The understandin' of it rose in the wind that come up quick and blew across the yard.

"I love ya' Mom."

Thursta's eyes watered.

"Someday, I'll take Bolen's industry with me, and grow a big garden like his! Someday, I'll can tomatas' like you do, and learn not ta' speak sa' quick."

She peered up at Thursa.

"Don't worry 'bout Bolen. He ain't got nothin' to give ye'. He's too scared of his momma' from back when he was a little boy and he took all of what he had to give on the road and left it out there so she couldn't come near it.

Anyways, I've got grandmaw Drusa's and Fallon's and Mercy's Healer ways ta' rely on. Ya' passed 'em on ta' me, and I thank ye' fer' it. When I git' older, not by much, I'm goin' back ta' the mountains, fer' I ain't through learnin' from 'em."

Her tone changed and she spoke in a stern voice, one wise beyond her years.

"Ya' set me free ta' go when ya' let West set me on the floor fer' three days. I couldn't have left ya' before that. So ya' had ta' do it ta' set me free from ye'."

Thursta's heart thundered with hurt and guilt. She heard the warning and the underlying forever hurt behind the words. Tears rained down her face. Emerald studied the tears. They were true and not a chemical mix from somethin' else. Many times she knew things like that. Thursta knew that intense look, for she had grown up with it. Emerald spoke sternly again.

"Ya' set me free all the way when ya' made it up ta' me by goin' in the woods ta' show me who ye' are, and how ta' survive the new path I now hafta' travel. You carry the true blood of the pioneers and their understandin' of Nature. You are my Ward Bond! You know, Wagon Train?"

She grinned and waggled her sharp little chin at Thursta.

Thursta stared at her, not knowin' how ta' feel. Emerald came from her heritage. She was a child of beliefs and centuries old Healin' and Knowin's passed down, warshed in her family's blood line. She sighed and settled into acceptance. Healers never belonged completely to their family. Emerald was of her heart. She set in a different place in it. She'd endured Bolen, and her hard life was made easier 'cause of Emerald bein' there. She went forth each mornin', knowin' her heart kin was just a look, a laugh, a smell, a young voice away.

Emerald stepped away so Thursta could memorize her profile. She did a little hop, skip and jump and looked around. Robins, blue jays, little brown wrens in the old pine tree in the front yard, chirped and circled above her. The sky was a rich, bright blue, tellin' of a hot day. Gold wheat rippled in waves in the fields around her. The ground was warm, the green grass neatly mowed. Life was good, big, rich, and terrible.

The wind stopped blowing. A littler breeze surrounded them. In it stood Fallon and Mercy, Drusa, and their long line of Healers.

The decision had been made. She would leave, and soon. That decision would keep her learnin' and lovin' deeper than she ever wanted to. It was that a' way for she was Bolen's child too, a child who liked stayin' away from others and travelin' in her own insides. She wanted, just like he did, ta' view the world outside as a hobo just passin' through. She understood his surprise and disappointment each time he got on the road and it carried him back to the same old place. She had watched his heart take a fell swoop each time he thought one of his boys might leave him, like he had left his mother.

"Bolen had ta' father me, so's I could have travelin' blood in me mixed with yours. You've suffered fer' it, I know, but ya' did good."

Thursta stared at her.

"No. I don't know the reasons for the others. Jist' me. But there were reasons, fer' sure."

Bill and Joanie's car came slowly down the road, dust billowin' behind it. The car drove between the two pine trees, and pulled up where they was standin'.

"Someday, I'll need ta' know what you and Bolen had to give up, so's ya' could live in this place. That'll take goin' back there." she warned Thursta before she turned away.

Thursta watched the car go down the road. She turned and went back in the house. She shook her head to clear it, grabbed the cast iron skillet and slammed it down on the stove. "I don't know a damn thing!" she muttered, grabbing the biscuit bowl.

Bill's car pulled out onto the highway. Bill and Joanie looked back at her and smiled. Then they looked ahead and sang together, "I've got a home in glory land that outshines the sun, look away beyond the blue!"

After a minute, Emerald started singin' along with them.

Many terrible life stories are carried in silence, remaining alone for decades. No one wants to hear the horror of it, especially the new children. But once in awhile, someone tells theirs anyway, risking all to unburden themselves before they die. Before the story returns in another perverse form to haunt someone. This is such a story- told in reverse for survival and many other reasons.

Sometimes it is the Trickster who helps us survive. This novel addresses only the gentle gray edges of the Shadows that hovered along the borders of Light and Hope, Shadows that did not enter often nor stay long because Angels, Flare's, Pitchure's, Sunlight and and a few Good Women with their skimpy, limpy, never ending laughter and love warshed sheets 'til they were snowy white, cooked vegetables 'til they were green and bright, and told fanciful stories cause' they knowed laughter allus' sends the devil on his way.

So here's to the women and children who survived, sometimes defeated, but never destroyed, by the men who made their poverty filled childhood-and lives-a living hell and an unnecessary war zone. Bravo!

About the Author:

Patsy Stanley is an artist, illustrator and author.She has authored both nonfiction and fiction books including novels, children's books, energy books, art books, and more. She may be contacted at <u>patsystanley123@gmail</u> or questions and comments.

Books by Patsy Stanley

Novels:
Addition Jones
An Older Wine
Emerald Hawks Flight
Avalon Blues Quest

Children's books:
Christmas Stories From the Crone's Castle
(author illustrations)
The Dreadful Noises of Landoshar
(author illustrations)

Native American:
Red Leaf
The Green Mountain Shaman

Muse Art books:
The Zen of Three Zines
The Zen of Leota and the Laundromat

Metaphysics:
The Mental Body
The Spiritual Nature of Atomic Structure
Sound Energies
Shield Energies
Chakras, Meridians, and the Color Energies
The Elements

Avalon Blue's Quest

Avalon Blue, past sixty, hides the secret initiations holding her hostage, forcing her to remain a loner traveling the world in eccentric clothing of her own design. In Winter's Lee, a small northern fishing village, she meets Lucian and Melanie, cousins and best friends who have settled down, planning to be bored and lonely until their demise from old age.

That is, until an unexpected, muddy, squalling little messenger flings itself into their arms, bringing the gift of a new emotional, imaginative, journey involving Shamans, animal totem, tattoos and a mysterious island into their lives.

An inspiring, humorous story woven through with ageless spirit magic, a story in which the ageless, never ending expansion of the soul meets love in daily life.

Addition Jones

Addition Jones fled Cross Grove as a young man after the town accused him of murder. No one ever heard from him again. Now middle-aged, successful, and wealthy, but still haunted by his old life and his ridiculous name, he decides to return to his hometown to put his past to rest.

With great malice and intent to do as much harm as he can, Grady Miller flings the name Addition Jones and what he did to him in his daughter Nell's face, then dies.

Nell grabs on to the name and sets out to right the wrongs her father did to Addition Jones. He returns home to find her living on his property, and a battle between good and evil, love and hate begins, played out between two lonely outcasts and a town that doesn't like to forgive its own sins.